I0588001

THE SWEETEST DAY

THE DELUCA FAMILY BAKERY SERIES BOOK 1

BLAIR BRYAN

READ MORE BY THIS AUTHOR

Use the QR code below to access my current catalogue. **Teal Butterfly Press is the only place to purchase autographed paperbacks and get early access.** Buying direct means you are supporting an artist instead of big business. I appreciate you.

https://tealbutterflypress.com/pages/books

Also available at Barnes and Noble, Kobo, Apple books, Amazon, and many other international book sellers.

Find My Books at your Favorite Bookseller Below.

Books by Ninya

Books By Blair Bryan

To all the curvy girls who have been told their entire lives they are too much.
You're not.
You're perfect just the way you are.

ONE

I always thought I was the luckiest girl in the world. My childhood was literally sugar-coated growing up at DeLuca's Family Bakery—a place where magic was made and powdered sugar-coated life in a pristine sweetness that made everything more manageable. Constructed of charming hand-carved antique bricks with wide plate glass windows capped with pastel awnings, our bakery was storybook perfection, straight out of Hansel and Gretel without the cannibalistic witch. Inside, little round bistro tables and antique caned chairs were arranged in curved rows to give each customer the best view of the kitchen, and the illuminated fully-stocked pastry case was always empty by noon.

DeLuca's was famous for its cannolis—a title my dad, Marco, won during a throw down with a world-famous pastry chef in the nineties. The sun-streaked photo of my pops with his arm slung around the neck of a scrawny redheaded celebrity chef still hangs on the wall in the dining room, and we proudly stake the claim that we make the best cannolis in Illinois.

The bakery is a part of me. In my childhood it was a living, breathing being. I grew up there, always in the kitchen with my grandparents, Nonna and Bumpo. The scents of fresh baking bread and vanilla beans are seared into the fabric of my soul. I grew up in a world of whisks and rolling pins and discovered that food can absolutely be called love.

DeLuca's marble countertops and wooden floors were the backdrop of all my grainy childhood home movies, lovingly recorded by my parents. I took my first rickety coltish steps there, falling to the floor in a pile of chubby baby thighs and coal-black hair. My dark-haired mustachioed Pops would scoop me up and immediately reward me with ticklish kisses and a cookie. Our bond was lovingly constructed in sugar and is as sweet as it gets. I am a daddy's girl through and through—a literal chip off the old block. Pops was dark, chunky, and funny as hell. His deep laugh boomed, filling the crevices, a sound that reverberated through any space he inhabited. Always the life of the party, he loved to sing and dance around the bakery, humming and whistling while he worked.

When the mood struck him, he'd sweep my mom, Lorraine, into his strong arms and spin her around the kitchen, crooning sweet Italian love songs into her ear while she protested. All the while, her delicate fists were balled and beating on his massive chest while she giggled and squirmed.

It was a carefully choreographed cry that always fell on deaf ears. As I grew older, I understood she was playing a part, putting up a fight when he did it, but not a real one. Instead, it was a playful skirmish where she called him a rascal and chastised him by saying, "Marco, stop getting so carried away." He'd just laugh and spin her faster until she yielded.

Their ritual required her to protest in vain while he laughed into the crook of her neck. An outcry she didn't really mean, because deep down, Mom always wanted to be carried away, but she wouldn't give herself permission to do it on her own. Dad was a professional level carry away-er with a playfulness that melted Mom's defenses.

My earliest memories are of sitting on a stool next to my dad all dressed in white, watching him carefully measure out the ingredients and then dump them into the commercial mixer. He would hand me a galvanized tin scoop, and I would happily shovel out flour by the cupful onto a scale, with liberal amounts of it fluttering to the ground like snow.

Usually, Mom would interject into the fun and say, "Gionna is too little. You are wasting so much." She could sometimes be a buzzkill like that, not because she had a bad bone in her body, but because it was physically painful for her to waste anything. It was a trait that instantly bonded her and Bumpo together, united by their tireless mission to reduce waste and preserve bakery profits.

She applied the same focused earnestness to her own physical appearance. Meticulously maintained with religious salon visits, her blonde hair was always smooth and braided to keep wayward strands out of the kitchen. She was thin and seemingly weak to look at, but when it came to raw grit and determination, pound for pound, the woman was a force to be reckoned with. My mom was smart and focused. Like a tiny chihuahua, her bark was always far worse than her bite. I didn't get much from Mom in the looks department; I vastly favored my dark-haired, dark-complected dad, but we shared the same icy blue eyes and we both embraced the brutal end of honesty.

Mom was the kind of person who ironed her t-shirts and tucked them into white mom jeans, her self-imposed daily uniform at the bakery. Fashion-less denim with a waist so high, it must have grazed her nipples. If she ever heard me utter that description aloud, she would probably shoot me a look and tell me to stop being vulgar, which would only serve to spur me on to say even more offensive vulgarities. With a mom like mine, being cheeky was the ultimate act of rebellion and the source of much personal glee. I was good at it. Spouting off outrageous phrases to shock and awe my mother was one of my favorite pastimes. I'd say nearly anything to get her goat, and she'd roll her eyes and laugh at me.

"Oh, Gionna. You're being so ridiculous."

To which I would respond, "Yes, Mommy. Yes, I am. The *most* ridiculous." And I would tuck my chin to my chest, pandering to her and batting my thick eyelashes at her beguilingly until she melted, which she always did.

In my late twenties, Mom tried to fix me. She decided it was her responsibility to transform me into someone who could get a man. Almost like you could set a trap and ensnare one like a wayward rabbit or some poor, unsus-pecting bear. Just put a pot of honey out and wait. It didn't work that way, and it was exhausting because being the honey requires things of a woman like shaving and waxing and plucking, and I just didn't give a shit about any of that.

When I turned thirty, I initiated plan B and froze some of my eggs. Originally, my carefully curated life plan included getting married and having kids in my twenties, and I added two children to the vision board. I would have a boy and a girl spaced precisely three years apart. It's true, I can be kind of a control freak, but that dream faded away the day I hit the big three-o. I panicked with the biological clock ticking so loudly in my ears it was hard to hear anything else. After lengthy research and secret doctor appointments, I decided to invest in a back-up plan. Just to buy me a little time, in case the right guy finally walked into my life. I never let Mom in on the secret, because she was like a dog with a bone when she wanted something, and she wanted grandkids more than anything else in the entire world.

As the years drifted by, I started to doubt my desire to be a mother in the first place. You sure as hell don't bring a baby into the world with even a whisper of uncertainty. I didn't feel that primal ache anymore, so my little eggs were frozen in time, floating in a sea of liquid nitrogen without her knowledge. She probably wished she'd had a few more kids, maybe had the six that Pops wanted instead of pinning her future on me. That way she would have been virtually assured of armfuls of grands at our regular Sunday dinners.

I'm the third generation of DeLucas to work in the bakery, and at forty-two, it was looking like I would be the last with no realistic options on the man horizon and no real pressure or desire to change that fact after my last heartbreak. It was difficult growing up surrounded by two generations of successful lifelong marriages when my own love life had crashed and burned. Admitting failure, I had given up at finding the love they'd found. I didn't believe that kind of love existed in my generation, where most men were looking to maintain the loose tie to scratch a horny itch while they waited for something better to come along. In my mind, real love was a unicorn, a mirage, a farce, and instead of focusing on that useless soul sucking mission, I decided to stay in my own lane.

Mom was cleaning up after the morning rush, bent over the table and scrubbing hard before sanitizing as cleanliness was one of her most beloved virtues. She caught my eye, and I winked at her, and then watched her pick up Mr. Manzetti's bowler hat from the ground, dust it off, and then place it back on the table for him. Mom always took care of people in her quiet way. He was one of my favorite regulars who had been coming to DeLuca's five days a week ever since I could remember.

"Thank you, my dear. You are too kind. May I trouble you for another original cannoli?" He always asked so sweetly it was hard to tell him no, but he was a diabetic and a touch forgetful.

"Mr. Manzetti!" I admonished from my post at the pastry case. "You know the rules. Check your blood sugar first, and then we will see if you can have another cannoli."

"Yes, warden," he moaned with a mischievous twinkle in his eye before he turned away to discreetly test his sugars, and then triumphantly waved the monitor in the air at me. "See, Gionna! One-seventeen!"

"You know that's only three away from a no," I warned. My feet were tired, shoved into the black crocs on my feet. I pinched at the tension in my back with my fingers. After I turned forty, the random list of aches and pains multiplied, and I avoided the doctor like the plague after he wanted to have a discussion about my body mass index.

"Technically, that still makes it a yes." He smiled, his face crinkling up like crepe paper. With a shock of white hair and always dressed impeccably in a suit jacket, cardigan, and corduroy pants, he carried the newspaper and spent hours working on the crossword puzzle just to keep his brain sharp. "Three letters, last one is a Z. Clue is they come in last."

Crossword puzzles always stumped me and then made me feel stupid with their pithy wordplay. The morning rush was over, so I had a second to mull it over when my best friend Aubrey breezed by with a warm-up for his coffee.

"Easy—it's X, Y, Z," she sang out as she flitted by the rest of the tables like a hummingbird, tipping a stream of our Italian dark roast into each remaining patron's cup.

Aubrey was beautiful, and that was part of the reason Mom hired her to work at the bakery. In the early days of the Starbucks coffee empire insanity, Mom was smart enough to recognize a lucrative opportunity. One she could leverage to charge handsomely for the black gold we carefully percolated into tiny coffee cups. Espressos, Macchiatos, cappuccinos, Americanos—all the coffee drinks that ended in O required us to hire a barista, and that's where Aubrey came in. She was a single mom with two littles now, Owen and Stella, and she made a killing in tips at the bakery. Still beautiful and thin even after two pregnancies, she was the kind of girl with an insane metabolism and the type I used to loathe in high school that could eat her weight in ice cream every night without the worry of even a dimple of cellulite.

You couldn't hate Aubrey. It was physically impossible. When she hit you with one of her adorable smiles, and you focused on the smattering of freckles that dabbled across her nose, you melted. It didn't matter who you were. You were powerless against her charms. She was the classic dictionary definition of cute. I have no idea why buttons are the standard measure of adorableness, but Aubrey truly was cute as a button.

I, on the other hand, was a little fluffy. I was thicc, closer to three Cs than two, big-boned, voluptuous, a curvy girl, all those adjectives people use to dance around using the word fat. It was like my entire body was inflated. Every one of my features was bigger than everyone else's. After trying every diet pill and diet plan known to man to starve myself, and it changing nothing, I accepted the reality that I was simply destined to take up more space.

You have never been truly miserable until you have tried to stick to a low-carb diet when you work full time in a bakery. My week going keto was the longest seven days of my life. At night, I would dream about cupcakes and buttercream and wake up drooling with my stomach growling. I say a week, but it was more like forty-eight hours. Forty-eight of the longest hours I have ever endured that ended with an epic sugar binge I would be embarrassed to fully detail. Sometimes, you have to decide if the misery is worth it, and I decided it wasn't. It was evident buttercream tasted better to me than skinny ever felt.

Maybe I was a touch cynical, but I was content and deeply settled into my comfortable life. It was fate that made me a pastry chef, being born into the DeLuca family. It was also fate that brought Foster Valentine through the doors of my bakery. I wasn't looking for love when it found me. Mom always said that is exactly how it would happen. She was right.

TWO

I swear if you cut me open, pastry cream would be found running through my veins. Mom didn't even want me to go to culinary school. My ever-practical mother thought it was a waste of time and money.

"If you want to make pastry your life, you don't need to get a degree. Your father can teach you everything you need to know."

I argued and pleaded and begged, and in the end, I had to leave home to pursue my culinary degree without Mom's full blessing. At eighteen, I wanted to set out on my own path and not be only limited to the bakery. I wanted to know everything about food—the savory and the sweet, the acidic and the salty. The elusive umami. Desperate to carve out my own career away from the shadow of my family, I enrolled in culinary school.

Pops would send me care packages that made my roommates swoon, and carefully tucked into the boxes of butter cookies and lemon tartlets was always nearly fifty dollars in cash, in small denominations. It was obvious that he was secretly sending me the bounty from the tip jar without Mom's knowledge. These singles and fives were interesting to explain to the lady at the power company. She always looked me up and down when I presented her with an envelope full of them. Immediately concluding that I was not a stripper, she would quizzically stare at my body, her brain desperately trying to compute the equation in front of it. Where does this chubby honey standing in front of me earn stripper money?

After culinary school, I convinced Pops to expand into wedding cakes. I was eager to carve out my own identity at the bakery, to forge my own success instead of living on the coattails of my parents and grandparents. Armed with the facts and figures I knew I needed to win Mom over, I delivered a PowerPoint presentation that knocked their socks off, and so my parents took a gamble on my idea. My biggest win was convincing Pops to install enormous picture windows between the dining room and the kitchen to give our patrons more of an *experience*. It wasn't just the luscious smells they stood in line on the sidewalk an hour before we opened to enjoy—the savory tang of the fresh-baked, sun-dried tomato and garlic focaccia. No, they came to watch us bake and create. It was like a theater in the round. People would come for the cannolis and stay for the show. Keeping them adequately caffeinated was nearly a full-time job for Aubrey. Mom was also savvy at pushing the stacked honey-baked ham sandwiches and Nonna's famous Minestrone soup the closer it got to lunchtime.

I was booked out for a year for custom cakes, and in the most coveted Midwestern bridal month of all—June—I was contracted years in advance. My cakes were sculptural and one of a kind. They were not just something beautiful to look at, they also tasted incredible, and that was what had the phone ringing off the hook. Brides relished the craftsmanship and attention to detail, but their papas loved the way they tasted, made with farm-churned butter, stone-ground organic flour, and free-range eggs. I sourced the best ingredients on the market and paired them with perfect pastry execution, and it yielded stellar results. Marketing is easy when you combine a one-of-a-kind, world-class product with glowing testimonials. An impeccable reputation ensures your schedule will always be packed with minimal effort.

I loved being a wedding cake designer because every cake was different. It was an artistic expression, yet required thoughtful consideration of the sugary mechanics. A beautiful cake is a disaster if the structure doesn't hold up and it falls onto the floor. Engaging both sides of my brain was a skill I thrived at and something I craved. I enjoyed my work in a way that few people get the opportunity to experience, and I tried to never take that for granted. To have a vocation that you are passionate about and successful at is a dream come true and makes every day easy to roll out of bed. Work was never a chore; it was something that I was lucky to be able to do.

After work was another story. It was when the loneliness crept in. During the days, my work kept me busy and happy, but at night, there was this nagging suspicion that something was missing, a growing void that was becoming harder and harder to ignore.

That day, I was sculpting with sugar, a delicate, finicky substance that was hard to control, and fragile like glass. Sugar work mandates obsessive measuring and regulation of the temperature. Swing a few degrees one way or the other, and it's a disaster. You can end up with a sticky mess that never hardens or a form so fragile, looking at it will make it shatter.

A little gold bell tinkled when patrons entered the shop, but I had been conditioned to the jingle, and tuned it out years ago. The sound just became part of the chorus of noises and voices in the bakery and coffee shop, an under-score of warm murmurs, laughter, and cutlery on dishes. I was hyper-focused on the thermometer, dressed in chef whites, with striped black and white chef pants and black non-skid crocs. It was ugly as hell but built for comfort. My long dark hair was braided and tucked up into a hair-net, and I wore a zebra print headband. It was the only bit of personality and flair that Mom allowed me to wear because it had a purpose— hair in a pastry was the kiss of death for a bakery.

I poured the blue liquid sugar into the mold, then anxiously waited for it to set up. Patience is not a virtue I embrace. I got a little ahead of myself and pressed it out of the mold too quickly, and the thin crescent shape I was casting cracked.

"Shit," I whispered to myself and then walked out to seek comfort from Aubrey. I needed a break. Sugar work is intense and requires complete focus and patience. It will burn you out.

He walked in like he owned the place, cocky and tattooed. Caught off guard by his confidence, I felt an unexplainable surge and a noticeable energy shift in the room. Tall and thin, his hair was a blond mohawk that fanned out slightly with the tips dyed a royal blue. His scruff was very neatly trimmed, giving off an edgy rock and roll vibe. The man obviously knew his way around a razor. I've always loved scruff on a man. That yummy, dirty sexiness just makes me weak in the knees. He wasn't the kind of guy that usually saw me. Trust me, I am not whining about it, it was just the way it was. He was the type who saw girls like Aubrey.

He stood, feet planted in a wide stance, one arm wrapped around his body and his other elbow resting on his wrist as he absentmindedly stroked the scruff on his chin, analyzing the pastry case and the coffee menu. He rocked back and forth on the balls of his feet, and there was an underlying hum to him, a magnetism that I can't accurately describe, but I felt the pull toward him deep in my core. He radiated energy and excitement. Studying him, I tried to guess his age. Late twenties? Mid-thirties? There was a feistiness and fire to him that didn't exist when men got a little longer in the tooth. Closer to my age, forty knew how to beat the hell out of a man and take away his will to live. Life hadn't gotten its mitts on him that deep quite yet.

"Gionna!" Mom called, snapping me out of my dazed reverie. I shifted quickly and adjusted the front of my coat before tugging on my headband. "Aubrey is getting slammed. Step lively now and help her out." Mom was in her bakery best—white jeans with a pink DeLuca's logo t-shirt; for some reason, she insisted we all look like frosting. I had to give the woman credit, though, because she was pretty smart when it came to the business and branding. In typical teenage rebellion that I never fully outgrew, getting away with wearing black pants made me feel powerful in the way a fifteen-year-old feels when she successfully sneaks out of the house wearing too much makeup.

I walked closer to the pastry case, and his dark eyes swung to meet my icy blue ones. My eyes were by far my best feature, and I spent too much money at the salon on eyebrows and lashes. It was my one splurge, trying to play to my strengths and draw people's focus from my body to my eyes. Some of my friends were getting their first streaks of gray, but my thick coal-black hair was steadfast in its stubborn Italian heritage and refused to give up even one strand. I had a nice rack, an ample booty, and a tiny mole dotted a space between my cheek and lips, a trait made desirable by Cindy Crawford in the nineties.

He cocked his head to the side and addressed me seriously, his forehead furrowed with intensity. "Are your coffee beans fair trade?"

"Yes," I answered proudly. "All fair trade, organic, and eco-friendly." It was something Mom fought me on initially, but culinary school opened my horizons to the plight of the workers in the third world countries that harvested the beans. I forced her to watch painful video after painful video until she finally said, "Okay! Enough." And from then on, we only sourced the best gourmet coffee beans that were roasted locally from farmers who were paid a livable wage.

"I'll try a double espresso and two original cannolis."

"Great choice," I said, and then I felt like an idiot saying something so lame that my cheeks pinked up.

"Aub, can you make this gentleman a double?"

"Gentleman?" He winked at me. "I can honestly say that is the first time I have ever been accused of that." He leaned against the glass counter filled with crispy, delicate cannoli shells. His arms spread wide as he ogled the offerings.

"Looks like you and the case might need a minute alone together," I teased.

His eyebrows arched up as he grinned. "Man, what I wouldn't do to her if I got it. Former fat kid here," he said and then trailed off, thinking he offended me.

"Professional fat kid here," I joked, trying to laugh it off.

His eyes swept back to mine, and the gaze was so powerful I shifted uncomfortably.

Aubrey broke the moment, and for a second I wondered if it had even occurred at all. "Double espresso for?" She prompted him for his name, something we never asked for, so I was surprised when she did.

"Foster. Foster Valentine," he offered proudly and then turned back to me. "It's not fair that you know mine, but I don't know yours."

I stood stunned and with my mouth agape. Frozen, and unable to utter a syllable.

"Gionna," Aubrey answered for me. "Her name is Gionna, and she is an artist with pastry. This girl is making the most highly sought-after wedding cakes in all of Chicago." She enthused hiking a thumb toward me.

I flushed red again at the praise. Aubrey was always a kick-ass wing woman. Whenever I felt a little insecure or unsure of my skills, Aubrey came to the rescue, singing my praises and forcing me to believe in myself, but Aubrey could lay it on thick. And she was laying it on extra thick now.

"Well, maybe not *all* of Chicago," I mumbled humbly, feeling a rush of heat.

"Is that right?" he mused. "Can't say, being single, that I am in the market for a wedding cake, but if I hear of someone needing a cake artist, I'll be sure to pass the information on."

"Thank you." I plucked two empty cannoli shells from the case and turned away, pulling the pastry cream from the refrigerator. Hearing him declare he was single gave me an unexpected little thrill deep in my belly.

At DeLuca's, only after a customer made their selection of the cannoli shell, did we pipe in the pastry cream. One of the things Bumpo insisted on from the beginning was that no cannolis of his were ever going to be served to a customer soggy.

"Filled to order even," Foster remarked. "Brilliant!" He clapped his hands and rubbed them together excitedly. "It's those little touches and respect for the freshness of the ingredients that make the biggest difference. Chain bakeries will never understand. I love it."

My hand shook as I felt his eyes bore into my back. I tried to suck in my stomach and stand taller while warmth flushed my body.

What in the hell is going on here? Why is this guy having such an effect on me? You're being an idiot. Stop it.

Finally, I finished piping the cream into the shells and then broke off a mint leaf and added it to the recyclable cardboard container before turning around and handing it to him with a flourish.

He smiled and handed me his credit card.

Foster Valentine. He was serious. There it was, printed in bold block letters.

"Your name is...ah, unusual," I said, trying to make

small talk in a desperate attempt to draw this interaction out as long as possible.

He laughed, which made him even more irresistible. Long, straight white teeth. Full lips. My heart quickened in my chest.

"My mom is kind of a nut, a lovable nut, but a nut." He explained fondly. "I was born on Valentine's Day, if you can believe that." He laughed at himself and my heart fluttered.

"Seriously?" I asked. "Valentine's Day?"

He grinned again. "Seriously," he repeated, confirming his birthday.

"It suits you," I said and then wished I could take the words back. Pluck them from the air one by one, and swallow them whole.

What is wrong with me? What did I even mean by that? God, I'm so lame.

"Does it now?" He sounded intrigued and teasing, leaning in closer to me. His dark eyes glinted mischievously. Devilishly handsome, he was toying with me and enjoying it. I was having a hard time putting more than one thought together in front of him.

"I have no idea what I'm saying right now," I confessed.

"Ah...rendering women speechless," he bragged. "It's kind of my superpower."

"Of course it is," I answered. I was sure this kind of thing happened to him all the time. Women fawning all over themselves to get some of the white-hot spotlight of Foster Valentine's attention.

"What's yours?" He leaned in even closer to me and tapped his ear. "Don't worry, it'll be our little secret."

"I don't have one."

"Liar," he sweetly admonished me. "Everyone has one. Guess I'll have to come back to figure it out."

"Guess you will." I beamed and handed him back his credit card. He added a ten-dollar tip, scribbled his signature, and then handed the receipt back to me. I was shocked by his generosity.

"Wow. Thanks."

"You're most welcome, Gionna. It was beautiful to meet you." My name sounded more dazzling when it was formed with his tongue and lips. Three syllables birthed from his handsome mouth. Then he grabbed his coffee and cannolis and walked out of the bakery, and I swear the light dimmed and everything else paled the moment he disappeared. Foster Valentine saturated the space he inhabited with vivid technicolor and the brightest sunshine, and when he left, he took it with him. It was a phenomenon I had never seen or felt before, and if I had never met him would not even have known existed. Now that I did, I was jonesing for another hit.

THREE

Nonna was busy rolling out dough and humming to herself when I got to the bakery in the morning. The bakery was always quiet at four am. It was my favorite time of day, before the hustle and bustle of customers and the whirring and hisses from the coffee bar got started. Four am was serene and peaceful, a calm before the chaos of our morning commuter rush.

In her glory days, Nonna was Luciana, a buxom dark-haired Marilyn Monroe look-alike. She had the kind of silicone-free curves that songs were written about and wars were fought over. Half of a century later, Nonna was short and square. Glasses sat on her round, upturned nose tethered to a crystal lanyard that she never used since she wore them all the time. I once asked her why she wore the lanyard at all, and she said sometimes a girl just needs a little sparkle. On her fourth finger was an enormous diamond, the one Bumpo bought her right after he was diagnosed with cancer. You could have knocked me over with a feather when he presented it to her on one knee the

Christmas before he passed, asking her to marry him again. After we helped him get back on his feet—kneeling is *not* for the elderly—we all stood in shock with mouths agape at this over-the-top extravagance. No one was more stunned than Nonna, who pressed her hands to her chest, and with tears in her eyes, nodded yes. He burst into an adorable rendition of the Beatles classic, *Lucy in the Sky with Diamonds*, dancing her around their living room. They could still glide on a dance floor, arthritis and all.

He went quickly, so fast it was mere weeks from the diagnosis to the funeral. Before he passed, I asked why he did it, and he said, "I need to see my Luci sparkle from my cloud in heaven." Thinking about it now gives me chills. That's what true love is supposed to be.

I loved to page through their old photo albums at home. Seeing Nonna and Bumpo in their glory days, they were charismatic, dark-haired beauties. Nonna had quite a body on her back in the day. The women in my family are very blessed in the mammary department. Myself included, and I played up that asset often, knowing that boys loved boobs and were willing to overlook many other flaws if you had a nice set of tits.

Tits. I always hated that word. Nonna's had been flattened by gravity and likely were wrangled into place only by her thick, strappy cotton brassieres. Nonna had a sharp wit and a dirty mind, but she was old enough that she had completely stopped caring about what other people thought. She would say whatever came to mind with zero filter. Nonna made me snort coffee out of my nose more than once, and I cherished our time together at the bakery in the mornings before Pops came stumbling in with Mom before the morning rush.

"Nonna, do you think I will ever find someone who will love me like Bumpo loved you?" The question surprised even me, shining an uncomfortable spotlight on the fact that maybe I wasn't as content as I convinced myself I was.

She continued to roll the dough into thin, perfect circles. Her thick fingers moving swiftly, she dusted the surface with a handful of flour by flicking her wrist above it. Her fingers flew through the task, nimble and dexterous, from all those years of rolling heavy wooden pins at the bakery and squeezing out pastry cream between layers of delicate petit fours. Her knuckles were gnarled and bumpy from arthritis, but it never slowed her down and she never complained.

"Yes, *Mia Bella*. Once in a lifetime, every person gets a chance to find a perfect love. The key is to be prepared for when it shows up and to recognize it when it does." She launched into a story to illustrate her point that I had already heard a million times, but I treated like it was brand new every time she told it. These were little concessions I made to make Nonna happy. It was such a small price to pay for a woman who lit up every time she laid eyes on me.

It was a parable, where the man readied himself to receive the king, who was to come and dine. Three times, a person knocked at the door, and each time he refused them and sent them away. It was supposed to teach you the lesson that what you are asking for might show up at your door one day, looking nothing like you thought it would. A good lesson, but one that I had committed to memory the first dozen times I'd heard it.

She scattered more flour over the marble work surface,

which had been installed to Bumpo's exact specifications decades ago and brought over from the old country. "You are so beautiful. You deserve a man who spoils you with his time and attention." Nonna always saw me as perfect. "When was the last time you had relations?"

I blushed.

"It's the most natural thing in the world, *Mia Bella.* You have to get the poison out." She winked at me, her dark eyes glinting mischievously.

I snorted. The poison.

"I do okay, Nonna," I said, then thought about that statement. Actually, I'd been in a significant man drought for a while now. When I wanted to get laid, it was easy. I could always find a willing partner. The problem was that they seemed to get clingy afterward, which I could never stand. So, I was on hiatus. Not looking, not needing, just focused on work.

"A woman has needs. She is like a flower ready to bloom." She looked me over. "You are bursting with femininity, *Mia Bella.* Surely, there is someone who can tend to you."

Tend to you.

The concept was laughable. Most men I met couldn't even tend to themselves, let alone had enough effort left over to tend to a woman.

"You know there is a matchmaker that can find you a strong Italian boy."

Italian boys were the worst. So much bravado and machismo crammed into their DNA. Jersey Shore wasn't as far off base as people thought. Although depicted in a caricature style, there were glimmers of accuracy woven through it. Italian men were notoriously flirty and possessive, and they were very concerned about appearances. It was more than a little off-putting, and so I steered clear.

"Or a beautiful Italian *girl*, if that is what you are into."

"Nonna!" I chastised her, laughing at her audacity.

"What? There is no judgment here. I just want to see you happy."

"I'm definitely into men," I said and shook my head at her, then walked away. Definitely. And then his face popped up as I again walked through our painfully awkward interaction yesterday in my mind, this time rewriting the dialogue and gestures to something sexier and wittier. As I pulled out the cake pans to begin baking the cakes, my mind wandered as my fingers worked on autopilot.

Where was Foster right now? What was he doing? Who was he doing it with? And the most important question of all, when would I see him again?

FOUR

Foster Valentine intrigued me, and his scruffy good looks popped into my brain more than I would ever want to admit. It had been a minute since I'd had a crush. That's what I thought it was at first, just a childish infatuation; at least, that is the story I told myself.

Across the room, Aubrey made the after-commuter rush rounds to warm up our customers' coffees, lingering at the table of a not unattractive muscled bald man. He reached out to touch her arm, and my eyes narrowed. I was overprotective of my girl and wary of anyone who came into her life. My interest piqued when Aubrey threw her head back and laughed, then returned to the pastry case and began filling it with the last of our daily treats. Perfect rows of red macaroons, chocolate-dipped cannolis, and frosted sugar cookies remained. In two hours, the case would only contain crumbs.

I took a sip of espresso and pointed my pinky at the guy she had been talking to. "Who's the beefcake?"

"Beefcake? I hadn't noticed," she said, trying to play it off, but I knew better.

"Liar!" I sweetly chided her.

"Okay, fine, according to societal standards of beauty, he could probably be considered *mildly* attractive." She reasoned. "His name is Tony. He found us on *Trip Advisor* and has visited twice this week already." She grinned a grin that revealed he might be more than just your average customer.

"Looks like he doesn't just come here for the cannolis."

"What do you mean?" she asked innocently.

"I'm pretty sure that man wants to sample *you*."

"Nah." She waved it off and abruptly changed subjects, turning the conversation back to me. "You've been quiet all morning. What are you daydreaming about over there?" Aubrey was the queen of calling me out, and I both loved and hated her for it.

"Nothing much," I said, trying to duck her scrutiny. The bell rang at the door, and I scanned the customer coming in. My heart leapt in my chest a little each time, hoping to see Foster Valentine strolling through the door again.

"Hmm," she said, wrapping the apron strings around her waist twice before tying them tight. "If I had to guess, I would say it's that boy you met yesterday. He was into you big time."

"No, he wasn't," I argued, but part of me was secretly praying what she said was true.

"I'm pretty adept at picking up clues from the male species, and he definitely was flirting with you."

"He probably does that with everyone. You know, the

type that skates through life on his charisma and charm," I said cynically.

"I do," she confirmed. "That type has impregnated me more than once." She declared laughing at herself.

"At least, you have two of the sweetest kids to show for it."

"True. And I wouldn't change that for the world." She tossed the dark brown coffee beans into the grinder, and it whirred loudly, pulverizing the beans down to a fine grate. Then she tapped the powdery grounds into a pristine filter on the machine and pressed the button to percolate. Almost instantly, the aroma of fresh dark roast coffee filled the air; it was one of my favorite scents in the entire world. I closed my eyes and inhaled deeply, not hearing the door bell tinkle.

"Sleeping on the job again, I see," a warm voice called out, and my eyes snapped open.

"One taste and you're addicted, I see," I shot back flirtatiously, unable to stop a huge goofy smile from spreading across my face that was already starting to flush with warmth.

He pressed his hand to his heart. "The first step is to admit you have a problem. And I am man enough to do that." He held up his right hand solemnly. "My name is Foster Valentine, and I am an espresso addict."

Aubrey sauntered over and took his coffee order. He stopped to address her quickly, but his voice changed. With Aubrey, he was all business. He was always polite, but the teasing tone was removed; his flirty banter with her was nonexistent. Sensing that shift surged unexplainable joy through me. I was used to interactions with boys going the opposite direction. They were usually chatty and flirty with Aubrey, and cool and business-like with me.

He studied the pastry case. "I am going to have to work my way through your menu, so you should plan on seeing me every day for the foreseeable future."

My heart leapt with joy at his declaration. Every day? Now, *that* was something to look forward to.

"Do you live around here?" I asked conversationally as I pulled out a fresh kraft brown container and waited for him to order.

"Are you angling for an invite to my place already?" He waggled his eyebrows as a smirk slid across his features.

I shook my head at his foolishness and laughed at his antics. "No," I insisted, lying to us both.

"I just got out of culinary school and landed a sous chef job down the street at The Ivy."

"That's awesome," I replied, instantly regretting my choice of phrase that made me sound like a hormonal teeny-bopper.

That's awesome? That's all you've got? My usual sparkling wit and personality were seriously lacking in the presence of Foster Valentine. But in my defense, it *was* awesome because it gave us mutual interests and a common ground.

Aubrey appeared with his coffee cup wrapped in a thick warmer band with our logo on it.

"Thank you." He grabbed the cup from her hand and then turned right back to me.

"What can I get you?" I asked.

"Well, that is a loaded question," he teased, his eyes twinkling with amusement. "How about you surprise me?"

I studied the case and then picked three different cannoli shells and a slice of flaky baklava. Pops wasn't Greek, but the baklava tasted like he was, and it was proclaimed the best in the city by more than one restaurant critic. I turned my back to him and pulled out the pastry cream. My eye caught Nonna's, who had suddenly stopped working and was completely engrossed in watching my interaction with Foster through the plate glass window while she nibbled on a biscotti. She nodded like she was giving permission and winked with a little shoulder shimmy that made me giggle out loud.

"What's so funny?" Foster asked, oblivious to what she was doing.

"Nonna is what's funny," I said, turning back toward him with the takeout bag in my hand.

"Is that your grandmother?"

"I think that's the technical term, but she's the least grandmotherly person you'll ever meet."

"I'd *love* to meet her," he stated.

"I don't think you're ready for all of that," I admitted. "She's an acquired taste."

He laughed. "You are so lucky to be surrounded by a family like this."

"Not sure if lucky is the right word," I joked. My family was loud and boisterous and always digging around in my life, but they always meant well.

He handed me his credit card and left another amazing tip. "See you tomorrow, Gionna DeLuca."

"Can't wait, Foster Valentine." I smiled and watched him walk away, admiring his crisp chef whites and the way his shoulders filled out the chef coat. He was thin but sinewy, probably strong as an ox, but he didn't look it.

"Guuurrlllll." Aubrey dragged the word out so it went on forever. "That man is so into you." She sidled up, putting her arm across my broad shoulders.

"Nah. He's just a flirt who's addicted to our pastry cream."

"How about we make this interesting? A little wager, perhaps?"

"What do you have in mind?"

"If I'm right, Auntie Gionna watches my lovable little demons for a weekend. If I'm wrong, then I will come organize your closet."

Her offer *was* interesting. My walk-in closet was jam packed and should be featured on *Hoarders*—it was where clothing went to die. Because my weight had fluctuated so much for so many years, I stored full wardrobes in it from size 10 to size 22.

I offered my hand. "You have a deal."

Let's just say, Auntie Gionna had to pay up. Aubrey was right.

FIVE

Once each month, I had a long-standing dinner date with Pops. Mom's palate wasn't as adventurous as ours, so she usually opted to enjoy a simple night alone at home with a glass of wine and a bubble bath instead. Tonight, we were trying out the new Indian restaurant called Curry Casa. We walked into the most magical cumin and marsala infused air, making my stomach growl instantly. Hiram, the owner, welcomed Dad warmly and escorted us to a table with an orange linen tablecloth, insisting his chef had something special for us to try.

"Bravo!" Dad clapped his hands together, excited to be a culinary guinea pig. Trying new places and new foods was thrilling for us both, and it gave us a chance to catch up outside of the bakery. Even though I saw him every day, it was these dinners where I had his complete focused attention that I cherished and looked forward to.

Pops always ordered enough food for seven people, a fact he hid carefully from my mom, paying with cash and sending me home with most of the leftovers. He always loved to try multiple menu items and would take iPhone photos of each dish and write up very long and detailed accounts of his dining experience that he would faithfully post on Yelp. Dad was an honest reviewer but understood that a restaurant could have an off night. So, if he didn't have anything good to say, he just chose not to return rather than gleefully bash a fellow business owner on social media. He only reviewed places he adored, and because of this fact, had built a network of restaurateurs who loved him and treated us like gold everywhere we went.

First up was an appetizer plate with Mirchi Pakora, hot peppers that had been battered and then fried, and garlicky naan coated liberally with cilantro. People either love or hate cilantro, and I was firmly in the love it camp. Even going so far as to put a little in my beer sometimes if I was feeling particularly frisky. Hiram also brought over an order of poori, softball-sized airy bread that was completely hollow inside. I tore into the pillows of air and dragged their crispy fried edges through a dipping sauce that tasted of spicy yogurt and peppers. The cool dipping sauce and the crispy dough provided a lovely textural contrast I savored.

"You seem so preoccupied lately," Pops said as he stuffed his cheeks with the chicken pakora that Hiram brought next to the table.

I took another couple of bites of the peppers and smiled up at him.

"Gionna." He waggled a finger at me. "You are hiding something. I know you." He smiled.

"I do not know what you speak of, Father," I denied, laughing at him. I only called him Father ironically. As far as I was concerned, there was nothing substantial to report yet. I met a cute boy, that was all.

Thankfully, Hiram appeared at the table again, and I was able to wiggle out of his sweet interrogation. He was dressed in traditional Hindi kurta pajama and waited patiently with a pad and paper to take our order.

"We will start with half of a tandoori chicken and the shish kebabs, goat curry, and shrimp vindaloo."

Hiram nodded his head eagerly. "You have made excellent choices," he confirmed in his melodic lilting voice.

"Hiram, I bet you say that to all the guys," I teased.

He bowed deeply and smiled again. I have always loved Indian culture because there's a calm countenance that runs through their veins that is vastly different from most Americans' frenetic energy. I don't know if it is their beliefs in karma and the afterlife, but for whatever reason, they are sweet, kind, and gentle people.

We waited patiently for our dinner to come while we shared a bottle of Cabernet Sauvignon. I smelled the cork while Pops swished the wine around his glass, deeply inhaled its burgundy loveliness, and then took a generous sip from it. He turned his warm eyes back to me and pulled my hands into his on the table. Ever since I could remember, we had begun hundreds of father-daughter dates like this, my hands warmed by his substantial palms with long, tapered fingers. It is a nurturing ritual that instantly calms me down—the poor woman's Prozac.

"Are you happy?" Pops asked the question like he always did. It was the same one our dinners always began with.

"Happy enough," I answered. "You have given me a

great life. I have fulfilling work that I enjoy and am surrounded by people who love me. To ask for anything more seems greedy."

He squeezed my hands. "That is true." He paused quietly before continuing. "But something is missing."

"What do you mean?"

"Your heart is still closed off," he said gently.

"Where is Hiram with our food?" I asked, anxiously laughing off his intensity, my neck flushing and becoming itchy under his scrutiny.

"It's been a long time," he continued.

"I know, Dad. I have finally gotten to a place where I feel like I am going to be okay on my own."

"That's good. Brett left your heart scarred and broken, and you needed time to heal it." He stroked the back of my hand and continued. "You have done that, *Bellissima*." He always used my childhood nickname at times like these. "But now, don't you think it might be time to take another chance?"

I pulled my hands out of his, narrowed my eyes, and pursed my lips in mock protest "Wait a second… I see what's happening here. I am on to you, old man. You are trying to butter me up for information. Mom put you up to this, didn't she?"

He smiled sheepishly, and his cheeks pinked up a little. "Your mother loves you and just wants you to be happy."

"I know that."

"She is worried about you being alone."

"Alone?" I laughed. "I have you and Mom and Nonna and Aubrey and Stella and Owen. I am *never* alone. My life is literally packed to the gills with people," I explained, trying to convince him, but my words sounded hollow even to my own ears. "It's better to be alone than trapped in the wrong relationship."

"That is true."

"You spoiled me. Having a father like you, the bar is set really high for any man, and I've found that most of them don't want to make the effort."

He sighed.

"I don't think the kind of old-fashioned forever love that you and Mom have and Nonna and Bumpo had is out there waiting for me."

"Be careful what you say, *Bellissima*. You will always find what you believe. Don't limit what life wants to give you with your own thoughts."

"You might have a point," I finally admitted, taking the time to square the napkin in my lap before continuing. "But every time I put my heart out there, it gets stomped on. Eventually, you have to stop the self-abuse."

"Love is always a risk," he agreed, "but when you find the right partner, it is a risk worth taking."

"That is so easy for you to say. You and Mom found each other in high school. My Prince Charming seems to be running about two decades late," I teased him. "Besides, I am not some weak-minded maiden who needs saving. I have a life that I fought for—that I'm proud of. At the moment, I am not sure how much space I have in it for anyone else."

He nodded in understanding, then clapped his hands together to signal the end of the interrogation. He always knew how to impart wisdom and then let it go instead of beating me up with it. I sipped thoughtfully on the wine and swished it around with my tongue, carefully considering his words.

I studied the fine black hairs that covered his forearms and the gold bracelet that had been Bumpo's and now ringed his wrist. My dad was one of the good guys, and at that moment, it hit me just how amazing he was. With childlike glee on his face, he popped a fried pepper into his mouth. They were starting to make me break out in sweat along my hairline, but Pops was eating them like they were candy.

Bollywood music cued up, and I heard little finger cymbals first. A trio of belly dancers sauntered into the room, making figure eights with their hips and shaking their bellies. In and out, their abdomens sucked in concave and then rolled rhythmically reptilian. Long, orange silk scarves ran from their fingertips to the floor, and a beautiful dark-haired beauty came and offered Dad the end of her scarf. Ever the ham, he got up from his chair and proceeded to follow her into a train as the other dancers each pulled someone from the surrounding tables. The music swelled and their hips were shaking and gyrating, and Pops was belly laughing, in his element, enjoying being part of the show. He always loved a stage. Five minutes later, he returned to his seat, a light sheen of sweat coated his face from the effort, and a huge smile was on his face.

"You better not tell your mother I did that," he joked. He never hid anything from Mom; she would just roll her eyes and throw her hands up in the air like, *What are you going to do? Men will be men.*

I got a little courage and said, "Can I ask you something, Dad?"

"Of course, *Bellissima.*"

"You and Mom seem so different. How does it even work?"

"It's not about finding someone that is exactly like you. It's finding someone you can't live without, that pushes you to be better than you ever were by yourself." He took my hands in his again. "Look for a partner in every sense of the word. You have to be a team, pulling toward the same goals, working toward the same reality." His thumbs brushed across the backs of my hands, and I didn't dare interrupt him because I wanted to understand.

"The bakery was not my dream. It was Bumpo's, but with hard work and dedication, Lorraine and I made it our dream. Your mom is amazing at marketing the bakery. We have seen such growth since she's taken over. I'm really proud of her," he gushed, his dark eyes crinkling at the corners. There was a hint of the handsome boy he had been tucked into his deeply lined face that was softening in the last few years. Recently, the white at his temples had increased dramatically, and his hairline was receding further backward every year. It was a follicle battle that was fought and surrendered pore by pore.

"And I'm really proud of you, too, Gionna. I know at first, we fought you on the wedding cakes and didn't think that it would be a worthwhile pursuit, but it has paid off handsomely. You are so much like your mother. So smart. People come from all around to see and taste your cakes." He was bursting with pride. It made me puff up a little at his remark, and I felt tears prickle at the corner of my eyes. Pops was a sentimental man, the kind of guy that wore his heart on his folded-up sleeves. It was one of the things I loved most about him.

"Did you know our custom cake commissions are up

twenty-two percent this year?" I bragged excitedly. It felt incredibly validating to find success on my own, and I bathed in the warm glow of my father's pride. "Knowing you are proud of me fills me with such joy. So, yes, Pops, I would say I *am* happy, after all."

"Cheers to my brilliantly talented and beautiful daughter." He held his glass up to toast, and I reached across the table to tap mine to his.

Hiram appeared with a cart loaded with all our selections. The basmati rice was a beige cloud to soak up the spicy richness of all the other flavors—garam masala, curry, mint, yogurt. All the exotic spices crescendoed in a symphony in my mouth. Pops scooped up thick, fragrant chunks of chicken with slivers of naan he ripped apart using the naan as a makeshift shovel. He'd close his eyes and savor each bite slowly, letting it linger on his tongue, and then joy would break out across his face. He was a man who knew how to devour life. He never rushed but took great pleasure in food that was beautifully prepared and served with a flourish.

"How lucky are we?" he asked me, then refilled my wine glass, always making sure I got the last strong pour left in the bottle before dribbling the bottom dregs into his. He had a servant's heart. Pops had ruined me, teaching me that there were men out there who were kind and generous beings with huge hearts. When you grow up with a dad like mine, it changes everything.

SIX

The next morning, my neck got whiplash from checking the door. Every time the bell tinkled, I swung around hoping to see Foster Valentine walking through it. Like Pavlov's dog, the jingle made me practically salivate in anticipation. This out-of character behavior was very distracting, and Pops was the first to take notice.

"Hmm. Why all the sudden interest in who's coming through the door, G?" His teasing voice was deep and warm like sitting in the sun.

"Just waiting for my next appointment."

"Of course." He smiled a small knowing smile, winked at Nonna, and continued to braid the dough. Cracking an egg into a ramekin, he scrambled it with a whisk, swirled a silicone brush through the egg wash, and painted it across the top of the buns.

My eyes wandered over to the table where Stella and Owen were coloring quietly. They were often in the background, Aubrey's sweet kids that I loved like my own. I pulled two fresh sugar cookies from the case and walked them over to the kids whose eyes lit up when they saw my offering. Spending time with Auntie G was any kids' fantasy, because I found endless ways to sneak them treats.

I sat down next to Stella, who handed me a red crayon and pointed to a place I was allowed to color.

"Thank you, my love," I said, kissing the top of her head. "It looks like you got a couple more angel kisses overnight." I snuggled closer and touched two freckles that I didn't remember seeing the last time I played this game with her.

"What are their names?" she asked, her little voice sweetly spellbound that I made the effort to name every freckle on her face.

"Esmerelda and Gordy," I said and then kissed her cheek in the exact place I knew she was the most ticklish.

She giggled and squirmed away, which only made me hug her tighter and blow a raspberry in the last remnants of soft baby skin that was disappearing on her neck. "You think you can get away from me?" I teased and swooped in to blow another raspberry.

A miniature Aubrey, Stella had tiny features, warm eyes that were slightly too close together, and a smattering of freckles across the bridge of her nose. At four, she was the youngest and the sweetest.

Owen was more serious. He had seen some dark things in his short life, and a few of the guys Aubrey dated had left a mark. He was an old soul, much more mature than his seven years, and incredibly protective of his mother. He observed everything, endlessly keeping track, ever watchful, and with a maturity that made most adults uncomfortable. It was a coping skill that was carefully crafted from painful lessons learned at the hands of strange men. His brown hair was thick, and his glasses made him appear owl-like.

"O, I made your favorite," I sang out, sliding the plate of cookies closer to him and waiting for a response. It seemed like he was always afraid to show his cards, and as a result, he kept so much of himself hidden. His first few years on the planet had taught him one thing—do not show too much excitement or glee because when you do, bad people take things away. "Come on, buddy. Auntie G is gonna need a smile."

He rewarded me with a silly grin, showcasing two gaping holes where his front teeth should be. They had been knocked out on the pavement when he was a three after an angry push from a man Aubrey was living with. That night was seared into my soul, Owen's face covered in blood and his hair sweaty from screaming, and Aubrey sobbing as I drove them to the hospital in our delivery van. It was a secret that I shared with Mom and Pops. I wasn't one to break confidences typically, but it was obvious that Aubrey needed some back-up. She needed my support and that of my family if she was truly going to make it on her own without a man. She kicked him out, and from that day on, Owen and Stella joined us at the bakery.

It turned out to be a win-win all around. Mom and Pops got the grandchildren they were never going to get from me. The wounded, empty desperation left Mom's eyes when Owen and Stella started hanging out at the bakery every day while Aubrey worked. They were sweet kids who never asked for much and easily folded into our daily lives. Nonna would bring Stella into the kitchen, tie a little apron she had sewn for her around her waist, and teach her how to cut out sugar cookie shapes. Pops loved to teach Owen how to use the scale to weigh the flour and how to run the commercial mixers with the bowls so large he could almost hide inside when we played hide and go seek.

The bell tinkled again. This time, a platinum blonde who had to be my prospective bride walked through it, giving my cover story a little more weight. She strode in, her stilettos tapping a morse code across our maple floors in a cloud of Chanel, with ivory hair in a huge back-combed halo. Dripping with large diamond studs that matched the three-carat stone on her finger, she was tiny and perfect, like a walking Barbie doll dragging a gorilla man behind her. It was always amazing to me when a woman was able to wrap a man like that around her finger. He was at her beck and call, killing himself to please her, effectively proving civilization didn't evolve as far forward from the caveman days as we once thought.

"Amara and Christopher?" I called out, looking at my clipboard. It was the day I did wedding consultations and tastings. Wedding season in Chicago runs high and hot, May through October. I'm booked every Friday and Saturday during the season and spend all week knee-deep in gum paste and edible glitter. November to April is a manageable two to three events each month that allows me time to recharge. I was getting close to wrapping up another successful wedding season and having some extra time on the weekends to myself.

Brides were a fickle and funny bunch, sometimes

reduced to demanding shrews that were power-drunk on their Daddy's money. You almost needed a Ph.D. in psychology to figure them out. It was a love-hate relationship. Although most of my brides I adored so much they practically became friends, there were a couple each year that were difficult and impossible to please. No matter what feat of sugar wizardry you were able to pull off, it just wasn't good enough. I didn't want to jump to conclusions, but I was picking up early signals that Amara was falling into the second camp.

"That's me," Amara declared, an off-hand comment that accidentally revealed that this wedding *was* all about her. During consultations I took my cues from the bride, gathering intel to help me win her over. I settled them into the small tasting room that was adjacent to the kitchen.

"Can I get you a coffee or anything to drink?" I asked her, trying to break the ice.

"Yes, please. A non-fat coconut milk cappuccino and an espresso for him." She waved at Christopher with the back of one hand while she tapped out a text, not making eye contact. I briefly wondered if he *could* speak or if he was mute.

As I walked out of the tasting room, my heart dropped. Foster had just walked in the door, and I was going to miss the opportunity for an interaction with him. He would have the chance to become smitten with Aubrey, and I would likely lose him forever.

He smiled at me, his face extra cute and extra scruffy today. It made his warm brown eyes pop even more, and I felt my heart pang with jealousy that I wouldn't get to talk to him. The disappointment surged through me. I gave him a small wave and then brought the drinks back to my couple. On the table was a thick pink binder that Amara was rifling through, containing pages and pages of cake ideas torn from magazines. She pushed the binder over to me, and I flipped through the pages, but none of the designs were consistent or cohesive or gave me even a hint as to what she wanted. They were all over the place, pristine white and deep, dark chocolate. Oodles of flowers and minimalistic gold leaf. I paged through the entire cake section of her binder and then smiled at her and slid it back. She had obviously been planning this wedding since she was seven, decades before Pinterest, just waiting for the right guy to show up.

"Let's talk about your event." I pulled out my notes with a smile. "Give me an idea of your style and what kind of wedding you are planning."

"I just did," she said, tapping the binder.

I nodded. "Those visuals are *very* helpful, and I appreciate the time you've taken to compile them. You have impeccable taste!" I was pandering to her, but you had to. Brides were some of the most sensitive people on the planet. "I have so many ideas, in fact, I need a bit more information to drill down exactly what you are really looking for. Is your event formal or casual?"

"Formal, at St. John's Cathedral."

"Can you describe your dress?"

She glanced over at a bored Christopher then leaned in conspiratorially closer. With one hand, she covered her mouth and spoke in a hushed tone. "Traditional and long with lots of sparkle. Champagne colored. White doesn't work with my skin tone."

I glanced at Christopher, who was so engrossed in his

phone, not even paying attention to the description at all. He was a statue in a chair tuning us out completely.

"Does your event have a theme?"

"Winter Wonderland." She proudly declared.

"And your wedding date is *June 14th*?" I asked, emphasizing the last three syllables, shocked the irony of the statement was completely lost on her.

"Yes." She gushed, "I know it's unusual and unique, but I adore the winter. I just didn't want to take the risk of having my event get ruined by an ice storm. So, Mom and I were talking... and brainstorming... and it just came to us." She spread her arms out wide and high as she transformed herself into an evangelical preacher. "Winter Wonderland." She paused for effect and looked at me, waiting for a reaction of awed reverence. I just couldn't lower myself enough to give it to her, so she continued. "Everyone is going to be talking about this wedding forever. We might even be featured on *The Knot*. That would bring a lot of publicity to your little bakery."

I bristled at the term little, but being featured on *The Knot* was something that made me salivate. It could literally guarantee massive overnight success if my cake was breathtaking enough. With a feature on the *The Knot*, the top wedding blogs would come calling, and I could name my price and handpick my clients.

"What are the wedding colors?"

"Ice blue and silver."

And will Elsa be appearing at the reception and belting out Let it Go?

I pinched my lips together to prevent that question from slipping out. My mouth could be big and unpredictable, like the rest of me.

Pulling out my sketch pad, I started tracing out a tiered traditional cake stacked high with thick swatches of cascading crystals in between the cake layers. I added extensive snowflakes and edible glitter. It took me several minutes, and then I turned it toward Amara. "This is what I am thinking. A traditional fondant cake with extensive sugar work. I'll create handmade snowflakes and peonies and dust them with edible glitter and sparkly sugar. The snowflakes will spill down the cake, spiraling down into a cluster around the base of it. I'll hand paint the fondant a metallic icy blue that fades to white, giving the cake tons of sparkle and shine from any direction it is viewed. In between the layers will be rows and rows of crystals, back-lit to maximize sparkle, add height, and increase the wow factor."

"It's so beautiful." Amara clapped her hands. "Ooh! I have an idea!" she exclaimed. "When we cut into the top layer, would it be possible to create the effect of diamonds spilling out?"

"That's really challenging because texture and moisture become a major issue with sugar work. I don't like to tell my brides no, so let me do some tests and see what I can come up with." I thought some more. "We could suspend it from a cake swing, covered in crystals and draped in icicles. It would look like it was floating; it's a very theatrical presentation."

Her drama queen eyes widened in response as her dark red lips curved up into a smile. "Yes! Oh my God. I love that idea."

"I'll need to coordinate with your wedding planner to get the necessary structure in place."

"Of course." She nodded.

"We could also create cake pops that coordinate and a bar of other winter wonderland inspired treats. Think icy blue macaroons and white sugar cookies frosted in edible pearls and your colors. It could be an entire dessert experience for your guests."

"Yes!" She exclaimed. "That's exactly what I want. An *experience*."

I started to assemble a custom cake quote.

"You know, I don't offer this option to every bride that walks in the door, but you seem to be planning a once in a lifetime event." I leaned closer to her and watched her eyes widen in excitement. "We could create a custom cake flavor for you. Kind of like custom cocktails, but in cake form." I smiled, adding just the right modicum of detached excitement. Custom and discerning were the words to Amara's heart.

"Ooh, I like the sound of that," Amara eagerly agreed.

"It would require a couple more tastings to get it just right, but when you want your wedding cake to be talked about long after it's gone, I would highly recommend going this route. I reserve this option for our most prestigious clientele only, and because of the extra labor required, it's limited to the first ten commissions of the year."

"We have to have that!" Amara's eyes flashed. "Right, Christopher?" The word prestigious revved her up like I knew it would. I inherited Nonna's gift for reading people, and in business, it was a huge advantage.

He grunted in an ambiguous response that I couldn't decide was positive or negative.

"Let's taste some flavors," I offered, and hearing that, Christopher perked right up and finally roared to life. Until then, he had just been a husky lump of masculinity filling a chair. I walked into the kitchen and pulled out the cake plate I had prepared this morning with all of our flagship flavors and icing options. I set it on top of a silver tray with long crystals, knowing she would fall in love with the presentation. I added a little glittery crystalized sugar to the plate for extra glitz. With a chick like Amara, there was no such thing as too much sparkle.

Aubrey appeared at my side with a post-it note in her hand. "You missed Mr. Handsome."

"What do you mean?"

"Don't play innocent with me, G."

"Fine, he's mildly attractive," I mumbled while I arranged the red velvet and champagne flavors on my plate.

"Then I guess you don't want this." Her hazel eyes flashed as she dangled a loose sticky note in her hand.

"What's that?" I licked a drop of buttercream from my thumb coyly and then washed and dried my hands again.

"Just seven little numbers Foster Valentine asked me to give to you."

"No way," I said as a little giddy thrill crept up my insides, flushing me from the inside out.

"Way," she answered with a grin.

"I thought I would have lost my chance with him forever when your sweet ass walked into his field of view."

"He only has eyes for you," Aubrey stated. "Got to give it to him, the man has good taste."

She handed me the note and walked back out front, the swinging door opening and closing in her wake.

Six words were scrawled on a pale yellow note: "I

need to ask you something" along with his number. I studied his handwriting looking for clues. It was scribbled quickly, each letter was a deep slash carved into the paper.

I smiled and tucked it away in the pocket of my chef's coat. Suddenly, this day and this meeting got a lot more tolerable.

SEVEN

After work, I began my two-minute commute home. I lived above the bakery. So, each day at three pm, I turned off the lights, closed the shop, and crept up the creaky stairs lit by a single yellow incandescent bulb on a long chain. The apartment was my refuge when, three years ago, I had to swallow my pride and come home with my tail between my legs after my engagement ended. I was grateful I had a place to land and get myself together; I know many other women aren't as lucky. The best part about living above the bakery was that, if insomnia struck, I could sneak downstairs and roll out gum paste flowers for a few hours. The busier my career got, the more sense it made to settle into the apartment permanently instead of taking on the extra expense incurred from renting and commuting.

I loved my neighborhood in the heart of what used to be Little Italy so much that it started to feel like home to me. There were a few restaurants and shops like ours that survived the colleges sprouting up around us like weeds in the seventies. The building has been in my family for generations, and I am pretty sure Nonna and Bumpo went at it on the old furniture that used to fill the apartment by the way she longingly gazed at it when I told her I wanted to redecorate. I didn't have the stomach to test out that theory with a blue light; some things you just can't unsee, and I had no desire to be scarred for life.

The front door had been coated in about forty layers of paint. From time to time, depending on the level of humidity and how long the ovens had been on in our kitchen below, the door would stick and I had to kick the bottom corner to open it. My floors sloped and felt spongey in certain areas, like any property that is over a century old, and was probably filled with ghosts if you believe in that sort of thing, but to me, it was easy and free. Allowing me to live cheap and funnel most of my money into a mutual fund that was as temperamental and moody as a hormonal prom queen.

Two large picture windows let in warm swatches of light in the living area and overlooked Taylor Street. Loft style, the apartment had a lot of the original architectural charm intact—exposed ductwork and rich warm bricks that covered one wall of drafty original windows topped with leaded glass. I lovingly caulked them every winter to stop Pops from moving forward with his renovation plans. They were just too beautifully flawed to give up on, shooting rainbows of prisms to the floors and ceilings in the morning sun. Old paint-covered radiators lined the living room, and in the winter, I would warm my down comforter on them before slipping into bed.

I loved the apartment. Even though it was on the small side, it contained everything I adored. After reading Marie

Kondo's book, I sparked joy all over my place, but I had to draw the line at talking to my t-shirts. With the exception of the disaster that was my walk-in closet, everything was neat and orderly. I bought into her advice that it all had to have a place or it had to go. I had a few well cared for houseplants, was recovering from an addiction to air plants that I suspended from glass globes with fishing line in my windows, and my sofa was covered in pillows and thick, hand spun chenille throws. Sinking into them at night was like getting a hug at the end of a long day.

I walked past the shelves with the layers of family photos that I carefully curated in colorful hand-carved frames. Bringing home dusty flea market finds, I would lovingly transform them with pops of lime green and turquoise, hot pink and purple. I loved picking through vintage shops and antique stores for unique picture frames. Then I would cover them in bright colors and insert a photo of someone I loved. Superstitious to the end, I always touched a couple of them every time I walked by as a good luck token to remind me where I came from. From his place on the shelf, Bumpo smiled up at me, his craggy face lit up with a toothy smile. Mom and Dad's wedding photo in all its late seventies faded glory rested there, shiny and happy, a vision of two hopeful kids in love.

I turned on the gas burner and put a panful of salted water on the stove. It was a Cacio e Pepe kind of night. I pulled the sticky note out of my pocket and studied it for a second. The old school way he formed his A's, taking the extra time to draw the curvy line and then a loop at the bottom was endearing. It was the same way Bumpo made his A's on the old school order forms we used to use in the bakery before we embraced technology. I sighed and set it on the countertop. Everything in me wanted to call, but I hesitated and second-guessed it. Should I wait, make it look like I lived a vibrant, busy life? The note sat there mocking me while I weighed all the options in my head. Do I wait an hour, a day, a week? Would it look desperate if I called before five? Would he even be off work? I pulled a bottle of Prosecco out of the refrigerator and uncorked it, watching the bubbles break free from the glass bottom and rush to the surface.

"Alexa, play my Nonna playlist."

The big band music struck up and filled the silence with blasting trumpets and moody saxophones. These were the songs that made up the background track of my childhood. Vivid memories of Nonna's warm kitchen rolling out pasta dough and pinching gnocchi while the driving drums and orchestra crescendoed. Bumpo would come in to critique our work and then spin Nonna around the kitchen until she was laughing and breathless. Oftentimes, they would forget I was there and kiss passionately until it was awkward. Their love burned so brightly it transported them into a world where nothing else existed. Growing up with that example set a high standard. If I had done more soul searching, I might have concluded that their archetype of perfect love was the reason I was still single after four decades. I just never found someone who looked at me the way Bumpo looked at Nonna.

There was always the void of silence to fill when you lived alone, something that took me a long time to get used to, but eventually, I got so accustomed to it I even began to crave it. Living alone suited me. I didn't need or require a lot more human interaction. At the end of a long day serving customers and corralling the insane expectations of the occasional bridezilla who thought the entire world revolved around her, all I desired was peace and quiet.

The water was finally boiling, so I added the pasta and stirred the furiously bubbling cauldron, setting a wooden spoon across the lip of the pan to prevent boil-overs like Bumpo taught me. I pulled a wedge of Parmesano Reggiano out of the refrigerator. Cheese was my lover, and I am not ashamed to admit that I spent an obscene amount of money at the Old World Cheese Shop on the corner. I looked at it as my way to support a small business, and since my parents didn't make me pay rent, I had money to burn. Fancy cheese was one of my absolute favorite things to burn it on.

I pulled out the grater and dragged the cheese down it, over and over, in time to the music. Up and down, I shaved the block against the grate, tucking my fingers back as a lofty pile of grated cheese began to form. The recipe only called for half a cup, but my personal philosophy is that one could never have too much cheese. So, I continued to grate it, stopping after a generous cup was sitting in a soft pile on the cutting board. I added some frozen peas to the boiling water from the bag in the freezer during the last two minutes of cooking time, then pulled some parsley from the terracotta pot growing on the windowsill, ran it under the water, and chopped it into small pieces. The pasta was the perfect al dente, and I drained it carefully, reserving a cup of the pasta water in a glass measuring cup.

Off the heat, I added the drained pasta and peas back to the pot, then added the cheese, parsley, and three ladles full of the reserved pasta water. The starch in the water was the secret ingredient. It reduced the thick cheese to a luscious sauce that clung to each noodle like a jealous lover. Then I pulled the giant pepper mill from the countertop and cranked it over the pan. The fragrance of fresh cracked black pepper wafted up and tickled my nose with its sharp, spicy notes. Finally ready to eat, my stomach growled in anticipation. I pulled a large portion onto the plate, refilled my glass of Prosecco, feeling slightly like a national traitor when I didn't pour the prerequisite glass of red wine. If Nonna were here, she would chastise me publicly at this sacrilege, and then sneak me an extra glass of Prosecco behind Bumpo's back.

I pulled the remote out and turned on the TV and Netflix. Documentaries were my jam. True crime, planet earth, you name it. If it was a true story, I would watch it. I wasn't the kind of girl who let herself be caught up in fantasies and outlandish tales of passion and woe. I wanted real. I wanted honest. I wanted truthful. I wanted to be outraged that the fresh water was disappearing for the hippos in Africa, not consumed by glittery vampires in Seattle. I wanted to put the clues together and discover the innocence of a man unjustly accused of murdering his wife. Real mattered, and I wasn't interested in wasting time with my head in the clouds.

I twirled the fork using a large tablespoon to corral the noodles. Once, when I was eight, one of my friends had the audacity to cut her angel hair into one-inch sections on her plate in front of Bumpo. I never heard the end of that. He gawked in horrified silence as she shoveled spoonful after spoonful of offensive knife-shortened noodles into her open mouth, oblivious to his obvious dismay. His own mouth opened and closed in outrage, barely able to squelch his fury.

Bumpo had opinions about everything, something I inherited from him. My mouth cost me many things, but I never paid a price too high to stop the behavior. I adopted his belief, "If they don't understand me, screw 'em." I gravitated to the ones who got me, and so my circle was small but incredibly loyal. I didn't adhere to the typical fat girl stereotype of fading into the background; I took an unapologetic stand to be seen. I wasn't obsessed with counting calories and running to create a deficit to fit into the box the world wanted to assign me. I ate the delicious food and had sex when I found willing partners. I unabashedly enjoyed both with *all* the lights on and savored the hell out of it.

Life was predictable and easy, and I was content. Content was a trap because it probably made me play a little smaller than I should have. Content was safe and predictable. It kept me from putting my heart out there. I was happy enough with content, until I wasn't. In just a few short days and two chance meetings, it was becoming obvious I wasn't content anymore. Suddenly, I was filled with wondering, a little seed of wanting that two brief interactions with a stranger had planted deep inside me. A seed that he watered the last few days and then bowled me over with his sun. There was an awakening happening that I couldn't deny, a shift of thought, a door that had creaked and cracked open where it had once been dead-bolted and padlocked.

Damn you, Foster Valentine.

I held out all of seventy-four minutes. I blame the Prosecco, encouraging me to do naughty things that were totally out of character. I mean, not *completely* out of character, because I have to be honest, Nonna's naughty streak was alive and well in me. I enjoyed a good night of dirty texts, and it had been too long since I let myself indulge in one.

He needs to ask me something.

I took a sip and considered my opening line, deciding to keep it simple.

Me: So, Mr. Valentine, what do you need to ask me?
Foster: What? Who is this?
Me: Sorry. It's G. From the bakery. You left a note for me.
Foster: Well, it took you long enough.

I grinned triumphantly.

Me: Well, I know you probably never hear this, but I have other responsibilities besides texting back customers.
Foster: Is that all I am to you? A customer? Sad face.
Me: My favorite customer?
Foster: I'll take that... for now. Winky face.
Me: For now?
Foster: I was hoping you'd be able to show me around Chicago, take me to a few of your favorite foodie places. Show me the dives and the secret gems you can't find anywhere else?
Me: Why me?
Foster: You're a chef. A pastry chef, but it still counts. Winky face.

I sent him a middle finger emoji. He immediately responded with three laughing while crying emojis.

Foster: A sensitive pastry chef.

Another middle finger emoji.

Foster: A sexy pastry chef. Heart eyed emoji.
Me: Finally, you've landed on an accurate adjective. Quick learner.
Me: FYI I also earned my full culinary degree.
Foster: Well, now you have to say yes.
Me: It's a maybe.
Foster: How do I turn it into a yes? And not just a yes, but a hell yes?

Smiling at the screen, I considered my response. I typed it out, then erased it, then typed out another one and erased it, too. Finally, I decided to do things my way. No sense in hiding what I wanted and frittering around waiting for the man to make the decisions.

Me: You let me pick the place and you let me order the food.
Foster: Deal.
Me: I'll send you details in a couple of days.
Foster: Why you gotta make me wait so long? I suck at it.
Me: The best things are always worth waiting for.
Foster: You got me there. I have a feeling you are completely worth it.

Giddiness flushed up my chest, and I danced around the room hugging my phone to my breasts and smiling like an idiot. Feeling only slightly stupid that a boy in a text message had that kind of effect on me. I mean, I'm only human after all.

EIGHT

The next day, I zipped around the bakery, my mood light and buoyant. I was busy sculpting lavender hydrangeas for my next wedding. Hours would go by and I'd be in the zone, working quietly while I people watched our regular patrons at the bakery through the kitchen windows.

Miss Sophia was sitting in the corner of the dining room with her elderly wiener dog, Clifford. She was a retired dance school teacher who always floated through life gracefully, sitting in our caned chairs rim-rod straight with perfect posture. She had a uniform of long flowing dresses paired with ballet flats. Nonna confided that back in the day, she was on tour with the New York City Ballet. Her hair was softly curled and had roared past white into blue territory. Once a stunning beauty, her face had softened and sagged with age, and decades of laughter added soft crinkles near her warm brown eyes. She never left the house without lipstick, swiped on meticulously over her thinning lips.

The mornings were getting cooler in September, so she wrapped herself in faux fur and walked her little wiener doggy on a jeweled leash to our bakery where she always ordered tea with milk and honey, three biscotti, and an original cannoli. Clifford eagerly helped her out with the biscotti. He was a fat little man whose belly nearly brushed the sidewalks when he trotted proudly next to Miss Sophia.

Off the menu, I baked sweet potato and pumpkin biscuits for dogs. It was another stream of income I was experimenting with, and Clifford was one of my most valuable taste testers.

Needing to take a break, I pulled a white bag from the shelf and shook it open, then added four biscuits, folded the top down, and walked it over to her.

"Miss Sophia, you look beautiful as always," I called out to her.

"Oh, dear, you are too kind."

"I have a few treats for my man Clifford." I smiled and shook the bag. Hearing his name, Clifford immediately perked up and raised up on his hind legs in full beggar mode.

"You spoil us," she said graciously and then wiped her watery eyes with a balled-up tissue.

"Let me know which he prefers," I said. "He could be the face of our new dog treat line."

I bent down and scratched him under his chin. "Who's the best boy?" I said in my dog voice. Cartoony and singsongy, it was the one I used to speak to all dogs. His tail wagged, and I pulled him into my arms to pet him as he snuggled into the crook of my neck. Clifford was an excitable lover who eagerly tried to cover my face with kisses.

I walked over to Mr. Manzetti at his usual table, one that gave him a full view of the people on the sidewalk. "How are you today? Mr. M.?" My hand landed on his shoulder.

"Finer than a frog's hair split four ways," he replied.

"Well now, that is mighty fine." It was part of our usual shtick, but his voice was wavering so I studied his face. His eyes were tired and just didn't have the usual spark. "Are you okay?"

"Just running a little high," he admitted sadly.

"I am sorry to hear that," I said and squeezed his shoulder. He placed his hand on mine and squeezed back gently.

"You are such a sweetheart for always checking in on this old fool."

"Like it or not, you are family," I corrected him, knowing that he stayed at the bakery every day because, after his wife passed, he sank low into a depression. He needed a place to go to be near people so he didn't feel so empty, and at DeLuca's, he felt a little less alone. Nonna convinced him to come and stay as long as he liked. They developed a fast friendship forged from a shared understanding of grief from the devastating loss of your soulmate.

I grew up watching him dote on his wife, proudly opening the door for her with a sophisticated flourish when they came every Sunday after church. He would pull out her chair so she could get seated and comfortable, and often beat me to the punch on refilling her coffee cup. They sat together, always holding hands across the table while they worked on word finds and crossword puzzles. Nonna confided they lost several babies, yet refused to let those painful circumstances make them bitter and angry. It explained the sad sweetness in their eyes that never really left. An agony that fused them together and only made their commitment to each other stronger.

Mr. M took care of his wife the way Bumpo took care of Nonna, the way my Pops took care of Mom. "You know what I've decided?" I declared. "They just don't make men like you anymore," I told him, and he smiled.

"It *is* a different world, but there are a few true gentlemen that remain. Of that I am certain," he said, still clutching my hand.

"I'd love to believe you, but I have seen so much evidence to the contrary." I countered cynically.

"Believe it. You have to believe; that's the only way your heart will ever find one."

"Well, I used to believe in Santa Claus, and look where that got me," I joked, and he laughed.

"I still believe," he said. "Because the alternative is accepting that there just isn't any magic left in the world, and I refuse to accept it."

Hmmm. Did I still believe in magic?

The bell tinkled and yanked me back as a power couple burst through the door. They had to be my eleven o'clock. I studied them for a minute. A familiarity quivered and I struggled to place it. Then the truth rushed in and my heart sank.

Was that? Shit. It was. Benji.

I forced a tight, professional smile onto my face and walked over to greet them. "You must be Laurel?" I asked sweetly as his eyes settled on mine, and I noticed a glimmer of painful recognition fill them.

"Yes," she said, smoothing her hair. "And this is Ben." She waved a hand back.

"Actually, we've already met," I said. "You're never going to believe this, but we went to high school together."

"Really?" She sweetly looked back over at Ben. "What a small world!"

"But he was Benji then," I offered, wishing the ground would open and swallow me whole. I was starting to overheat and flush. I was certain my cheeks were reddening and sweat was prickling at my hairline.

"Benji?" She laughed. "How dreadful."

Yes, he was.

His hair was graying at the temples, and his eyes were lined by crow's feet, but other than that, he looked like a moneyed slightly more sophisticated version of the guy who destroyed me in high school.

He nodded sheepishly. I wondered if he was walking through our mutual memories the same way I was.

Being fat in high school is a curse, where it's so important to fit in and belong and look like every other leather bomber jacket-clad teenage girl out there. My confidence was fragile and paper-thin and seesawed day to day, depending on if Benji Anderson noticed me. Benji was the co-captain of the basketball team. At six-feet tall, blond and gorgeous, he had his pick of girls who lined up with their freshly applied Bonnie Bell lip-smacker waiting for their chance with him. I wasn't even on his radar and was so inexperienced it was pathetic. I practiced kissing my pillow at night, waiting for the moment I would have a chance to plant one on someone in real life.

His sixteenth birthday was the social event of the year. His parents invited the entire class to their estate, which had a pool and a hot tub. I starved myself for a week to fit into a swimsuit a size smaller and had spent hours in the changing room trying them on. Begging the Lycra and spandex to transform my body into something smooth and less lumpy. I kissed the scale that registered ten pounds less the day of the party, giddy with pride that I was physically smaller and lightheaded from not eating.

When I got there, the party was in full swing. His parents were nowhere to be found, so a few bottles of Mad Dog 20/20 were making the rounds. Everyone was staring when the bottle landed at me, and feeling the pressure, I took a long sip. I guzzled the sugary sweet grape flavor that barely concealed the burn of the booze. It hit my empty stomach quickly, making me feel more at ease, more attractive, and more bold. An hour and three more long sips later, the empty bottles were used to play a riveting game of Seven Minutes in Heaven. On Benji's turn, he spun the bottle, and after five lazy circles, it landed on me. A thrill burst in my belly, but I stayed seated, waiting for him to act.

His boys hooted and hollered, pushing his shoulder and chanting his name, "Benji! Benji!" They eventually quieted down and whispered in his ear, an act that should have made me leery and uncomfortable, but my first buzz chased any normal concerns away. I felt amazing and pliable, sexier, and more mature. Mad Dog made me ooze with confidence. Accepting his fate, he got up and walked across the rug to me and pulled me to my feet, a gesture that I immediately misconstrued as chivalrous and sweet because it was something I had seen Bumpo do for Nonna hundreds of times. I gathered myself up and gingerly walked to the closet with him, squeezing my glutes and feeling all the eyes burning in my back as my heart pumped with excitement. I couldn't believe my luck.

Benji Anderson was going to kiss me! My first kiss! With Benji Anderson!

I was giddy and nervous, the liquor making me giggly and fidgety. He pulled the door shut, and in the darkness, I waited while my eyes adjusted. The anticipation of his touch crackled energy through me. He reached out in the dark and pulled me toward him, brushing my lips with a brusque kiss. His lips were hard and unyielding, but I didn't care. I was kissing Benji Anderson, and that was all that mattered. I felt his hand on mine and then he pulled it toward his pants. In the dark, I heard the zipper unfasten and then I felt his fingers push me down onto my knees. My hands found his hips and then walked down to his limp penis. I'd never felt one before and was amazed by the soft smooth skin, but also confused because I thought it was supposed to be harder.

"Put it in your mouth," he said, pushing the back of my head toward the head of his cock.

"Okay." I touched him with my hand, feeling it start to harden and feeling a rush of power from having this effect on Benji Anderson. In the back of my mind, there was an alarm bell ringing, but I pushed the caution away. To have his focused attention right now was everything. Having no idea what I was doing, I licked and licked, not paying any attention to anything else. Focused on the task in front of me, wanting to do it well. Wanting to prove my worth to a guy like Benji.

He was in my mouth when a crack of light burst into the closet. I jumped, and he pulled out, laughing as I blinked into the bright light, looking around and trying to get my bearings. The booze on the empty stomach made me feel like I was floating. His friends hooted and hollered and carried on, jostling each other for a better look. The full lights snapped on. Disoriented, I looked over my shoulder into forty-two pairs of eyes. The laughing is what I remember. Loud and obnoxious, my face reddening in shame as I struggled to find my feet. The Mad Dog made me unsteady, so I stumbled forward tipsy and nauseous. Benji disappeared into the throng, laughing as he high-fived his teammates, then walked out to the pool, leaving me there. I grabbed a bowl of cheese balls and locked myself in a bathroom upstairs away from the party sounds and then laid in the bathtub, crunching away. Handful after handful, I tried to fill the growing emptiness inside. It gnawed at my ribcage, and ten minutes later, the grape liquor and orange cheese balls rushed up and into the toilet. I retched and retched until I had dry heaves. The beginning of a headache was pulsing at my temples as hot tears washed down my face. Two hours later, I was sobered up and riding home, quiet in the van next to Pops, looking out the window, wishing I could disappear. Dreading Monday when I would have to go back to school and see those forty-two pairs of eyes again.

I shook my head to clear the memory. This was a job. The party was a million years ago, and I could pull myself together like a professional woman does and treat this like any other wedding cake consultation.

"Follow me," I said to them and sucked in my stomach as I walked them back to our consultation room. Seeing Benji reverted me right back to that awkward chubby sophomore momentarily, and I hated that event still held power over me. "Can I get you an espresso or a coffee before we start?"

"No, thank you," he said, refusing to make eye contact.

"Okay, let's get started then." I forced cheery professionalism into my voice. It was too sharp and bright, but I hoped it sounded confident and like the voice of someone who had completely forgotten how she was humiliated at his sixteenth birthday party. "Tell me about your event."

I took detailed notes as I studied Laurel. She was blown out and thin with full lips. I briefly wondered if Benji was still as terrible a kisser as he was at sixteen. Peppering my questions with smiles, I sold my services and the bakery. I focused on Laurel exclusively; to be fair, that was not out of the ordinary. This was normally how I approached many cake consultation appointments. But for some reason, I felt like I had something to prove. That I had to show Benji that he didn't win, that I was secure and happy, living my best life in Chicago, and the events of the past weren't even on my radar.

"What do you think Benj—Ben." I corrected myself, flushing pink.

"To be honest, this is more Laurel's wheelhouse. I'm just here for moral support, and she bribed me with cake." He smiled at me, revealing perfectly straight, brilliantly white teeth.

I started to sketch out ideas. "I was thinking a pristine white cake covered in gum paste butterflies and hand-crafted stephanotis."

"Ooh!" Laurel was nodding excitedly. I pulled out the album of professional photographs of cakes I designed and offered it to her. "You can take a look at my cake portfolio of custom cakes I have created for past clients, but I can assure you that each cake is completely one of a kind, unique in every way."

"Perfect," Laurel said as she studied and flipped

through the pages. "It's like art. You're so talented," she gushed. "I don't have an iota of creativity in me; it's all spreadsheets and quarterly reports over here."

Damnit. I wanted to hate her, but she was enthusiastic and genuine with her praise and had warmed up considerably since she sat down. It was hard not to like her.

"Well, I wouldn't even know what to do with a quarterly report," I admitted, smiling at her. In spite of everything, she was winning me over, and I found myself wanting to create their cake. "How about we do a tasting next?" I offered.

"Finally, my time to shine!" Ben said and smiled at me again, trying to butter me up. He clapped his hands and rubbed them together in anticipation.

"I'll be right back."

I walked to the kitchen and started to assemble my tasting board, carefully labeling each choice when Aubrey sailed by.

"Remember that asshole Benji I told you about from high school?"

"God, yes, that was brutal, G," Aubrey commiserated.

"Guess who is seated in the tasting room right now?"

"No way!"

"I am stifling the urge to spit in these samples," I admitted as I added a couple of white gum paste flowers. "But I have to tell you his fiancé is such a sweetheart that I might end up taking on this commission."

"Seriously?" Aubrey knew my ability to hold grudges was legendary.

"Stranger things have happened." Finally ready, I pulled out the tray, added three bottles of water, and walked it carefully back into the room.

"Here we are!" I said too enthusiastically. "Let's put these in your mouth!" I blurted before I could stop myself as my eyes leveled on Benji. He looked away uncomfortably, and I felt a little immature powerful surge at the small victory. He remembered.

Laurel blinked at me, and her forehead wrinkled slightly.

I laughed and rolled my eyes at myself. "So sorry! There I go again, making it awkward. I meant let's find your preferred cake palette." I hastily passed out forks, and the awkward comment was quickly forgiven when the buttercream hit their systems.

"Oh, God," Laurel exclaimed, her eyes closed. "So good."

They dove into all the flavors with wild abandon, making loud appreciative noises of delight like little kids. It was mildly adorable.

"I love them all," she said.

"Seriously, you can't go wrong with any of them," Ben agreed. "Truly." He implored me with his eyes.

"Thank you. We can make each tier a different flavor if you'd like, or we can take it a step further and create a custom flavor for you."

"Can we talk about it?" she asked. "There are so many options, and I am a little overwhelmed, to be honest."

"Of course," I said, then turned to the closing part of my presentation. "So, the final bit of paperwork here is our contract." I shuffled the papers together. "You can take this with you and look it over."

"Can you hold the date for us?" Laurel asked. "Just until we decide exactly how much we need and what flavors we'd like?"

"I'm so sorry," I said. "I wish I could, but the only way to lock in a date is with a signed contract and deposit. Until that is completed, a wedding date is available. I'm sure you understand."

"Can we reserve the date and work out the details later?" Ben asked, and I felt the rush of victory. He reached out to squeeze Laurel's hand, and she nodded. "I think you've blown... I'm sorry," he stammered, apologizing, and then quickly continued. "I think you've *amazed* us both with your presentation." Ben looked down and avoided my eyes completely.

"In that case, we can sign a contract that locks in the date, you can pay the deposit, and we can fill out the rest of the details later. We can finalize the design and cost once you've had more time to think it over. After we lock in your date, we turn away other couples that inquire about it, so just understand that your deposit *is* non-refundable," I mentioned.

He looked over at Laurel. "What do you think, babe?"

"Let's do it! I have a good feeling about you, and DeLuca's came so highly recommended." She beamed at me, and I smiled back.

Ben pulled out his Am Ex and handed it to me. "Thank you, Gionna." His voice was warm and felt almost like an apology.

Swiping his card wasn't as cathartic as I thought it would be, but being chosen by Ben(ji) and Laurel to create their wedding cake was a satisfying moment of redemption I never saw coming.

NINE

The next day, a huge bouquet of yellow roses arrived with a note.

A million apologies and it wouldn't be enough. I was terrible to you in high school. Thank you for being a better person than I was and pushing past our history. Laurel couldn't stop raving about your work. With sincere gratitude, Ben.

This sweet note and stunning floral display flew in the face of the unequivocal truths I governed my life by. People don't change. When people show you their true colors, believe them. Once an asshole, always an asshole.

"Who are those from, Gionna DeLuca?" I heard his voice behind me, and a flush of warmth rushed through me.

"One of my clients."

"I wish I got declarations of appreciation like that," he said. "Do you like flowers?"

"It was a beautiful gesture, but I'd rather have a potted plant than for someone to murder flowers and send them to me to die."

"Ha! Cynical. I love it." He gazed into my eyes. "I will make a note of that for future reference."

"If you really want to get on my good side, air plants are the way to my heart."

"Is that so? I want to know all the ways to your heart." His words softened at the end, melting my defenses.

I rolled my eyes playfully, grinning in spite of myself. "You're something else, you know that?"

"That's what I hear."

Aubrey sailed over with his espresso in a to-go cup. "Thank you, my dear." He studied the pastry case. "Is that a new flavor?" He pointed to the macaroons.

"Good eye. It's mint with a dark chocolate filling. We also did a limited run of peanut butter and jelly. I'll add one of each to your order."

"Perfect, and a couple of pistachio cannolis?"

"Already ahead of you."

"You always take great care of me," he said, looking deep into my eyes, leaving so much unsaid I shifted uncomfortably. "Two more days," he said. "Are you counting them down like I am?"

"No," I lied.

"Dagger to the heart." He clutched his chest, his goofy antics making me grin again. He waved and then walked away, and I returned back to making gum paste flowers, daydreaming about Friday night.

TEN

The day of our meeting—I couldn't quite call it a date; it was purely two professional foodies sharing a meal and talking shop—there was a little niggle of something I couldn't put my finger on, a truth yearning to emerge. It surfaced and then disappeared like a whale in the ocean, leaving me confused and destroying my illusion of contentment.

My morning passed like it always did as I filled cannolis and wrapped up pastries for office meetings and did deliveries while my mind cranked and whirred in the background, churning out answers to questions I was afraid to ask.

What was this? More importantly, what did I want it to be?

Nothing, I decided. I wanted it to be nothing because to be something would shake things up when I had finally gotten them settled.

That night, Aubrey knocked on the door at my apartment as a formality before sailing through it. "It's me!" she sang out. "Holy shit, G! Did your closet explode?"

"What?" I asked in a daze, trying on what looked like outfit number thirty-nine from the cast-offs littering every flat surface. I whipped off the shirt and sat down hard, wearing only my bra and a skirt. "I'm a lost cause." I wrung my hands, looking in dismay at the mess around me.

"True story." She laughed. "But I love you anyway."

"I'm probably reading way too much into this," I said. "He's just new in town and wanted to find the good eats, so naturally, he'd ask the fat girl," I reasoned with my usual self-deprecating humor.

"I call bullshit," Aubrey said. "You and I both know it's more than that. I mean, look at this place. These are not the actions of a woman who doesn't give a shit."

"Why do you always have to call me out?" I wailed. "I love you for it, but still." I picked up a wad of clothing from the table and chair and handed it to her. "Help me," I begged.

"Okay. First, tell me where you are taking him." She started to lay out the options and created a discard pile. Picking through the pile of jeans and shirts carefully, one by one.

"Well, I was thinking the food truck by the Stadium to start, for a little ball-park style amuse-bouche. And then I was planning on heading to Alexander's for the entrée—mussels or seared scallops—and finish with a trip to the Sweet Life, that new hand-rolled ice creamery."

"Are you walking?"

"Yeah, definitely. They are all less than a mile apart. It

will give us a chance to get to know each other a little better instead of trying to cram into a dirty taxi or having to ask Pops to borrow the delivery van. I'm trying to keep this on the down-low. You know how excited my parents get when they think I am dating."

"Oh, God. Yeah, I know. Okay." Aubrey walked around the room, pulling out platform heels, a pair of dark jeans, and a fitted plum-colored top that was ruched at the waist but had flowing sleeves that capped at the wrists. It was a cute splurge I had forgotten about that I found on the sale rack last year. I never had a chance to wear it, since I hadn't gone to any places that dictated more than a t-shirt lately. She handed them to me.

"You're not wearing that bra, are you?" She asked as she took in my sad ancient sports bra, shaking her head in disgust.

"What? Why not? It's not like he's going to see it anyway."

"Did you shave your legs?"

"Yes."

"Then he's probably going to see it."

"What kind of trollop do you take me for, woman?" I exclaimed with false outrage, and then we both lost it and laughed our asses off. We both knew, if the situation was right and the drinks were a flowin', I could be a very loose woman. Again, I blame Nonna's hot blood racing through my veins. You just can't fight biology.

She flung a lacy black plunge bra at me, with a push up I didn't need, but that made the girls look fabulous.

"You have great boobies," she said, making squeezing gestures with both her hands.

I shimmied my shoulders at her and winked.

"After breastfeeding a couple of kids, mine are just sad, empty sacks now."

"Stop it! You're gorgeous. And those two minions of yours were totally worth the stretch marks and sag."

"This one is different," she accused as she watched me pull on the top.

"No." I tried to deny it.

"Liar."

"Okay, fine. You're right." I exhaled heavy and hot. "Jesus, I don't know what's wrong with me. For some reason, he gets my motor running. Seriously, in a way that it hasn't run in a really long time."

"Really, G?" Aubrey said dreamily. "That's so awesome. It's about time someone amazing walked into your life."

"I'm trying not to get my hopes up too high, but it's really, really hard."

"That's what she said," Aubrey deadpanned, and it made us both giggle.

I rolled my eyes.

She laughed at me and then uncorked the bottle of wine that was perpetually in my refrigerator, poured herself a glass, and then tipped the bottle toward me. I reluctantly declined.

"Wine makes me slutty," I confessed. "I need to have all my wits about me around a man like Foster Valentine."

"That name," Aubrey said.

"I know. It's crazy, right?"

"It's like a celeb or a sports-caster," Aubrey pondered.

"I'm fluttery as shit around him. That scruff and those

eyes." I sighed dreamily. "I want him to rub his cheek against my collarbone and leave my skin raw from where he's been."

"Holy shit," she said again, fanning herself. "Do you hear what you're saying?"

"I do and it's terrifying."

Aubrey pulled her phone out of her pocket and smiled down at it.

"What's happening over there?" I asked sweetly.

"Oh, nothing."

"It doesn't look like nothing." I challenged her.

"If it becomes something, you'll be the first to know."

"I better be." She was distracted, not even paying attention to me, so I snapped my fingers in front of her face. "It's okay to have fun, but we both know you are too trusting. I just don't want to see you get hurt."

Her eyes flashed at me. "Not every man is Brett."

That was a sting below the belt, and I recoiled as her sucker punch landed.

"G." Aubrey reached out, trying to soften the blow.

"No. You don't get to say something like that and then act like everything is fine."

"You're projecting your hang-ups on me."

Therapy-speak always made me rankle in anger. I stomped to the closet, searching for a jacket, needing to dispel the energy of the rage that was building.

"Look at Marco and Lorraine, and Bumpo and Nonna." She begged, walking toward me, closing the gap as angry tears formed at my lash line. "True love does exist. It doesn't look anything like the bullshit fairytales our parents read us, or the Barbie movies we were forced to watch, but I choose to believe there are good people in the world that can love you if you give them a chance."

"Well, I guess I'm a little more gun shy and jaded," I spit back at her. "That's what happens when you get your heart ripped out by the man you thought you were going to marry."

ELEVEN

B rett. It's no coincidence his name rhymes with regret. Of all the regrettable things I have done in my life, he takes the cake—and this girl knows cake. When you think of men that are classified "players," you think slick, abs for days, devilishly handsome, a person who skates by on looks and charisma. They are the manipulative snakes that are easy to spot a mile away. That's what guys like Brett are counting on. My Brett was a traveling regional salesman who came through Chicago on a bi-weekly basis. He was soft in the middle, endearing, and easy to talk to. He was able to hide in plain sight under his chubby teddy bear persona, but he was as cunning as a fox. Looking back, I feel like such a fool. It's embarrassing to admit how naive I was.

Our courtship was a whirlwind of first date butterflies, long romantic dinners, compliments, and gushing sentimental declarations. I was living inside a fluffy rom-com snow globe and didn't even know it, thinking that he was the ticket to my happily ever after. Brett would blow into town every two weeks, where he would dazzle us with his easy smile, make us laugh at his jokes, and take me on the most enchanting dates I had ever been on. During the week when he was gone, he would text me sweet gushy messages, and we would talk on the phone until three o'clock in the morning the way teenagers do.

You hang up. No... you hang up. Puke.

Absence does make the heart grow fonder, but no one ever tells you it also makes the heart grow dumber. Being showered with attention from the wrong guy can fool you into thinking he is the right one. The addition of long-distance love goggles make the truth harder to recognize.

Three years ago, I witnessed the most romantic proposal, and shockingly enough, it happened to me. I was working my regular shift at the bakery when Brett surprised me by walking in on a day he wasn't even supposed to be in the city. God, I used to love surprises, but Brett destroyed them for me.

He waltzed in and raked a hand through his sandy-colored hair, smiling wide as his eyebrows danced, a fun loving gesture that always melted me. It was at the tail end of our morning rush. I finished serving the last few customers, distracted by his presence, and became confused when I watched him lean over to speak to a dark-haired man who had an acoustic guitar strapped to his body. The guitarist began to strum the most seductive soft notes on his guitar, coaxing beautiful sounds from it like a lover, as I walked out from behind the pastry case. My brow wrinkled up in concentration, trying to decode the reason for the impromptu concert that was unfolding right in front of me. Smiling like a loon, I struggled to put the pieces of what was unfurling together, but the most astonishing moment of all was when Brett opened his mouth and began to sing—*in Italian.* The audience gasped as his warm bass tenor rippled and pulsed through the dining room—he was so good! Hairs stood up on the back of my neck, and my heart swelled with pride at his hidden talent. I was completely bowled over.

Brett sauntered toward me as the sweetest notes resonated from deep in his diaphragm and lulled me into a warm cocoon of captivated joy. He'd swung for the fences and hit a home run with his grand romantic gesture. I took his hand as he twirled me to a chair in the center of the room while crooning into my ear. His warm breath caressed my neck, sending tingles down my forearms. Nonna came out of the kitchen, her wrinkled hands laced together in front of her chest, mouthing the words to the love song that she knew by heart, as she rocked from side to side, her filmy eyes glossy.

Warm morning light flooded the bakery and danced across the tables in time to the music. It rushed into my heart, warming me from the inside out. I was living every little girl's love sick fantasy. A boy was serenading me publicly, declaring his love in not just one, but two languages. Rich and deep, his voice reverberated from wall to wall, holding us all spellbound, prisoners to its beauty. The patrons in the bakery formed a loose circle around us, smiling at me. I didn't understand the lyrics, but they gave me goosebumps anyway. Tears gathered at my lash line; I was speechless and stunned at this amazing surprise reve-lation. From the corner of my eye, I saw Pops pull Mom close to him, and they swayed to the music. He whispered in her ear, kissed her temple, and she smiled sweetly. When the last few notes dissolved into the air, there was awed silence, and then fervent applause burst from the crowd.

I wiped at the corners of my eyes and laughed uncomfortably, hyperaware I had become the center of attention as Brett appeared in front of me. Dressed in a wrinkled tan suit, his face was beet red and slightly sweaty from the physical exertion of singing. He winked at me and reached out his meaty hand to mine, and then in one small gesture, he dropped to his knee as the audience gasped and my eyes widened.

"Gionna Maria DeLuca, I love you enough to learn Italian. You have captivated me, heart and soul. Would you do me the honor of becoming my wife?"

My hands flew to my mouth, my pulse quickened, and my stomach fluttered. He opened the box to reveal a stunning three-carat diamond engagement ring resting on a satin pillow that sparkled in the light.

Oh my God. This is really happening.

Aubrey's jaw dropped and matched mine. Our relationship had escalated quickly, but it's easy to call it true love and fate when your man sings to you in Italian. I didn't even hesitate.

"Yes!" I pulled him in for a kiss, and we stood as the bakery erupted in applause around us, the patrons and my family hooting and hollering. Mom and Pops ran across the street to the liquor store and came back with ten bottles of champagne, and we toasted in coffee cups. It was an amazing fairytale moment in the middle of an average week of my average life, making me feel like a princess. I wish I had remembered that fairytales are fiction. It would have saved me so much heartache.

———

It started off innocently enough. First, it was forgetting his wallet on our double dates. Then, it progressed to the occasional emergency need for money when he was on the road and had his wallet stolen or he had driven off without his ATM card. Then, I started to suspect that cash was disappearing from my apartment, mostly my daily haul from the tip jar in ones and fives and fistfuls of change. The amounts were small enough that I explained it away, made excuses, and doubted it, telling myself I must have counted wrong. The unfortunate truth is that I saw what I wanted to see and found endless ways to lie to myself about what was really happening. No one is perfect, I'd tell myself when the occasional niggle of doubt surfaced. Then I'd push it back down, readjust the rose-colored glasses on my face, and go wedding dress shopping with Mom and Nonna. Did Brett helping himself to my change jar really matter when soon we would be married and combine our finances anyway?

The weekend of our couple's bridal shower, he sent a panicked text telling me he wouldn't be able to make it because his car broke down and needed a new transmission. I sent him the money because, in my mind, we were partners. We were planning our wedding and working toward coupling our lives. If he was stranded, why wouldn't I move heaven and earth to help him out so we could spend time together? Especially on the weekend of our shower? Looking back, I hate myself for being so weak, so naïve, and so easy to manipulate.

As a surprise, I started looking at real estate. I knew we couldn't raise a family in the one-bedroom apartment I was currently renting, so I started getting all my financial ducks in a row to see if we could get pre-qualified for a mortgage on my income alone. Early on in our relationship, he confided that his last serious girlfriend destroyed his credit and left him filing for bankruptcy. It would be more than five years before it dropped off his record. Brett's acting skills were so on point the night he told me that sob story, he actually shed tears! I rushed in to help like I'm prone to do and told him not to worry about it. We would figure it out. I loved him, and money didn't matter. I had enough for both of us.

The house of cards started to collapse a few weeks later. First, my bank called with shocking information. Two new lines of credit had been opened in my name and were carrying balances of over twenty-one thousand dollars. Horrified, this news filled my belly with lead. I was a girl who faithfully paid her entire balance every month to avoid finance charges at all costs. I remember gripping the phone so tight to my ear it started to ache, listening to the words. "It appears that you may have been a victim of identity theft."

I reached out to Brett, who suddenly became impossible to reach. After leaving message after message on his voicemail and sending endless texts, he appeared to have fallen off the face of the earth. I kept calling and was dumbfounded when his phone was disconnected. In shock, I kept the information to myself at first. Feeling like a stooge, I tried to track him down. I began an investigation that was full of dead ends. I filed a police report that went nowhere. Brett used an alias and didn't officially exist in any database anywhere. He was a ghost that disappeared into the ether with a lot of my money.

I went to the jeweler to have my ring appraised so I could sell it to pay off the debts and was flabbergasted to learn it was moissanite and practically worthless. The final death blow was when a routine physical revealed he had given me an STD. Sitting in the brightly lit office with my feet up in the stirrups, feeling dirty and used, I wanted to die. I burst into tears laying on the examination table, shivering from the cold, but mostly from the shame. My doctor treated it, and for all accounts and purposes, I was physically fine. On the outside, I was no worse for wear. But on the inside, at night when I was alone, I hated the gullible trusting face I saw every day in the mirror. I felt like such a sucker. So easily played by a scam artist and wanting to be loved so much, I bought into his lies and let him take advantage of me.

He destroyed my credit and he destroyed my heart, but most of all, he destroyed my belief that there were good men in the world. Telling my parents the truth was the hardest conversation I'd ever had in my entire life. I was so ashamed. It seared through me white-hot and all-encompassing. Their pity was an even more bitter pill to swallow. I vividly remember sitting in Nonna's living room, hearing the crunch of the plastic slipcovers as their stunned silence filled the room. Mom's eyes loomed up at me, huge and childlike, as Pops buried his face in his hands. Their faith in humanity took a hit, but it was nothing compared to the total destruction of mine.

To save money to fight my legal battle, I moved into the apartment above the bakery. I buried myself in my work, and it took a year, but I was finally able to legally prove he had stolen my personal information and opened these accounts without my knowledge. I found a lawyer, and thousands of dollars later, it was settled and I was able to move on. But not without a deep scar, not without suspicion and cynicism, and not without a chip on my shoulder a mile wide when it came to men.

I was going to stay in my lane. Love was off the table. There was no way I was going to give another man the power to destroy me like Brett had. Keeping men at arm's length, I was open to a friends-with-benefits arrangement, but nothing more. I would call the shots, so I would never get myself into a situation like that ever again. For the better part of three years, I did exactly that, and then right when I thought I had my life figured out, right when I thought I had everything under control, God laughed and sent me Foster Valentine.

TWELVE

It's true when they say some of the best days of your life haven't even happened yet. You don't know when you're going to have one of those best days because they start out like any other. You're out living your life, doing the things you normally do, and then right smack dab in the middle of all that sameness is a flash of lightning.

Weather in September in Chicago is unpredictable, but for once, the stars aligned and it was a seasonally cool night. My thermostat always ran a little high, but add the bundle of nerves that being around Foster turned me into, and it had the potential to make me a sweaty, pitted out mess. I was waiting outside the bakery, fanning myself with butterflies in my stomach.

This isn't a date. Relax.

I was lying to myself. If this wasn't a date, why was my chest fluttering at the sight of Foster walking toward me? Why did heat rush up my torso, and why did my cheeks burn?

As he got closer, a huge smile broke out over his face

and spilled light on everything—his eyes, the sidewalk, the clouds, my face. My entire universe brightened noticeably when he was in it. My belly somersaulted against my will, and I felt my pulse accelerate. Wearing a black butter-soft leather jacket and dark jeans, he was hot in an edgy way that felt effortless. My throat knotted up and my stomach stirred, from more than just physical hunger.

"Wow," he said when he was within earshot. "You clean up well." He opened his jacket, showing me a vintage Stones concert t-shirt, and asked, "Am I dressed okay for this?"

"Of course." Then I felt myself get swept up into his arms for a hug that made my stomach flip and my hands sweat. He was a magnet, and I was iron. This was a chemical attraction I couldn't deny, each particle of me aligning with a particle of him, inexplicably fusing us together.

I closed my eyes in his arms, and he rocked me from side to side, shimmying on the sidewalk. When I looked up at him, the corners of his mouth twisted up into such an irresistible grin, I felt myself getting swept away. It was a terrifying sensation that felt like a free fall. To steady myself, I breathed him in, inhaling his scent of cedar and soap with an undercurrent of lavender. The first trickles of fear swelled in my chest, and I pulled away quickly like I had been burned. His warm golden eyes leveled on mine, questioning, yet he remained quiet.

"You ready for this?" I asked in a tone I hoped sounded playful. My dating banter was rusty, sending my mind spiraling for witty remarks and coming up empty. I tossed a handful of coal-black hair over my shoulder, hoping it made up for how far short I felt I was falling.

"Absolutely," he said and took my arm, sending shocks

down my forearms to my fingertips that I tried to ignore as I led us toward our first stop.

"You've heard about the Chicago icons, deep dish from Lou Malnati's and an Italian Beef from Al's?" I asked, turning into tour guide mode, counting off each option on one of my fingers. "They are truly Chicago staples and should be enjoyed by everyone, but tonight, I wanted to share something a little off the beaten path." We walked up to a food truck parked outside of the stadium. "A Chicago dog with everything," I ordered from the window, and in five minutes, a paper boat with the meaty treat covered in pickles, tomatoes, dressed in a poppyseed bun, and topped with mustard and onions was placed in front of me. I pulled it out of the window, and we walked to the alley to get out of the wind. "The first bite is yours," I offered, my mouth watering already. "It's the snap of the casing, the spicy mustard, and the fresh crunch of the pickle that makes it incredible. Just an explosion of flavors in your mouth. The perfect bite." His eyebrows lifted as his lips curved up in anticipation.

"You have to feed it to me," he proposed, and I laughed at the suggestion, and then damned if I didn't find myself picking up that bun and hoisting it toward his open mouth like a trained seal. "Come to Papa," he said and then opened wide and took a huge bite. His cheeks puffed out like a chipmunk—an adorable chipmunk. "Celery salt," he said through his full mouth that he partially covered with his hand, then closed his eyes, savoring the experience like an orgasmic moment.

"Do you need me to leave you two alone?" I teased him.

He held up one finger, his eyes still clamped shut, a

huge smile breaking out over his face. This gave me time to study his face while he chewed. Not enough lines. Maybe thirty? He had a drop of mustard on his delightfully scruffy chin, and my finger ached to wipe it off. But I clung to the rest of the hot dog, waiting for him to come up for air. Finally, he opened his eyes and winked at me.

"You have..." My voice trailed off as I waved my other hand by my chin and then handed him a napkin.

"Such a slob! You can't take me anywhere." He laughed and wiped off the mustard. "Okay, your turn. Open your mouth wide and accept my meat." He barely made it through that ridiculous line before he dissolved into giggles and I joined in. Ordinarily, juvenile comments like this from men were met with eye rolls and irritation, but there was just something so sweet and adorable about the way his nostrils flared as he tried to hold back his laughter that melted me.

"Open and ready." I played along, and he placed the hot dog close enough for me to take a big bite. I moaned in pleasure, too, chewing thoughtfully and slowly, but not uninhibited enough to close my eyes. The snap of the casing and the crunch of the relish were a perfect pair. Normally, hot dogs were something I loathed, but a Chicago dog with everything on it was one of my weaknesses. That and I was starting to think maybe, Foster Valentine. "So good." I swallowed and handed him the bun.

He picked it up and stuffed the rest of it in his mouth. Shamelessly, like a little kid, eating as fast as possible so he could go out and play. He took a long sip of the vanilla Coke and tossed it into the trash in the can. "That was incredible. What is next?"

"A tiny little seafood joint that has the best seared scallops, shrimp cocktail, and mussels."

"Is there anything more perfect than a golden-brown seared scallop?" He asked. "It's the very definition of sexy. So tender and luscious slathered with luxurious pats of butter." Foster was practically drooling, lost in his own love affair with scallops.

"You get me," I enthused, trying to be funny, but there was a desperate sliver of hopeful truth embedded in it, too, that weakened me. There was an invisible tug of my heart toward his, like a string connected us, and it took my breath away.

"Tell me about yourself, Gionna DeLuca."

"What do you want to know?"

"All of it," he said, and I could tell that he meant it. The sweet truth of that simple statement forced another tug of my heart closer to his.

"You've been to the bakery. That's pretty much my life in a nutshell," I said. "You're the one who is the mystery."

"No mystery at all, I'm an open book. Ask me anything." His warm hand found mine and laced our fingers together. His skin on mine ignited a flame that felt reckless, yet I was powerless to pull back. I prayed my palms wouldn't start to sweat.

"How did you end up at culinary school?"

He laughed self-deprecatingly. "You'll be shocked to hear this, but it turns out I wasn't good at anything else. I was getting into trouble *in* school and out of it, and my mom thought I needed to stay busy so she got me a job washing dishes at a restaurant in town." He was quiet as he walked, then abruptly tugged me by the hand away from a deep crack in the sidewalk, the kind that usually sent me sprawling into a concrete face plant whenever I wore heels. Letting go of my hand, he pulled me in by the shoulders and drew me closer, even after the trip threat was far behind us. My body burned where it touched his.

Careful. Careful.

A distant alarm bleated out its obnoxious shrill warning tone in my head, and I skirted away from him and then gently dropped his hand, pretending to dig for something in my purse.

"I loved the energy in the kitchen." He shoved his hands in the pockets of his jeans and continued. "I was a busy kid, busy hands, busy brain. My poor mom, I was the very definition of a handful." He paused and looked off into the distance, thinking about his mom, and the sweetness made my heart pang. A man that loves his mom has always been a weakness of mine. He turned toward me and locked his eyes on mine, and with a wisp of a sad smile, confessed, "That kitchen saved me."

I cocked my head, searching his face that had gotten so serious. The doubts and the guilt washed across his features only for a moment before they disappeared again.

"The chef, if you could call him that, taught me knife skills and talked my mom into letting me try culinary school after graduation. She wasn't too excited to fork over thousands more dollars since I had barely graduated from high school, but I blossomed there. I finally took my ADHD meds regularly, and it helped me focus, and I graduated with honors." He smiled, effortlessly melting me and making me weak in the knees. "She was so proud of me. You know when you're screwing up, I mean royally screwing up, and everything you do is another disappointment to your parents? She had gotten so used to seeing me fail that when I finally succeeded, it healed us both. She's my biggest fan now. It's bordering on embarrassing."

"God, I know that feeling," I commiserated. We arrived at Alexander's, a tiny little seafood bistro that was booked solid for at least six months. Another generational family restaurant that flew the seafood in daily and had a very dedicated local following. I had to call in a favor to even get us a table.

I opened the door for him, and the first buttery notes of garlic yumminess hit my nostrils. Golden fresh-baked bread and the saltwater tang of the sea crescendoed into one enchanting scent that made my mouth water. Small round tables were covered in red and white checked tablecloths and lit with long tapered candles in hurricane lamps.

"Is this heaven?" Foster asked.

"No," I teased. "They'd never let hooligans like you in there."

Hooligans? Another grandmotherly word accidentally chosen but effectively highlighting the age gap. Good job.

Dmitri came forward with a mustachioed smile, genuinely interested in the man who was standing next to me. "Gionna, so happy to have you join us for dinner. How is Marco?"

"Busy as usual," I said. "You know Dad." He nodded graciously before his warm, inquisitive eyes turned to Foster, and I wondered how long it would take for him to report this sighting back to my dad. I was pretty sure it would happen between the appetizer and the main course.

"And who is this?" Dmitri inquired innocently, his eyes widening and faithfully recording every detail for the conversation I knew he couldn't help but have with Pops.

"This is my *friend*." I emphasized the word just long

enough for it to cool Dmitri's jets. "Foster Valentine." Foster stuck a hand out on cue with a quick smile. "He's new in town and I promised I'd show him all the local gems."

"Follow me, Foster Valentine," he said with his thick Italian accent, making Foster's name sound even more romantically surreal. He spun on his heel, and we stepped lively behind him, following closely as he led us to the best table in the house. I peeled off my coat, and before I could grab the chair, Foster appeared behind me, pulling it out for me. Dmitri gave a small appreciative nod and disappeared. I sat down, shifted forward as he pushed the chair in, and then pulled the wine list from the menu and studied it. One bottle caught my eye. A '78 Roblar Pino Noir at nearly $700 a bottle, it wasn't ever going to see the light of day.

"So, what's your vintage?" I asked.

"Is that your sneaky, yet effective way of asking my age?" he wondered, smiling. His rich brown eyes crinkled at the corners, reminding me of the way my dad's did. I flushed pink and then nodded and waited, sipping on my water to have something to do. He thought about it for a minute, sitting back in the chair and rubbing his chin with his hand like he did the first day we met. "I would say I'm a 1986 Poujeaux Bordeaux Blend. A robust red with an oaky finish that at fourteen percent alcohol by volume is guaranteed to get you lit with one single glass." I nodded appreciatively, understanding he was probably right on all accounts.

"Nice... and dangerous." I smiled, appreciating him embracing my silly wine analogy.

"I'm thirty-four," he said while gazing directly in my eyes. "How old are you?"

"Forty-two," I muttered through gritted teeth.

"Perfect," he answered in a way that put me instantly at ease and made my stomach flutter. "I prefer a woman who is old enough to know who she is."

"Men always tell you that until the stretch marks show up and you stop coloring your hair."

He glanced up at my hair, and I nervously tucked a stray piece behind my ear. Breaking his intense gaze, I looked at the menu like it was my job. He stared at me, and my chest constricted, tightening every muscle in my torso and making it hard to take a full breath. I was light-headed and fluttery all at once, complete intoxication in full effect sans vino.

He reached out and rested his warm hand on mine on the menu, and I froze. A fire was building in my belly that he continually stoked with his touches. Pulling back again, I studied the menu, trying to focus enough to select a wine, but every sense was focused on where our skin had touched. The heat still gathered there and had seared me, leaving a trail of fire where he brushed against my skin.

God. Did he feel this, too?

I tucked my hands carefully in my lap under the table to avoid overheating as Dmitri circled over to the table for our drink order. I decided on the house red and ordered a double order of seared scallops, a pot of mussels, and shrimp cocktail. Decisions made, I leaned back in the chair, trying to put inches between us, fighting the invisible pull toward him.

Like a moth to a flame. Where is that wine?

As if on cue, Dmitri appeared with the bottle of wine

that he poured into the glass. I swirled it around and took a sip. "Very good." The truth was anything that would take the edge off was appreciated. Every sense was elevated and acute. The fears and the hope were razor-sharp and debilitating and I ached to soften them.

He filled our glasses and then left the bottle behind.

I took a long sip and rejoiced in the warmth in the back of my throat loosening the knot.

The shrimp cocktail appeared next with a flourish—a large crystal goblet of ice with huge, succulent shrimp with bright orange veins that dangled precariously over the edge. A bright red spicy cocktail sauce was in a dish in the center.

"The cocktail sauce here is so good. The horseradish is grown at an organic farm Dmitri's brother owns. It's that sweet heat that is so perfect." I dragged a shrimp through it and popped it into my mouth, then pulled a lemon wedge from the dish and squirted it on the rest of them.

"I love watching you eat," he said.

Great, he's a chubby chaser. I knew he was too good to be true.

I shifted in my chair uncomfortably, which he noticed immediately, and took another long sip of the wine.

"Whoa—not in a weird, fetishizing type of way," he scrambled to explain. "Being a culinary grad, you've been taught to savor the subtle nuances of the flavors and have a more discernible palate. You enjoy the pleasure of it more. I love that I'm not sitting across from a date, watching her push salad around with her fork and never really eating anything."

My mind stuck on the word date, and suddenly, I was overcome with this massive desire to label our evening.

The wine had loosened the weight on my chest and pried open my mouth.

"We're on a date?" I asked cautiously, leaving plenty of room for him to correct me.

His forehead crinkled in uncertainty.

"Well, I know *I'm* on a date," he declared. "What about you, Gionna? Are *you* on a date?"

I couldn't help but smile. "Yes. I think I am."

"Good." Then he sipped on the wine and chased it with another tender bite of cold, spicy shrimp.

I exhaled for the first time that night. The relief of the clarification made the atmosphere lighter, and I could finally fill my lungs completely instead of taking small, peckish sips of air. My chest rose and then fell, and I studied him watching me, enjoying the simple food and wine in front of us.

"Tell me about the bakery? My boss said it's been in your family for three generations. That's really impressive."

"I'm really proud of my family," I gushed as the wine loosened my tongue and turned me into a chatterbox. "My Bumpo was a driven man fresh off the boat at Ellis Island. He started out selling cannolis from a street cart in his twenties. My Nonna would bake them in the kitchen of the house they shared with three other families. Times were really lean when he started, but Bumpo was a hard worker and an incredibly skilled salesman. That man could sell anything to anyone. Billy Mays had nothing on him." I smiled, fondly reminiscing about Bumpo. I missed him so much. Grief was an endless cycle that ebbed and flowed, and you never knew when it would knock your feet out from under you. I blinked the tears away that threatened to surface and took another sip of my pinot that was making it too easy to let him in and left me scrambling to lock my heart back up again.

Foster leaned in closer and studied me, searching my eyes for clues. I knew I was hard to read and that emotions flitted across my face like thunderstorms during Florida summers.

I broke the intensity of his gaze with another awkward smile and continued. "Bumpo scrimped and saved until he had tucked away enough money from the street cart proceeds to put a small down payment on a corner shop."

"That's amazing work ethic," Foster said, listening intently and sipping on the wine that was making me pliable and soft.

"He was a very ambitious man." I nodded. "My grandparents had to live in the bakery for a year to save money, and they slept on two cots pushed together in the small kitchen next to the ovens and showered at the YMCA. They sacrificed—like, really sacrificed, and within five years, Bumpo had made enough to buy the storefront next door and double the size of the bakery. He was able to double the oven space and added delivery service, and business exploded. I guess you could say, the rest is history." I shrugged with a grin.

"The dedication it takes to sacrifice like that is just nothing short of amazing," Foster agreed and popped another shrimp into his wide mouth that I was having a hard time not fixating on.

"His frugality was legendary. Bumpo reused paper towels religiously, oh, and dental floss, hanging them to dry in-between uses."

He laughed. "My grandma was like that. She saved

everything. Single socks just in case she came across another one that didn't have a mate, and she dusted her furniture with old pairs of underwear."

"They *were* the greatest generation," I joked. "But Bumpo took it to a whole other level. He repurposed his bath water to water the plants and then spent countless hours at city council meetings, campaigning for reduced water usage and garbage fees for the 'conscientious folks'."

"He sounds like quite a character."

"God, he was," I mused. "I miss him." I took another sip of the wine, emptying the glass. "I'm incredibly lucky. It took me too much time to truly acknowledge it, but Nonna and Bumpo's weird sacrifices paved the way so we could have more. And we do."

"It must be amazing to come from a family like that."

"It is. I never knew just how lucky until after he died." My tone hit a somber note.

"I'm sorry," he said and reached across the table to squeeze my hand. We sat in comfortable silence for a minute, and for once, I didn't scramble to fill it with words.

"You have to tell me the story behind your name."

He leaned in, his dark eyes burning into mine, the wine working its magic.

"Mom figured since I was a Valentine's baby, she'd capitalize on the fact." He continued. "Originally, it was my middle name. She was only sixteen when she had me, and she'd be the first one to admit she wasn't making great decisions back then." He smiled when talking about his mother; his expression softened, and I could tell he loved her very much. Seeing that, I relaxed.

"Whoa." It slipped out, and I hated that I sounded judgmental. "I mean, sixteen? That's so young."

"I think I definitely fall into the accident category."

"Your dad?"

He sighed and sat back in his chair, breaking the spell. There was pain there, and I was afraid to push or stay anything more. "I'm sorry. Too nosy. My mouth always gets me in trouble."

He brushed it away and then leaned in closer. "Let's just say he wasn't a very nice guy and the idea of traveling through life with anything permanently tying me to him was impossible to accept. I changed my name when I was eighteen with my mom's blessing."

I cocked my head to the side. We came from vastly different worlds, that much was blatantly obvious.

"I want to cook for you next time," he said, effectively changing the subject.

My heart surged at the words "next time." Another huge grin spread across my face, the joy making me flushed and looser. He pulled my hand into his and traced down the length of each of my fingers, sending shock-waves wherever his fingers connected.

Dmitri brought our bill, and he jumped to grab it before I could, placing his credit card in the leather folder. Then we stumbled out of the tiny restaurant and onto the street, warmed by the wine and the new warmth from the fire building between us. We walked quietly, and I felt him reach for my hand and then pull me into an alleyway. He pushed me gently against the brick wall, pinning me with his body, giving me nowhere to go except his arms.

The top of my head rested against the bricks as I looked up at him. He was a head taller, and I couldn't stop staring at his lips. They were full and pink, and I wanted to press mine against them. I licked my bottom lip and bit on it, trying to calm my hammering heart.

"Jesus," he whispered into the space between us. "You have to stop doing that."

"Doing what?" I asked, puzzled at his comment. Before I could ask another question, I felt the pads of his thumbs at my cheekbones as he pulled me in gently. His fingers laced into my hair, cupping the back of my head, and finally, his lips brushed across mine. Warm and willing. His kisses were soft at first, then I could taste the wine that lingered on his tongue that met mine when the kiss deepened. He pressed against me, and everything else fell away. All that was left were his soft kisses, becoming more urgent and needy. Then he pulled back, still cradling my face in his hands, his fingertips massaging my neck, sending shivers down my spine and making goosebumps prickle up my arms.

"You're really, really good at this," I breathed out, not ready to break the spell yet.

"I know," he said.

"And you're incredibly humble, too," I teased.

"It's confidence, sweetheart," he whispered and then pulled me by my hand back out onto the street where we walked the two blocks to the Sweet Life, watching as the pimply teenagers scraped our chosen flavors and mix-ins across a frozen slab of granite. The cream instantly froze and was scraped and rolled flawlessly into large rolls of creamy goodness.

"It's almost too pretty to eat." He turned the dish to the side to check out all the angles.

"Speaking of too pretty to eat…" I teased as I dipped a

long-handled spoon into the sculpture and then sucked on it long and hard, my eyes burning into his. Telegraphing the open invitation to replace the spoon with another part of his anatomy. Introducing him to Tipsy and Flirty, two of my most popular dwarfs.

"Damn," he said under his breath out of the earshot of the table of little kids next to us.

We finished our ice cream in record time and then stepped back out onto the sidewalk only three blocks from the bakery. In a daze, my feet barely touched the brick pavers. His hand laced in mine and felt like it had always belonged there. I walked slowly, wanting to savor the night, not wanting it to end, but too quickly, we were standing in front of the bakery. The lights from the glass cases illuminated the shop in a swoony romantic way.

"Do you want to come up?" I asked, barely able to put the words together.

He pulled me in for a hug, then pulled back and kissed me softly again.

God, I wanted him in my bed.

I said a little prayer of thanks that I was still wearing my ugly underwear. It gave me the tiniest pause when the wine was in my ear and screaming "Full speed ahead!"

"As amazing as that sounds, this is the kind of thing that you can't rush. Don't you think we owe it to ourselves to do things the right way?"

Confused, I looked up at him.

"When you find something this special, you protect it," he said. "I haven't felt a connection like this with someone in a really long time."

"But I don't wanna," I only half-joked, loving the way his eyes crinkled when he smiled. His eyes had flecks of gold dancing through brown irises. They were mesmerizing.

"Gionna, it will be worth the wait. I promise." He tucked a stray hair behind my ear, a gesture that equally melted me and unnerved me. The fear was building in my belly; I had wanted to keep things simple. Casual. I had allowed myself a fling, a bit of fun with an attractive guy. But the way he was looking at me and the promises he was making with his words and his eyes were telling me he had no intentions of keeping this casual. "But I am not letting you out of my sight until you agree to let me cook for you."

"When?"

"Next Friday?"

That was seven whole days from now.

"Don't worry, you'll see me before then. Your espresso calls my name in the morning." He pulled my hand up to his lips and brushed them across my knuckles, then tugged me into a dizzying twirl in the light spilling from the bakery. "Thank you for a great night, the first of many, I hope."

"Me too," I agreed, and I meant it.

He stood outside and watched me walk away. I ran up the stairs and then looked out the picture window, giving him a little wave. Once he saw I was safely inside, he turned, and I watched him walk away until he disappeared. The fear and doubt came rushing back the moment he was out of view.

Is he for real? Careful, girl. Slow your roll. Don't get carried away.

My fingers brushed against my lips, and I rubbed them across my chin that was slightly chaffed from his kisses.

Remembering how his lips felt urgently pressed against mine. Kissing was important, and he was incredible at it. I got undressed and washed my face before pulling my hair up into a bun on top of my head. It took me a really long time to settle down that night enough to be able to sleep. I finally drifted off with a smile on my lips, hugging my pillow tightly to my chest, wishing it was Foster Valentine.

THIRTEEN

After a short night, I was up and showered. Usually cranky, my attitude was softened by the blissful memory of the night before. Just recalling his lips on mine sent delicious thrilling ripples through my body, but I had to focus. Wedding days were always a pressure cooker for me. No matter how long I was in the business, they were always stressful. I'd have oddly specific night-mares where the wedding was happening and I hadn't even started baking the cake yet, or the icing was made of blood. Or the scariest one—at an outdoor summer venue, the finished cake started to precariously slide in the heat and humidity as I stood watching the destruction, twisting with anxiety while the bride raged next to me. It didn't matter how comfortable I was with the process or how long I had been doing this, I still woke up sometimes the morning of a wedding in a cold sweat. When you build a business creating a custom product for people on the biggest day of their lives, tension and stress come with the territory. I never half-assed it. Every cake was a chance to better my skills and to create something magical for the couples who entrusted me. My reputation was on the line at every single event. If you booked with DeLuca's, you could count on me to whole-ass it every single time.

Mom usually came with me to the venues because she has a very quiet and calming presence. She also provided a buffer between my nerves that were stretched drum-tight and the wedding planners who always seemed to run high and hot. In a crisis, my mom was a rock. She never got rattled, or at least, I never saw her show it. On the other hand, Pops and I had the same uncanny ability to get carried away on the drama train at the drop of a hat. She was a consistent transportation expert, driving like a turtle, slow and steady, while Pops had a tendency to slam on the brakes. I relied on Mom's delicate touch to get us there safely and with my precious cakes fully intact.

It took us thirty minutes to load the delivery van. First, I lined the floor of the van with two yoga mats. Their non-slide surface with just the slightest amount of cushion hugged my boxes, prohibiting them from sliding around. Each tier of the cake was carefully placed in its own new moving box from the supply stack I kept stocked at the bakery. I placed the box on its side and slid the cake in, then taped it closed to protect it from dust. Once all the boxes were in the van, I rolled up towels and shoved them between the boxes, then wrapped it all with bubble wrap. I surveyed my checklist one more time before I climbed in, and Mom closed the back door behind me. Mom navigated us to the ballroom while I ran over the sequence of the setup in my head. Putting the cake together on-site took several hours the day of the wedding, so I had gotten used to giving up every Saturday morning during wedding season.

Transporting the cake was always the trickiest part and where things could go horribly wrong. Pushing through the heart palpitations, I never could fully relax until we arrived at the venue. I had all my tools tucked into my wedding kit —a black leather duffel bag filled with a piping bag, flower nails, and everything I would need to make an emergency cake repair. Another box was filled with meticulously sculpted gum paste orchids and roses I had spent an eternity handcrafting. I amassed over a hundred hours of rolling them out, cutting the petals, and then embossing the edges to crinkle them, then carefully attaching the petals to the base. I built an assortment of unique flowers, every one slightly different, just as they are in nature. After they set up, I hand-painted the edges of some of the petals with gold edible paint. They rested delicately boxed in tissue paper, ready to be applied to the cake. I sat on the floor in the back of the van, cradling my cake like a newborn baby, keeping a hand at the ready in case the boxes shifted, carefully avoiding as much movement as possible. If a semi came at us and locked up their brakes, I would shield this cake with my body. I am not exaggerating; I would die before I let something happen to one of my cakes. The drive was uneventful until the van lurched forward as Mom stomped on the brake

"Sorry, honey," Lorraine apologized. "Jerk!" she muttered under her breath. I softened the jolting action with my body as the cake slid and then recovered as my heart pounded in my chest. Every mile she drove was tense. She eased back onto the gas again, and twenty minutes later, she pulled into the gated country club. By the time we arrived, my muscles were shaking from all the clenching.

The Sugar Hill Country Club's century-old sugar maples were on full technicolor display, sporting their mid-September full reds and oranges. The trees flanked the endless asphalt drive that meandered to the ornate front veranda. Mom finally put the van in park and opened the back of the van where I carefully untangled myself from the boxes and climbed out onto the asphalt.

It was a venue I had frequented often, and I strode to the ballroom confidently, scanning the mass of people that were engaged in various tasks like worker bees in a hive. Finding the Queen Bee was easy; the headset and the buzzing beehive of activity that swirled around her always gave her away. I say 'her' because most wedding planners are women with the occasional fabulous man thrown in the mix. Surrounded by florists and decorators, equipment engineers, and lighting companies, she barked out orders after consulting her clipboard. They were on a mission to completely transform the space and had only a few hours to pull it off. I always insisted on being on-site first thing, because in the pastry world, rushing the process ends in disaster. I approached it like a tactical mission, wanting to get in and out, completely set up before the florist was finished. My goal was to be completely set up with hours to spare so I never had to see a bride on her actual wedding day.

"I'm here from DeLuca's to set up the cake and dessert station," I announced when I had gotten to the front of the line of professionals vying for the planner's attention.

She glanced at the clipboard and pointed to a table dressed in a cloud of organza with a larger set of bar-height tables against the wall draped in the same soft fluffy fabric.

"Perfect," I said. "Thank you!" The lighting engineer had already adjusted the specialty lights, and an ivory-colored light washed across the face of the cake table. The back wall was painted with layers of dancing fuchsia light. It always amazed me how much event lighting could transform a space.

I am meticulous with my cake setups. A stickler for details and a card-carrying perfectionist. I corralled a shiny stainless steel cart from catering and pushed it outside to the van. Mom knew my method by now, and I was superstitious enough to never deviate from it. I needed to unwrap the boxes and set them on the cart myself. Being a control freak herself, Mom understood that if anything happened during transit, I wanted to be the one held responsible. She grabbed my emergency kit, waited until the cart was laden with boxes, and then followed me into the ballroom as I rolled the cake parts to the table.

I pulled out the box with the cake stand and opened it. It was aged gold leaf, ornate in a baroque design, and one of the many I'd collected over the years. I set it on the table and held out my hand as Mom placed the tape measure in it, like a surgeon with a scalpel. We developed a short-hand while working events together over the years that didn't require me to actually speak anymore. She knew exactly what I needed and when I needed it. Carefully, I measured from side to side to center the stand and double checked every measurement to locate the center point. Calculating the placement of the stand correctly was crucial because moving a cake was asking for trouble. It was a lesson I learned from devouring cake competition shows on *Food Network* while holding my breath as they transported the finished design to the table to win. The big takeaway was—never move a finished cake unless you have no other choice, or a hundred thousand dollars is on the line.

Mom pulled out the bottle of organic cleanser, squirted it into a blue microfiber rag, and meticulously cleaned the stand, wiping away all the fingerprints. I returned to the metal cart and opened the box with the bottom tier.

I carefully pulled the cake out while Mom held the box in place, the two of us working like a well-oiled team.

"Thanks, Mom."

It was a heavy cake. To save time on-site, the bottom layer was completely covered on the right-hand side in ivory gum paste roses and orchids, and the edges of each flower were dusted with gold. It weighed nearly ten pounds on its own. I rested it on the golden stand and exhaled for the first time after it had found its home.

One at a time, I added the next four layers, and then the hard work began. I pulled out the edible gold leaf and began placing it on the cake with a brush. It was slow going work that required me to commit to the final placement before I was ready. Second-guessing myself constantly, I lined it up, and with a shaking hand, gently brushed to adhere the gold to the cake. The gold leaf was as fragile as butterfly wings. Over the next hour, I continued to paint it on and cascade it down the front of the tiers diagonally to add a bit of layered sparkle before I would cover the rest of the right-hand side of the cake entirely with orchids and roses. I pulled out my piping bags filled with the frosting I had prepared and piped a rope design between the layers to tie them together.

When assembling cakes on a wedding day, I blocked out the rest of the world. Laser-focusing on the task at hand, I controlled the pressure and speed of the frosting piped out of the bag. I got into the zone—the pastry version of Tom Brady during the Super Bowl. I completely concentrated on the piping bag, unaware of anything or anyone around me. I slowly circled the cake over and over again. Being Anal Annie over here, I had prepped five full bags of icing for the task. I preferred to start each new layer with a fresh bag that I had obsessively prepared at the bakery that morning. No air bubbles or false starts would do. When I finally finished piping, I took a step back and surveyed the results.

"It's perfect, honey," Mom said. "The piping is flaw-less. You're like a machine."

I laughed at first and then welled up with pride. "It's really coming together, isn't it?"

"It is!"

"I mean, after I spend the next two hours of our lives adding orchids and roses."

She just smiled and continued to work silently next to me like an extra set of hands that knew what I wanted before I did. Starting at the bottom, I added flowers to the cake, one by one, poking them into the fondant with flower picks to secure them in place. I carefully stacked them in sweeping, staggered rows where each flower had its own place to shine. They covered the entire right half of the cake from top to bottom when I was finished. I stood back and then circled it slowly, looking for flaws or imperfec-tions. Then I was able to relax. The hard part was over.

Mom put together another multi-tiered stand and cleaned it until it gleamed in the colored light. She began to fill it with cake pops dipped in ivory glaze and then hand-piped with scrolling designs that looked like embossed lace. They were dusted with gold, making the lace design shimmer. I added bowls of madeleines and macaroons stacked on stunning crystal stands to give them height. White chocolate monograms were layered on another plate, it was a recent lucrative addition that my brides raved about. The wedding day was the only time in a woman's life her monogram suddenly surged to the forefront, so I rode the trend and developed a line of chocolates to fill that need. I was always looking for savvy additions to add to our product offerings, wanting to have something new to entice brides every year.

I added delicate petit fours, tiny squares of bite-sized heaven that were flood-coated with white chocolate icing and a hand piped lacy pattern. Then came the sugar cookies coated in iridescent edible paint. I snaked the organza and lighting through the table to give the gold and crystal stands a warm glow and stood back to survey our work. I glanced at my watch; three and half hours had passed in the blink of an eye, but it was finally ready and a show stopper.

I pulled out my phone and swiped it quickly for messages, and my fluttery hope was replaced by slight discouragement when I realized there were no texts from Foster. I pushed the disappointment away and took a few photos of the dessert buffet and the finished cake, then begged one of the floral assistants to take a quick photo of Mom and me standing next to it. A photo with Mom was an every-wedding ritual, and I loved walking back through them to see how far I had come as a designer. I would get professional photographs from the event planner eventually, but this photo was for me. I hugged her thin shoulders and looked over at her. She ignored me, sweetly smiling at the camera as her eyes crinkled at the corners. A few age spots dusted her cheeks and forehead, but she was still a beautiful woman. I looked back at the camera and gave her a little squeeze and smiled for the photo.

"You done good, sweetheart. It's another incredible cake," she said as she finished tearing down the empty boxes, preparing to go home.

I felt the phone vibrate in my pocket, and a little hopeful thrill shot through me. I pulled out the phone, and seeing Foster's name, smiled down at it.

Foster: Missed you today at the bakery. Aubrey said you were on site. Hope your day is going well. I know I can't stop smiling.

I tucked it back into my pocket and looked up into the unblinking inquisitive eyes of my mother.

"Who is making you grin like that?" she asked.

"Aubrey is just being a goofball," I lied. I was in denial that this thing developing between me and Foster was going to turn into something real that I would need to tell my parents about. I didn't want to get their hopes up or hurt them again. The sting from Brett ran deep and was impossible to forget. For now, I wanted to keep this secret to myself.

FOURTEEN

The next day, I floated into the bakery, barely sleeping all night long after hours of exchanging flirty texts and sexy banter with Foster. I woke up with my phone still cradled in my hand, red creases on my cheek, and a smile plastered on my face. I was giddy to start another day knowing that sometime during it, Foster Valentine would walk into my world.

"*Mia Bella*." Nonna immediately noticed a shift in me. "Who has got you shining like this?" Her eyes danced as she leaned closer, studying me.

I flushed red and smiled at her, pressing my lips together to keep the confession from escaping while she went back to punching and proofing dough. Nonna had a knack for reading people like tea leaves, especially me. I could never hide anything from her. I was struggling to keep this new and exciting turn of events to myself. It was a delicious secret that I couldn't help but spill. "I might have met a boy—a boy like Bumpo," I confided in a whisper. It was the first time I'd said the words out loud, and doubt bubbled up the minute they left my mouth.

Her crooked fingers clasped together. "Ooh! Bravo! Tell me everything. Leave nothing out." In Nonna's world, everything took a backseat to love.

I hesitated. "I don't want to jinx it."

She stopped what she was doing, quickly washed her hands and wiped them on her apron, and immediately came around to my side of the table. Nonna cradled my face with her satiny hands and brushed her nose in a butterfly kiss across mine. It was our thing, a loving gesture we both took joy in since I was tiny. Then she pulled back, still holding me close, to capture my full attention, and said, "If he is the love of your life, you can't jinx it. Nothing can keep away the heart that is yours."

She said that phrase to me many times before, and I dismissed it as a silly romantic notion, but this time, as I watched her wash her hands and go back to cutting perfect circles from the wide span of dough, I wondered if she might be right. There was a churning in my belly as I remembered the way his lips felt on mine. Reliving the moment transported by the roughness from his stubble combined with the softness of his lips. I closed my eyes as a swoony pang of pleasure flooded me, and then they popped open when a fresh twinge of doubt bubbled to the surface.

Nonna was smiling at me dreamily. "This one is different. I can tell. His soul has a hold on yours." She waved her finger at me knowingly.

A bolt of fear coursed through me, a nervous laugh escaping as I struggled to push the distrust away. "It's a little too early to say that," I explained as I preheated the oven for the first batch of cannolis.

"I assure you, little one, it is not. Nonna knows." She beamed at me, her face soft, and tapped her temple. "It is okay if you do not yet, but you will see."

She was so certain it was unnerving. Nonna was practically a witch with her clairvoyant ability to accurately foresee the future. I had never known another person so in tune with those around her, picking up the most sensitive shifts in behavior and being able to read people like a book. She was a human divining rod and never wrong.

Seeing I was becoming skittish and jittery, she changed tactics. "The boy that comes into the bakery every day, with the crazy hair?" she asked, looking for confirmation.

Sweet Jesus. Was it that obvious?

My cheeks itched as warmth flushed my face.

Her hand flew to her chest, and she clasped it there. "I knew it, my love."

"How?" I asked.

"The shift. I felt it, and apparently you did, too."

So, I threw caution to the wind. Instead of concealing all the torrid details of the first heart-pounding date I had been on in ages that actually had the potential to go anywhere, I recounted the night to her, minute by minute. Getting more flushed and animated as it went on.

She smiled so sweetly at me, savoring the revelation. She oohed and aahed at all the right places, completely spellbound, and I marveled at her ability to still believe in romance all the way into her eighties.

After I had spilled all the deets, she hugged me. Her thick body pressed against mine, her strong fleshy arms wrapping me in a hug that was so familiar and comforting. Her hugs were one of my favorite childhood escapes.

"You've waited a long time, *Mia Bella.* You deserve this. Open your heart and let him love you."

Tears prickled at my eyes. "I'm afraid, Nonna. I don't know if I can. Brett…"

She frowned and cursed under her breath at the sound of his name. "Let it simmer. Love is best when it simmers."

A burst of cold air hit the back of my legs. "What is going on here?" Pop's deep voice boomed, making me jump as he rolled in, arriving for work and seeing us dissolved into a teary mess. Mom was at his heels, watching the obvious display of emotion with interest but immediately went into store opening mode by turning on all the lights and starting to count the petty cash to open the register.

"Just giving my granddaughter a hug," Nonna answered for both of us, winking at me. She held out an arm and beckoned him with her fingers and a smile, and Pops was pulled into the group hug that ended with him kissing both of Nonna's cheeks.

"Good morning, Mama." Dad smiled. I always enjoyed watching Nonna reduce him to a sweet little mama's boy in her presence.

"Did anyone clean the bathroom yet?" Mom asked, destroying our mushy moment with sobering thoughts of dirty public urinals.

"Lorraine, come here first dear," Nonna requested and enveloped Mom into a warm hug. No one could refuse Nonna. "What would we do without you?" Nonna's praise made Mom beam with pride, and she gave the janitorial duties a brief hiatus. "Bumpo was always so proud of your mind for business." Mom and Bumpo had a special connection, and I knew she missed him terribly. A sad smile crept across her face.

"All the details, Rainey, how do you keep them at the tip-top of your mind? You've transformed DeLuca's into what it is today. I'm so proud of you." Pops praised her warmly, using Mom's nickname to butter her up. It was cute to see them in this light. It clicked that Pops had the same effect on Mom as Foster was having on me.

High praise this early in the morning was clearly making Mom uncomfortable, so she got right back on track. "Clean bathrooms are the cornerstone of a good review on Yelp," she reminded us.

She was right. Yelpers were notorious for barbecuing restaurants based on the cleanliness of their bathrooms. They reported any missteps with glee under the cloak of self-righteousness, so Mom pandered to reviewers. In her defense, it was probably a smart business decision, but it never ceased to annoy me. I mean, you can't make everyone happy. It's impossible. And unfortunately, the internet was filled with trolls who had nothing but time on their hands to make themselves feel better about their own shitty lives by destroying some else's.

The early morning passed slowly. Every time the door-bell chimed, my eyes would instantly dart to the door with a flash of fevered anticipation, and then I would look back down in disappointment.

I've been reduced to a lovesick teenager, and it feels so good, I don't even give a shit.

Around eight o'clock, Aubrey came over and sidled up to me, whispering, "Has he been in yet?"

I shook my head. "Not yet."

"I'm dying for details. You've been uncharacteristically quiet all weekend, and that's not like you." It was true, I usually called her for a post mortem after any date, but I was oddly driven to keep this one to myself.

"I'm a little gobsmacked. It was..." I struggled to find the right word. "...incredible."

Her eyes widened. "Well, I like the sound of that." A grumpy line of un-caffeinated patrons was forming at the register again. "Let's catch up at lunch."

With morning light streaming into the bakery, I pulled out my gum paste ingredients. Fall weddings were always cloaked in jewel box colors—rich burgundies, burnt oranges, and vibrant yellows. I had to make some real headway on the cake pops for the Magnuson wedding this weekend and prep the burgundy gum paste for the Miller cake the following week. Getting the dark burgundy color the bride requested just right had been a killer. I couldn't work at night, because under the kitchen's artificial lighting, the color looked muddy and brown. This was my third attempt, and since each one was made from scratch, every batch varied slightly in color to give a realistic varied effect that was more believable and pleasing to the eye. Nothing is perfect in nature, it's the imperfections that make flowers beautiful.

I separated the eggs, poured the egg whites into the mixer, and added powdered sugar, then turned on the mixer until it achieved a royal icing consistency that was like soft cream cheese. Then I started adding the edible powdered pigments. Achieving the perfect color was not an exact science, so I started by adding a lot of red, some blue, and a little black powdered food coloring, consulting the fabric swatch from the Bridesmaid dresses the bride had given me as a reference point. I continued to mix it and tinker with the colors, adding a few dashes of edible powdered pigments with names like stargazer, hot pink, and red rose and then a liberal squirt of burgundy color gel. It's a little dash of this and a little sprinkle of that, knowing it will dry slightly darker. After about twelve tweaks, the color was a perfect match.

I added the tylose powder slowly, waiting for it to clump in the mixer, then turned it out onto the marble countertop, rubbed shortening on my hands like lotion, and began to knead it. It was a little wet, so I added a dash of powdered sugar and continued to knead until it reached a pocked consistency that held its shape when I pressed it. I loved the physicality of kneading, the long strokes folding the gum paste onto itself and across the marble with the heels of my hands. Like meditation, the controlled movements were zen-like and almost had a Tai Chi quality. Finally achieving the right consistency, I wrapped it in a Ziploc, squeezed all of the air out, and put it into the refrigerator to mature overnight.

An hour later, after the early bird church crowd dispersed, the bell jingled and there he was. He winked at me, and my mouth curved into a smile that I had to conceal from my mom. Keeping her in the dark was my usual modus operandi because when she was privy to information in my personal life, she went into wedding planning mode. I quickly learned it was always better to keep her in the dark.

"The usual?" I asked. He grinned at me, causing goosebumps to break out on my arms. My fingers ached to rub against his scruffy chin.

"So, I already have a usual?" he teased as I folded one of our branded kraft paper boxes while I racked my brain for a flirty response.

"Do you see something that you like?" I settled on and peppered it with a smirky smile.

"Oh, I see *so* much that I like," he answered, staring at me intently, his voice dripping with sexy sweetness. It's amazing how infatuation can reduce a woman to a bumbling teenage-esque idiot full of clichés and flirty innuendo, no matter how old you are. That surge of joy deep in your belly when you lock eyes with the person you're interested in is a drug, and I was addicted. I pulled three of our freshest cannolis from the case and began to pipe the cream into the sleeves.

Glancing through the window, I met the watchful watery eyes of Nonna. She studied us, deeply engrossed and invested like she was tuning in to one of those terrible soap operas that she loved so much. Like telenovelas, they were entertaining insanity distilled into ridiculous sixty-minute storylines. She made a little scooting gesture with her fingers, encouraging me back to Foster with a huge knowing grin on her face and her sparse eyebrows dancing.

I shook my head at her and turned back to Foster, handing him the container of cannolis and his fresh espresso. He looked right at me and said softly just out of earshot of Mom, "I don't think I can wait five more days. Patience is not my strong suit."

"Someone told me good things come to those who wait," I proclaimed, then felt stupid repeating trite plati-tudes when all I really wanted to do was kiss him until my jaw was raw and chapped.

He pulled the box from my hand, and our fingers touched for the briefest moment, sending tingles through me. Making me wonder, if this was the effect that he had on my fingers, what would the Foster Valentine effect be on the other parts of my body?

Sweet Jesus, woman, cold shower time. You need to get yourself under control.

He thanked me politely and walked away as I eyeballed his butt in his jeans. Yum. He had those muscle dips on the sides of his sweet...

My sexy daydream was abruptly interrupted when he turned around, feeling my eyes burning on his back, and shot me a cocky smile. A few seconds later, the text notification rang on my phone in my pocket. I pulled it out and read:

> **Foster:** *I saw that. I'm not just a piece of meat, G. Winky Face.*
> **Me:** *True. You are a hot piece of meat, but you have other things to offer me. Many other redeeming qualities.*

I looked up from my phone and into the amused eyes of Mr. Manzetti, who had been watching our interaction with a soft smile on his face. I pulled the coffee pot from the burner and headed over to warm him up.

"Looks like you have a new beau," he said.

"How do you even...?"

"It may have been a long time since I've fallen in love, but I still remember what it looks like." He grinned up at me sweetly, an act that offered a fleeting glimpse of his teenage face.

"I only have eyes for you, Mr. Manzetti," I teased as his cheeks reddened. "Are you feeling okay?"

"Just a little tired, sweetheart."

"I'm going to get you a couple of cannolis to go, but only if you agree to test your sugars before you eat them." I squeezed his shoulder that felt frail in my hand.

"You, my dear, are an absolute angel."

With the breakfast rush over, I finally got to relax at lunchtime with Aubrey.

"So? You've been holding out on me! Spill it, sister." She leaned in, her adorable freckles popping against her ivory-colored skin. Dressed in white jeans and a pastel blue, long-sleeved bakery shirt, she took a bite of her sandwich. Nonna fed the staff every day. It was one of the perks of working at the bakery. Some days, it was gently simmered soups, lentils and ham with celery and carrot. Others, it was cranberry and turkey sandwiches on hand-kneaded cottage bread dusted with flour. The bakery was her family, and she lived to feed us all because that is how Nonna loved you, with artisanal peasant bread from ancestral recipes and hand-cut pasta from the old country. She put the comfort in comfort food.

I smiled, not wanting to tell her the story because it felt like such a decadent treat I wanted to keep to myself in case it was too good to be true. The more people I told, the greater the fear grew about it falling apart. I was afraid that speaking the words out loud too often, even to my best friend, would make Foster disappear like an incredible dream that is so vivid and real, but upon waking disintegrates into the bright light of dawn. Aubrey tapped her fingers on the table impatiently. "Come on, girl! You know

I have to live vicariously through you. I haven't been on a date in ages."

"You can get a date anytime you want," I argued.

"I know. It's my choice for sure. But dating is different when you have kids. It's not just finding someone to bang. It's finding someone to bang who likes to be called Daddy outside the bedroom."

I snickered. "Yeah, that's a tall order."

Her eyes widened and she pushed my shoulder impatiently. "Come on, girl. Spill it!"

I looked around to make sure no one was listening and then started recounting the events of the night. "It was incredible, Aubrey. I haven't been on a first date like that in so long." I paused, considering what I had just said. "Maybe ever." Still swooning, I laughed and continued. "I took him to the Stadium and for a Dodger dog, and then we had the most amazing seafood at Alexander's. We finished with hand-rolled ice cream at Sweet Life, which wasn't as good as the dessert I had in mind."

"What? You trollop!" She leaned in and licked her lips in excited anticipation that she was going to hear something scandalous.

"Down, girl," I teased her. "It was just kisses. The most incredible, heart-throbbing, life-changing kisses."

Aubrey sighed. "God, I miss kissing. And you have someone that knows how to do it well? That's the holy grail, woman, and you know it!"

"Ain't that the truth! I could seriously kiss him all night long."

"So, did you?"

"Of course not. I have morals—good Christian values." I barely got the words out of my mouth before

Aubrey burst out laughing, and I followed suit. We both knew that was a lie or, at the very least, a massive exaggeration.

"He's different, Aub." I paused; hearing myself gushy like this was brand new and strange. "He said he didn't want to rush into being physical because, when you find something this special, you don't want to do anything to jeopardize it."

"He actually said that?" She dropped the spoon in her hand stunned. "Wow."

"I didn't think guys like him existed," I confessed and swallowed a spoonful of soup before continuing. "I'm letting my hopes get up, and I'm so excited to see him again, but this little voice in the back of my head wonders if there's an ulterior motive."

"Like what?"

"I don't know." I stirred the soup absentmindedly.

"Is he using you to weasel his way into the DeLuca Bakery Dynasty?" She was joking, but I felt a small stab from the word "using." "Wait, I didn't mean it like that," she said quickly.

"I know, it's fine," I claimed, "but I wonder what he sees in me. A guy like Foster can have any woman he wants. He could have you."

"You need to tell that voice in your head to shut up. You're a catch, G." Aubrey reached over and squeezed my forearm. "He wants *you*."

"He does." I squealed at the thought, grinning like an idiot. "He doesn't know what he's in for. I'm what you call a handful, Aubrey. Maybe more than a handful." I grimaced self-deprecatingly and pinched the extra skin by my belly.

"You better stop that. You're beautiful. Stop trying to convince people otherwise."

Comments like those are why Aubrey is my best friend.

"So, we ended our date, and he said that he wouldn't let me out of his sight without agreeing to cook me dinner. That's the plan for Friday, but it seems like forever away." I took a nibble from my sandwich. "When he walks into the bakery like he does every day, it just gets my motor running." I fanned myself with my hand. "Do you think I'm being stupid and getting carried away?"

"Hell no! Enjoy it. Go get carried away! Those yummy new love excitement feelings are the best life offers. Don't talk yourself out of joy, G."

God, I do that. I talk myself out of joy all the time, telling myself that I'm just being practical. But what had being practical gotten me so far? Nothing. A very basic and humdrum life.

Now that the door was cracked open and I could see there was a promise of more, a reality more beautiful and fulfilling than I was currently living, it was hard to shut it and go back to living my normal life. I had a taste of what was out there, and I wanted more. I needed more.

"Okay, I won't," I decided, and then I said the two little words she always loves to hear. "You're right."

"Now you're talking." She smiled and then stole the pickle off my plate, and I was so giddy with the first bursting bubbles of gooey love that it didn't bother me at all. Normally, I am very protective of my food.

"Well, I have some news of my own," she said coyly, licking the last of the pickle juice from her fingers.

"Does it have anything to do with why you keep looking at your phone and smiling like a loon lately?"

She blushed slightly. "I might have a date."

"Might? You sexy little minx!" I pushed her shoulder playfully. "And who would that be with?" I asked.

"Remember Tony?"

"Mr. Muscles who sat in your section for hours, Tony?" I asked, teasing her, and she beamed and focused on the screen, looking like she wanted to reach through it and stroke his cheek.

"How long have you been talking to him? You seem a little too infatuated already." I studied her narrowing my eyes. "Are you catching feelings?"

"Of course not. It's strictly a catch and release program over here until the kids are older." I couldn't tell if she was saying that to placate me or not; the only arguments we ever had were over the men she dated. "But Mommy yearns for some fun. Do you think you could watch the kids some night soon so I can have a night out?"

"Absolutely. As long as I can sugar them up."

"You're the one who will have to deal with the fallout if they are up until midnight on their sugar high."

"Good point. I didn't think of that." I rubbed my chin, trying to devise a new plan. "Pizza and arcade it is."

"You're the best, G. It's so hard to date when you have kids," she cautioned.

Aubrey had no problem getting asked out. At the bakery, it happened at least once a week. What she did have problems with was picking a good guy. She had a type. Bad boy, muscled and tattooed, dark and manipulative. Ones that always treated her like shit.

I studied her examining the phone. She was glued to it,

and that was never a good sign. She always seemed to forget herself when she was involved with a man.

"Go forth and get the pipes cleaned. It will be good for you," I made the sign of the cross in front of her. "But don't get too attached."

She sighed dreamily. "That is where I always go wrong. I go all in, too quickly."

"I know," I agreed, walking the delicate line of trying to look out for her but not wanting to ruffle her feathers. It always made her pull away. "Where is he taking you?"

"Not sure yet. Probably just gonna hang out at his place."

The radar went up. Anytime a guy just wanted to hang out at his place on a first date, it was a red flag. "You deserve someone who makes an effort, who plans an actual date."

She hung her head and smiled wanly. "We'll see." I knew that look; it meant she would accept what showed up. If there was one thing I wanted to change about Aubrey, this was it.

"Your type is bad for you, honey." I was trying desperately to straddle the line between pushover and judgmental twat.

There was a heavy exhale, and then she finally put the phone down and made eye contact for the first time in several minutes.

"I know. But I can't help myself." She fanned herself. "Sometimes, I just want to be taken by a man. Pushed up against the wall and kissed breathless. Part of me yearns to be man-handled a little bit." She lowered her voice and surveyed the waning lunch crowd then laughed and looked at her phone longingly again. I looked at my watch, noting it had only been thirty seconds since she set it down.

Gonna have to keep an eye on that.

———

Later that night with a glass of Chardonnay, I started digging. I googled Foster Valentine. I found his social media profiles and wandered through them for an hour. Looking for evidence that he was a liar. There were mushy posts with his mom, Wendy, on Mother's Day. Photos of his Culinary School Graduation. Artistic closeups of food looking good enough to make me drool. Delicate nests of angel hair, peas, bacon, and chanterelle mushrooms with a cheese crisp sitting diagonally atop. Perfectly seared steaks with billowy clouds of mashed potatoes and crisp spears of asparagus.

I clicked through photo after photo and then accidentally hit the love button on a photo from four years ago.

Shit! Rule number one, never drunk Facebook. Everyone knows that! Rookie mistake.

Fifteen minutes later, my phone jingled with the custom text tone I had assigned him earlier that evening so I didn't have to obsessively run to my phone to check it every time a notification rolled in.

Foster: *Looks like someone is doing some stalking. Winky face.*
Me: *You weren't supposed to see that.*
Foster: *What did you learn?*
Me: *You can sear a steak like no one's business.*
Foster: *I can*

Me: *You love your mom.*
Foster: *I do*
Me: *You have the need for speed. Three tickets in five years.*
Foster: *Okay. Guilty.*
Me: *You don't date much*
Foster: *Neither do you.*
Me: *Look who's stalking who now. Winky face.*
Foster: *Stalk away. I have nothing to hide.*
Me: *You're too good to be true.*
Foster: *Don't worry, I'm sure I will disappoint you plenty. Did I pass inspection?*
Me: *For now.*

FIFTEEN

For a curvy girl on a second date, deciding what to wear is an exercise in futility. Going through my closet, piece by piece, pulling out tops and jeans and squeezing into spandex, trying to shape-shift my body into a silhouette that was pleasing to the eye was a frustrating fool's errand. What happened if Foster peeled my clothes off and saw my spandex encased rolls? Foundational undergarments aren't sexy. The prospect of being naked for the first time in front of him welled up a flurry of fears I wasn't prepared for.

Screw it. I wadded up the Spanx and threw them into a wrinkled pile on the ground.

I'm just going to do me. Be real and he will either love it or hate it. Real women jiggle and have cellulite and enjoy sugar without the obsessive need to weigh and measure every morsel that goes into their mouth.

It was freeing to let go of the urge to hide and smooth out my imperfections for him. It took me over forty years to create this brand of chaos, and I wasn't going to let a man, even one who made me weak in the knees, turn me into something I wasn't. He was going to have to accept me as I was or I wasn't interested. I wasn't entirely sure if this bold way of thinking was because I was comfortable in my own skin, or a self sabotaging behavior stemming from my lingering insecurities after Brett. To be honest, it was a toss up.

I heard a knock at the door before Aubrey breezed in holding a bottle of champagne.

"Thought you might need a little liquid courage for tonight," she said and popped the cork, pouring two glasses and offering one to me.

"You know me so well." I pulled a maxi dress over my head that was cinched at the waist and showed off the girls to perfection. Aubrey came over and pinched the fabric under my breasts, then yanked the top down a little bit in front, vastly increasing the visible square inches of my cleavage.

"There, that's better!" She walked into my closet and pulled out a pair of platform heels and said, "Slip these on." Being a fashion disaster, I always did as I was told. She retrieved the curling iron from my bathroom, dragged one of the kitchen chairs over, and patted on it for me to sit down. Taking a bubbly sip, I arranged myself on the chair as she pulled each chunk of long hair up and softly curled it.

"Why does it feel so good when someone plays with your hair?" I mused but got no response. When I noticed she was looking at her phone for the fourth time in ten minutes, I asked innocently, "Are things heating up with Tony?"

"What?" She was distracted and accidentally touched

the wand behind my ear, singeing a little pockmark on my neck.

"Ouchie." I jumped, rubbing the burn with my fingers.

"Oh, God. I'm so sorry," she said, tucking the phone back into her pocket and continuing to curl my hair.

"Are you okay?" I asked, my hand in a defensive position shielding my neck from future burns.

"I'm fine."

I'm fine. The two most passive aggressive words in the English language. I knew she wasn't fine. I'd had a front-row seat to the Aubrey show for the last six years. During that time, I watched her sell herself short when it came to men, over and over again. It wasn't quite time for an intervention about Tony yet, but it was obvious he wasn't going anywhere. Keeping my head statue still, my eyes flicked over to hers as she worked quietly.

"Your hair is so thick and pretty," Aubrey offered, trying to butter me up with a weak smile.

"It's a blessing and a curse, babe. Takes forever to dry even after the stylist thins and texturizes it."

Twenty minutes later, she handed me a mirror, and I tossed my head from side to side, admiring the view of smooth black waves that cascaded down my back. "You are a magician with a curling wand! Dang, I suck at being a girl." I frowned playfully and batted my eyelashes at her.

"You're *beautiful*," she corrected and then pulled out the phone again after a flurry of notifications rolled in seconds apart. Her eyes widened briefly, and then her lips set in a hard line.

"Are you sure you're okay?" I asked again. "I have to run, but can we talk after the rush tomorrow?"

"Sure," she mumbled absentmindedly, then began to

text feverishly, tapping out aggressive letter after aggressive letter.

"My Uber is here. Can you lock up?" I asked and gave her a quick side hug, grabbing the bottle of wine I wanted to bring to Foster's on the way out.

Twenty minutes later, I was standing in front of a door at the address I had been given. It was the sage and garlic scent filling the hallway that confirmed I was in the right place. I looked down and straightened my dress, yanked it down a few inches to make Aubrey proud when I retold the story later, and knocked hesitantly. Hearing footsteps, my pulse quickened, then the lock scraped against the strike plate and the door opened. Foster appeared behind it with a devilish grin. He grabbed my hand and yanked me inside as I gasped in surprise. Then he pushed me up against the wall and kissed me as ripples of warmth rushed through my center.

"That's one hell of an appetizer," I whispered still breathless from his kiss. Bubbly always made me a little reckless and flirty.

His apartment was a typical bachelor pad. A one-room studio that had shabby furniture that looked like it had mostly been claimed from sidewalk left-behinds when renters moved in the city, but at least it was clean. That was one of the most impressive parts. In my limited experience, most single men were notorious slobs. I would have to inspect the bathroom later, but so far so good. You can tell a lot about a person by the way they live.

Foster was wearing a plain white V-neck t-shirt with a kitchen towel slung over one of his shoulders, faded dark Levi's that looked so broken-in and molded his skin, and faded black Converse sneakers. His sinewy forearms were covered in tattoos. Black ink snaked up strong arms covered in soft man fur with symbols that faded in and out. I longed to examine the designs, to walk my fingers up them, inch by inch, while I explored the canvas that was his body, but it felt too intimate. There was a seed of menacing fear forming in my belly. A "this is too good to be true" sensation that made me ache to pump the brakes. I pushed it away and said instead, "It smells amazing in here."

Foster laughed. "I'm happy to hear you say that. Because I have to tell you, cooking Italian food for an authentic Italian girl is a pressure cooker. I mean, if I get this wrong, this relationship is doomed."

"Relationship?" I repeated timidly. Bracing for his reaction, I silently begged for his confirmation, not realizing until that moment how much I wanted to hear him confirm this wasn't a fling to him.

"Yes, Gionna," he answered calmly with another endearing smile that sent me spinning on the merriest merry-go-round again. "I don't do anything halfway. I don't play games, and when I want something, I usually get it."

Whoa.

My throat knotted as a giddy swell of happiness unfurled inside me, flooding every pore. A man who knows what he wants? I hadn't come across one of those in the wild in decades.

But why me?

It was the question I yearned to ask, but afraid of what the answer would be, I kept it tucked away deep in my heart. It was getting harder to deny the growing ache within me and the little voice that egged me on whispering, "Oh my God, this is it. He could be the one."

I handed him the bottle of wine, and he looked at it lovingly, studying the label. "Oh, this is amazing. I have been dying to try this vintage, and it will pair perfectly with our gnocchi." He looked up. "How do you know so much about wine?"

"Well, between culinary school and being Italian, it's pretty much part of our factory settings."

"Have you ever been to Italy?"

"Not yet. I've always wanted to go, but I've never had both the free time and the right guy at the same time to make it happen."

"Sounds like something we need to put on our bucket list."

"Wow, someone's already planning our bucket list? You've got it bad," I teased.

He looked at me with nothing but sincerity in his warm eyes. "Yep. I think I do." Five little words that made my stomach flip and make figure eights in my belly. Changing subjects, he clapped his hands together twice and asked, "Will you do the honors?" He pointed to a corkscrew on the countertop and two glasses in the wine rack. "I need to focus on our dinner."

I uncorked the wine and poured it into an aerating decanter to let it breathe. Since I had a few minutes, I walked over to a rustic cabinet that housed an old turntable. Inside the glass drawers were hundreds of old-school vinyl albums. I walked my finger down their spines, sorting through the albums one by one like I loved to do at the vintage record store a few blocks down from the bakery. I carefully examined his collection, smiling as I saw all the old school big bands that Nonna introduced me to that I loved so much. It felt like a sign. I pulled out a Frank Sinatra album that Nonna had lusted over; it was incredibly rare and impossible to find. "Oh my God! Can we listen to this? I've been combing through every record store in the world to find a copy for Nonna." I hugged it to my chest with excitement.

He chuckled at my infatuation. "Absolutely, baby."

Baby. A syrupy term of endearment that made me throw up a little in my mouth when I heard other people say it, but for some reason when it was directed at me, it gave me a jubilant thrill.

I pulled the record out of the sleeve carefully, holding it by the edges, and slipped it gently onto the turntable. There was a short scratching noise as I softly placed the needle on the record, watching it swirl and spin as the first few notes cued up. Then I poured two glasses of wine and sat down at the table, watching him work.

The butter sizzled as I studied him at the stove, deftly chopping fresh herbs and garlic. His hand held down the tip of the blade as he minced them into impossibly uniform tiny pieces. He lifted the stainless steel pan in the air and swirled it in theatrical circles to coat the bottom with the butter, then he tossed the hand-rolled gnocchi into the boiling salted water, and billowing steam rolled into the air. After a few minutes, he drained the gnocchi and then dumped it into the skillet with the herbs, coated it with sauce, and finished with a pat of butter. He served the gnocchi on two immaculate white plates, even taking the time to wipe off the sauce dribble on the edge before bringing it to a well-worn dining room table and lighting a candle.

"Wow! The candlelight treatment? You're pulling out all the stops." I flirted shamelessly, leaning closer to him.

"I'm an old-school romantic. Can't help myself." He smiled, slightly pre-occupied, and I melted into a puddle on the wooden chair I was sitting on.

"Ooh! The bread. I almost forgot." He rushed back to the oven, pulling a loaf of garlic bread out, and returned to the table with the bottle of wine to refill my glass.

"This looks incredible," I gushed. "I can't remember the last time a man I wasn't related to cooked a meal for me."

"Well, that just breaks my heart," Foster said. "A woman like you deserves to be spoiled."

I had no idea how to respond to his statement. A deeply seeded pang of unworthiness shot through my heart, rendering me speechless.

"You're gonna want to save some room for dessert," he offered.

"Dessert too? Is it my birthday?" I teased.

"No, silly, that's just the way we do things around here." He raised his glass to mine, and the crystal chimed. "To us," he affirmed earnestly. "To the first of many nights with incredible food and amazing company."

"To us," I repeated softly, daring to dream that there would be an us.

I scooped a spoonful of gnocchi to my mouth and closed my eyes with ecstasy as I delicately chewed and swallowed, savoring the velvety texture on my tongue. "Oh my God! Gnocchi like this and you're not even Italian? Don't ever repeat this, because I will forever deny I said it, but this gnocchi is better than Nonna's."

Pure joy broke out across his face at the compliment.

"Really? Take another bite," he urged like he didn't believe me.

I scooped another spoonful into my mouth, making loud *mmm* noises. The brown butter sauce was luscious, so perfectly savory with crispy browned bits of pancetta and fresh cracked pepper. "It is perfection. I stand by my initial review, but you must carry that secret to your grave."

He exhaled loudly, laughing in relief. "I was so worried it was going to be sub-par I almost scrapped the idea completely, but I was in too deep to change course."

"Truly some of the best I've ever had. If you turn around, I might lick this plate," I said, looking deep into his eyes unabashedly, the wine shoring up my confidence.

Or I might lick something else.

Candlelight is seductive, transforming everyday objects and people into romantic works of art instantly. The glow glistened in his eyes that drew me in like a moth to a flame. I couldn't stay away from him; I couldn't fight this attraction. The pull was intense and all-consuming and forced me to release my worries and penchant for practicality, encouraging me to fall. Our gazes tangoed seductively, taking small sips of each other and then darting away, still shy and unsure.

Let go. Stop clinging to the life you know and open yourself up. Fall into his capable strong arms. The music filled the air with the occasional chimes from the dishes and silverware. He reached across the table and held my hand, sending shockwaves down my arm.

My plate was empty. "Do you want more?"

"I better not," I said "But your gnocchi is incredible— light and fluffy. The texture was a spot on." I kissed the tips of my fingers and gave him a chef's kiss.

"Glad you liked it. I've come a long way since culinary school. The first month was brutal. I almost dropped out."

"Really?" I asked. "You don't seem like the type who gives up easily."

"I thought one of my instructors had it out for me. He made Gordon Ramsay look like a Sunday school teacher. Everything I prepared, according to him, was shit...inedible...not even fit to give to a dog, but I was cocky enough to think that he didn't know what he was talking about."

I sipped the rest of my wine, watching the candlelight wash his face in amber and yellow tones. I couldn't remember enjoying an evening as much as I was enjoying this one in a very long time.

"We butted heads hard, but it was one of those *Mr. Miyagi/Karate Kid* moments. Where he was having me wax on, wax off, which only frustrated me. But eventually, it all came together. After I graduated, he hired me as a sous chef in his new restaurant and became like a father to me, something I desperately craved. My dad was... difficult," he offered in explanation as a sad shadow passed over his face, darkening his eyes. Immediately, I knew there was much more to the story than he was ready to tell me.

"I'm sorry to hear that." The words sounded emptier than I wanted them to. I reached out and squeezed his forearm, and the touch sent a rush of heat to my face. "I have been spoiled by having a dad like mine."

"You're one of the lucky ones," he said quietly and took a sip of the wine. Lost in a different time, his lips pressed together as he fell silent.

I panicked seeing him disappear in front of me to a painful place that I couldn't follow him to, and blurted,

"So, what happened to *Mr. Miyagi*?" I was eager to change the subject and pull him back from the bleak abyss.

"He got sick. He was diagnosed with colon cancer last year. But his final act of love was to find me a job in Chicago. He called in a favor with one of his contacts that opened a new Michelin-starred restaurant in the city." His eyes met mine intently, his glossy and more serious, then offered a quick smile. "And tonight, it has led me to have a beautiful evening with a gorgeous Italian girl that I never would've met otherwise." He pulled my hand to his lips and kissed it, an act I'd seen Bumpo do a million times and I melted. "Things always happen for a reason."

SIXTEEN

The first Wednesday of the month was dedicated to a long-standing movie night tradition at Nonna's house. It was the night Aubrey and the kids, Mom, and I gathered for the classics. Occasionally, we'd get to slip a contemporary movie in the mix, but for the most part, we indulged Nonna's love for the old school black and white films.

I stood in Nonna's warm, sunny yellow kitchen that hadn't changed since Bumpo died. It was a bittersweet time capsule, filled with doilies, spider plants, and black and white family photos that snaked up the stairwell. White eyelet cafe curtains were tied together with a red sash, and honey oak encased the cabinets. She stood at the antique white gas stove, shaking popcorn kernels into a heavyweight Dutch oven that had been passed down from her mother, added a dollop of butter and another one of coconut oil, and placed a lid on top of it all. Within minutes, the first kernels started popping, and she shook the pan continuously over the burner with jerky movements to keep the popcorn from scorching. The popping sound intensified until the entire pan was filled to the brim.

I pulled out the ever-present chunk of Parmesano Reggiano from her fridge and the grater. No one else could be trusted to grate the appropriate amount of cheese. Nonna dumped it into a huge bowl, and I grated cheese over the warm popcorn that melted instantly the second it hit the hot kernels, like snowflakes on concrete in April.

Mom was busy getting glasses out of Nonna's cupboards that she filled with Italian sparkling soda. In lemon and grapefruit flavors, it was bubbly and refreshing and paired nicely with pan-popped popcorn and Red Vines —never Twizzlers. Once the snacks were prepared, I would gather every blanket and pillow that Nonna owned and spread them out on the floor to snuggle with Owen and Stella. I loved movie nights at Nonna's.

Tonight, I had a helper. Owen helped me stack so many pillows in Stella's arms you couldn't see her, and then he guided her to the living room like a seeing-eye dog.

"Where's Stella?" I asked loudly. "Stella?" I said louder, making a game of looking around for her. A small muffled giggle escaped from the pile of pillows. "Stella!" I looked around, acting very distressed. "I wish my Stella was here!" It only made her giggle louder.

"Auntie G! I'm right here!" she exclaimed, dropping the pillows on the floor in a huge pile. I didn't make eye contact and looked up at the ceiling.

"Stella! Where are you? I can hear you, but I can't see you!"

I felt her little hand grip mine and tug on it as I continued to make a show of looking everywhere but at her, and it only made her giggle louder.

"Here I am!" she said, dissolving into another pile of giggles.

Finally, I dropped my gaze to her, and then I threw her down on the pillows, dropped to my knees, and tickled her. Owen stood off to the side, wanting to get in on the fun, but always on the peripheral cautiously observing. I tugged him into my arms and tickled him, too, blowing a raspberry into his neck until he laughed.

I looked up at Aubrey engrossed in her phone again, and she sighed and put it away before throwing me a weary smile. She went to the kitchen and helped bring out the tray with drinks and treats with Nonna and Mom in tow. We all assumed our regular positions. I was leaning against the sofa with one of the kids tucked into the crook of each arm with a popcorn bowl sitting in my lap. Mom and Nonna perched together on the love seat, and Aubrey sat behind me on the sofa. I pressed play, and the opening credits of *Casablanca* filled the screen with its dramatic musical underscore. Over the next hour, the kids ate their weight in popcorn and Red Vines. The later it got, the less they moved until they were finally silent and sweaty, laying against me. I gently lowered them each down onto a pillow and tucked a blanket around them, then turned back to the movie.

Classic black and white movies are a guilty pleasure that Nonna passed down to me. Bogart in his trench coat and deep voice screamed masculinity and contrasted brilliantly with the breathy sweetness of Ingrid Bergman. They were dramatic as all get out, with a lot of lingering sultry looks and sighs of woe. Not to mention, the golden age of Hollywood fully endorsed smoking as a sexy habit by having actors light one up every five minutes, emphysema be damned! Classic films sucked me into this dreamy vintage land of make-believe. *Casablanca* was the kind of over-the-top romantic storyline that made Nonna swoon, but had the kind of melancholy ending that made it tolerable for me to watch.

Twenty minutes to the end, Aubrey suddenly bolted up, jarring me out of my sweet, swoony revelry. "I have to go." I put the movie on pause and turned toward her, concern flooding me.

"What? Why?"

"Tony needs me. Can you watch the kids?" Panic washed across her features.

"Is everything okay?" I asked, wanting more information as I sat up and followed her to the closet, where she was quickly putting on her coat.

"I can't explain right now."

I pulled at her arm. "Aubrey, talk to me."

She looked at the phone again, ignoring me. "Can you watch the kids or not?" she asked again more urgently.

"Sure, I guess. Can we stay here tonight, Nonna?" I asked, and Nonna agreed. "I'll bring the kids to the bakery in the morning."

And you will have some explaining to do.

I bit back the words as she gathered her things up quickly and left without another word.

"That doesn't sound good," Mom said. "Have you met this Tony?"

"Only in passing at the bakery," I said.

"I'm concerned." Mom knew Aubrey's penchant for attracting the wrong guys. "She's been secretive about this one, and that is never a good sign."

"You're not the only one," I agreed. She was doing it

again, dropping everything to wrap her life around the guy she was interested in. I knew where this ship was headed, even if she was in denial. I exhaled and then pressed play to resume the movie while the kids slept on, oblivious to their mother's dramatic exit.

The final scene played and Bogie told Ilsa to get on the plane, that she would regret it if she didn't. "Maybe not today, maybe not tomorrow, but soon and for the rest of your life." I looked over at Nonna, who was wiping away tears with a crumpled-up napkin. The music score cued up dramatically, and then it was over and the credits rolled.

"They just don't make love stories like that anymore," Mom said as she gathered up the empty bowls and glasses.

"That's because it's all make-believe," I said. "People are more cynical these days."

"That's true, and that makes me sad." Nonna scooched forward on the sofa, the plastic slipcover crinkling under her thighs as she struggled to get to her feet.

"It's just reality," I told her as I offered her my hands and pulled her up to a standing position. "That kind of old school romantic, staring into each other's eyes, kiss me before I die drama, isn't real life. It's not sustainable."

"*Mia Bella*, your generation is so skeptical," Nonna chastised gently stretching as I helped Mom clean up the kitchen.

"Real love is quieter," Mom explained to me as she hand-washed the dishes. It was absurd; Nonna didn't believe in the practicality of dishwashers, but she was a stanch believer of happily ever after. I stood next to Mom drying them with a white flour sack dishtowel that made me think of the one that was perpetually hanging over Foster's shoulder. "Real love is deliberate and a choice. It's fighting through the good and bad days as a team, not the heart-stopping theatrics that are portrayed on screen."

I nodded considering her words.

"People think it has to be this big climactic moment, this huge revelation, but they're wrong. Love is forged in the tiny moments of life. The conscious decision to put the happiness of another person above your own. It is simple and easy, not the heart-pumping insanity that is depicted in movies, and that's the problem. People are looking to be swept away by passion—and real love, the kind that sustains you for decades is steady and true. It isn't flashy or heart-throbbing—it's calm and constant. That's why most people don't recognize it as love when it comes into their lives."

"Is that the kind of love you have with Dad?"

"Yes," she said. "And the kind of love I hope you find." She dried her hands and looked at me. "I know how much Brett hurt you, but I can't help but hope that some-day, someone comes into your life that makes you feel safe and protected and cherished and loved." She reached out and hugged me. "Someday, you will understand why things worked out the way they did. Someday, even the heartbreak you endured with Brett will make sense, and the love that you find will fit into your life better than you could have ever imagined."

I was afraid to tell her I thought someday might have already arrived, so I kept the secret to myself. It was safer that way.

SEVENTEEN

The next morning, Aubrey came to work with her eyes tired and red-rimmed. The kids brightened up immediately and ran to her for hugs.

"You look like shit," I said.

"Thanks," she muttered and started to brew the first batch of house roast.

"Rough night?"

"Yeah, Tony is up for a big promotion at work, and he couldn't find his suit and needed help picking a tie. He's so nervous we spent most of the night talking."

"*That* was the big emergency?" I questioned instantly irritated. "The panicky way you tore out of Nonna's last night, I expected someone to be dead or at least maimed."

"Tony's a very driven man," she explained making excuses for him. "He's under a lot of pressure."

I had to turn away so I could roll my eyes without her noticing. There were so many things I wanted to say, but none of them would make this situation better.

"He said wants to take care of me and the kids, G," she offered.

"But you can take care of yourself, and you have us. Besides, you've known this guy for five minutes. It's a little fast, don't you think?"

The bell tinkled.

Speak of the devil.

Tony was dressed in a navy suit and shiny brown loafers, his bald head freshly razored and gleaming. He strode to the counter confidently as Aubrey let out a squeal and ran around the pastry case. She hugged him while his eyes slid to mine.

"Tony," I said evenly. Aubrey pulled back and looked at him with hearts in her eyes.

"Doesn't he look handsome, G?" she gushed.

"You look very professional," I choked out. It was the best I could do under the circumstances. "Aubrey says you have a big interview today."

"I do and I thought I'd stop by my favorite coffee house to get this day started right." He winked and smiled a cunning smile, and my eyes narrowed. I picked up the distinct feeling that I was being handled. He was buttering me up, like sweet corn in the summer.

"I think I was at a wedding last month and tasted one of your cakes. Does the name Caitlin Armstrong ring any bells?"

"The peacock cake," I answered.

"Yes!" He smiled, a tight gesture that looked forced on his face. "It was delicious. You should have heard everyone raving about it."

"That's nice to hear, isn't it, G?" Aubrey prodded as

she made his latte, desperately vying for my approval and working to bridge the gap between us.

"Yes," I agreed, "it is."

Aubrey handed him the coffee as a line began to form, giving me a break from interacting with him further. Already, the little amount of contact I had with Tony left me cringing and wanting a shower.

I watched as he kissed her goodbye and then grabbed her ass as if he owned her. It was vile behavior, but worst of all, he did it in front of Owen. After the line died down again, I went into the kitchen to find him scooping powdered sugar into the mixer with Pops.

"Who was that man?" Owen asked, his eyes wide behind his glasses.

"Just a friend of your mom's," I said. "No one you should worry about."

My words comforted him, and he visibly relaxed.

I wasn't really sure if I was lying to the kid or not.

EIGHTEEN

Our schedules didn't align for the next two weeks. I was in my final month of the wedding season and had overbooked myself. It was a pastry marathon of late nights and early mornings to the finish line.

"Finally, I get you to myself," Foster said as he pulled me into his arms and kissed my temple. "I missed you."

"You did?" I asked. Those three simple words dissolved my defenses. "Thanks for being so understanding."

"Of course. I love that you are so driven. It's super sexy." He smiled. "But my daily coffee runs to the bakery and our texting sessions will only sustain a virile man like myself for so long."

"Virile?" I chuckled. "Poor thing. Did you have to take matters into your own hands?"

"More than I would ever care to admit to my girlfriend."

"Girlfriend?" I sputtered on the word.

"Is that a problem?" he asked, his eyes leveling on mine.

"Not for me," I found myself admitting with a grin I couldn't control spreading across my face.

"Good, because I've been wanting to lock this down for a while now."

My heart burst open.

"Come on, *girlfriend*, let's go have some fun!" Foster pulled my hand into his for the long walk to Navy Pier. I loved showing him my Chicago, avoiding all the tourist traps, and frequenting the local bistros tucked away that made Chicago so special. It was like I got to see the city with fresh eyes, not the cynical, jaded ones that took everything for granted because I grew up here. He approached every outing I planned with the enthusiasm of a four-year-old, and it was easy to get swept up into his sense of adventure.

"Navy Pier is quintessentially Chicago," I said in my very best tourist guide voice as we walked through the arboretum, looking for the ticket counter for the Ferris Wheel.

The glass room was delightfully warm with palm trees and vines reaching their glossy green leaves up to the mosaic glass sky, and the gurgle of fountains and water features tinkled in the background. The atrium was fogging up from the Indian summer sun. October in Chicago is a fickle tease, weather-wise. It can be cold and rainy, might even snow, or could be unseasonably warm. You had to be ready for anything.

"Does this sound make you want to pee?" He laughed, cupping his ear with his hand to listen to the water tinkling in the background.

"You might want to hit the bathroom before we get on the Ferris Wheel then. Wouldn't want you peeing on yourself in the pod. It would ruin the moment."

He bought two tickets for the carousel and the Ferris Wheel, and we walked deeper into the park. He was like a little kid at the Navy Pier, taking in all the sights and sounds with glee.

"This is the perfect place to people watch," he said, looking around at the crowd. He nodded his head at an elderly couple walking down the pier hand in hand.

"That will be us in about twenty-five years."

"Think you'll be able to stand me for that long?"

"Jury is out, but all signs point to yes."

"Wait, did you become a magic eight ball all of a sudden?"

"God, I loved that thing," he enthused. "Literally used it to make major life decisions. It never let me down."

I rolled my eyes and smiled at him as we stood in line at the merry-go-round. The gate opened and we walked onto the ride, looking for our spirit animal.

He chose a donkey.

"Nice ass," I snickered as I leaned in from my majestic purple unicorn to blow him a kiss.

"Seems to be impossible for you to resist," he said boldly.

"Guilty," I agreed, and the old-timey carnival music whirred up as the animals pumped up and down the length of their poles. The wind whipped through my hair as Foster took pictures with his phone. Four minutes later, the ride was over, so we climbed down and stumbled onto the midway where popcorn was popping and cotton candy was being spun onto white cones until it looked like pastel sugar clouds imprisoned inside plastic bags. We got one of each, and he wrapped his arm around my neck, drawing me in. He stuffed a huge chunk of pink, feathery sweetness into his wide-open mouth and then pulled me in for a kiss, his tongue sticky and sweet on mine.

"You're so easy to be with, Gionna," he said, holding my hand in his.

"That might be the first time in my entire life I have ever heard that," I deflected with humor. "You might need to get your head examined."

It was darkening to dusk at Navy Pier. We sampled our way down the wares of the boardwalk and ended up in a private, enclosed pod on the Ferris Wheel as it glided up into the sunset.

"Wow. You can see forever up here," he said at the top of the Ferris Wheel. Lake Michigan was glowing in all its golden hour glory. The last rays of the sun reflected the water and sky into a mass of mirrored skyscrapers that dotted the skyline, transforming steel and glass into dreamy pastel blocks. Foster's hand was warm on mine as the soft blue of the sky started to transform into baby lavenders, blushing pinks, and delicious peaches as the sun slid deeper into the horizon.

"It's incredible," I agreed. "I can't believe I have never done this before."

The lights twinkled to life down below and sparkled around us as the darkness intensified the colors. My heart was bursting, and the strangest unknown sensations were flooding through me. It felt like I had been living an entirely different life. Everything I had known up to that point was in stark contrast to the fluttering of my heart in my chest. I know it sounds irrational and silly and like an immature girlish crush. But it wasn't. I could only classify it as love, the kind of love that has a sweeping thematic underscore soundtrack to it. The kind of love I didn't believe in anymore, yet was coming for me in waves. Powerful waves like a stormy ocean that knocked the breath out of me and made me feel exhilarated and terrified at the same time.

I laid my head on his shoulder as the Ferris Wheel lurched up, up, up, and then slowly jerked down, down, down. Foster kissed the top of my head as his thumb traced along the lines of my fingers gently, slowly, carefully like he was paying homage and worshiping me. I had never felt someone touch me with such reverence before. The ride finally stopped, and the attendant let us out of the pod. I stumbled out of the love bubble, disoriented until Foster's hand found mine and he pulled me close as we started to walk toward our waiting Uber.

The driver pulled up to my apartment, and I surprised Foster by tugging on his hand and dragging him out of the car before leading him up the stairs to my apartment. His eyes were wide as I winked at him and said, "I think it's time." Barely inside the door, I pushed him against the wall and kissed him gently. His fingers ran up my spine and traced the lines of my neck, finally lacing through my hair while his fingers massaged the back of my head. I pulled away, a little drunk from his kiss.

"Alexa, play my sexy times playlist." And the robotic voice echoed my command as I pressed my lips against his.

"Sexy times playlist?" Foster pulled back, sounding wounded. "And here I thought I was special."

I laughed. "You have no idea how few times I have

actually had an opportunity to play this playlist." I walked my fingers up his chest and leaned in for a kiss. "You, sir, are *very* special." I breathed into his neck and then pulled him into my bedroom. Slowly, I began to undress him, peeling the t-shirt from his body and depositing featherlight kisses on his chest, delighting in every muscle and bone. I kissed my way down the long length of his body until I found myself on my knees. I tugged on his belt buckle. His eyes darkened into liquid pools of desire as a rush of pleasure began to hum through my core. He reached down, pulled me to my feet, gently tugged my dress up and over my shoulders, and I stood there in front of him completely unashamed, waiting for his reaction. I was tired of hiding. I was tired of sucking it in. I wanted to get to the place where I was comfortable in my own skin in front of him. Where I could be naked and unafraid, and so I left the lights on.

For several agonizing minutes, I trembled slightly as his eyes walked up my body slowly, tracing every curve, searing it into his own memory, and the only emotion I could read as it streaked across his face was desire. He held out one hand to me, and I walked toward him slowly. His fingers dragged up my back in long, sloping circles, leaving no inch of my skin untouched. He kissed and caressed every inch of me, deliberate and purposeful, his movements controlled and slow. I pulled a condom from the box in my bedside table and handed it to him. Its very presence quieted the fearful chatter in my mind.

And when I couldn't take it anymore, and when I begged him to enter me, he laid me on the bed and we became one. It was like jumping off a cliff, falling into the great unknown without a safety net.

———

The sun rose the next morning, scattering pinkish light into the room when I woke up. I heard dishes clattering together in the kitchen and rolled over, my fingers searching for him only to feel the cool sheets, confirming Foster was already out of bed. The magical meaty aroma of bacon and freshly brewed coffee filled the air. I smiled to myself and stretched like a cat for several minutes on the bed, enjoying the slight ache from him between my legs. I finally put my feet on the floor and pulled on a baby blue tank top and pajama bottoms, and then padded out to the kitchen on bare feet.

His back was to me, and he was humming while he held the handle of the stainless steel pan and tossed its breakfast contents high into the air with a flick of his wrist, performing hash brown acrobatics, and then slid it back on the burner. Turning, he saw me and smiled. "Hello, beautiful." He closed the distance between us and snuggled into my neck, planting a kiss near my collarbone. "Hope it's okay that I rooted around your kitchen."

"Of course. If you're cooking me breakfast, there is no way I am getting in the way of that." I perched on a chair at the table and waited.

"Did you sleep well?"

"Surprisingly, I did."

He visibly puffed his chest out like the male birds I'd watched on Animal Planet. "Just another service I provide," he bragged, and I rolled my eyes and couldn't help grinning at his remark.

He poured coffee into a mug for me and walked it over to the table. A few minutes later, he divided what was in the pan between us, added a few slices of bacon, and set a steaming one in front of me.

I rubbed my hands together as the scent of caramelized onions made my mouth water. "This looks so good."

He walked his coffee over and sat down, and we started to eat. It was a scramble of sunny eggs, caramelized onions, and sautéed green peppers, with liberal amounts of thick bacon, and thinly grated crispy hash browns covered in cheese. When I took my first bite, the brunch angels began to sing.

"So, what do you want to do today?" he asked. "It's Sunday Fun Day."

"I haven't thought that far."

"Well, I have," he said excitedly. "Let's get dressed and go for a walk."

"On the streets of Chicago wearing yesterday's clothes? You sinner!" I teased him and inhaled another forkful.

"Well, I'm going to have to take one for the team until we get to the stage where I can leave more than a tooth-brush at your place."

My eyes widened, and I started to panic.

"What was that look?" he asked, leaning closer, concern painting his features. "Where did you go?"

"Nothing."

"That definitely was something."

"You scare me," I admitted boldly.

"Why?" He smiled innocently, with a slightly confused expression on his face.

"You move fast, you say things." I looked down. The truth made it harder for me to make eye contact.

His brow furrowed in concentration. "Hmm. I don't say anything I don't mean. What are you afraid of?"

That you'll lead me on, break my heart, shatter it again when it took me nearly four years to put it back together.

I thought, but said none of it. To give my fears a voice was even more terrifying.

"Tell me about your last relationship," he asked.

My eyes darted away from his, afraid eye contact would reveal my fears. "I don't think you're ready for that shit show."

"Try me."

"That's a conversation you have when you reach the bottom of a bottle of tequila," I muttered and stuffed another bite in my mouth to give myself something to do. The seriousness of the conversation made the food taste-less on my tongue. I swallowed hard and pushed the plate away.

I felt his warm fingers find my chin and pull it up so I could meet his warm, chestnut brown eyes. Kindness and concern, that was all I found there. "That's better," he whispered.

His delicious breakfast became a sickening, solidified lump in my belly. I wrapped my arms around my waist.

"Who broke your heart?"

I closed my eyes and sighed, digging deep to draw the strength to tell him the truth. "A fiancé who stole my iden-tity, opened credit cards in my name, and left town, but not before he gave me an STD." The excruciating answer sucked the air out of the room. I delivered the explanation harshly like I'd intended, daring him to flinch. Daring him to run away. Practically pushing him out the door myself. I believed it was easier if he ran away now before I got too attached.

"Whoa." He swallowed hard and jerked back like he'd been slapped. "When was that?"

"A long time ago," I said sadly. "He humiliated me, and I haven't really put my heart out there since."

"G," he began, holding out a hand and pulling me onto his lap. "I'm so sorry that happened to you. You didn't deserve that."

I clutched his shirt in my hands and squeezed into his chest, trying to calm the hammering of my heart. I breathed in his scent, trying to loosen the knot that was lodged in my throat. The weight of shame crashed over me. I was so close to breaking wide open, and I was terrified to let him see that side of me. The unvarnished, imperfect ugliness of my shattered heart that I had carefully stitched back together. His fingers traced circles on my back as he held me, and I felt my walls shift. I wanted to let him in; I just didn't know how.

NINETEEN

Early October sped by as we hid away from the prying eyes of my family for as long as we could sneaking around on the sly. Nearly getting caught more than once when he would slip out of my bed and down the dark sidewalk before I would have to get up and go open the bakery in the early mornings. That was the downside of the non-existent work and home commute. There was always the possibility of getting caught, and when we did, I would have some explaining to do.

I was running on adrenaline and coffee and not much sleep. It is amazing how those two things can sustain you during that sexy, lusty time that is the beginning of a new relationship. We were consuming each other, and I had never felt more satiated. Foster was my food. Somehow, someway, he wormed his way in and, in record time, stole my heart. As cheesy as it sounds, I was a smitten kitten. Everything was new and precious. Suddenly, life had more meaning, flowers were more beautiful, and food tasted richer. I surprised myself with the intensity of the feelings

I had for him. It was like something deep inside my soul finally shifted into place. I was humming to myself, actually freaking humming, something I never do, when Mom appeared.

"You're in a good mood," she accused gently, sniffing out the source of my happiness like a bloodhound. It wasn't her fault. Since Brett, I kept them in the dark for as long as possible when it came to my personal life. I was afraid to tell Mom and Pops I had met someone because the more people I told, the more it would hurt when things fell apart.

I smiled at her and continued to stir the mint green frosting for the sugar cookies. "What? Can't I be in a good mood?" I asked, bating her at the marble counter where Pops was punching down dough that had proofed and was the size of his head. He always watched us like he was enjoying a night at the cinema, never a participant, but an interested observer. His eyes landed on mine, and I smiled at him, too. Hell, I was so giddy, everyone was getting my full Positive Patty treatment.

Aubrey walked into the kitchen, and Mom pounced. "You must know why Gionna is so happy," Mom implored her.

"What do you mean?" she asked innocently, lying through her teeth with a beautiful smile on her face.

God, I love that chick. She always has my back.

"Nonna?" Mom moved on from Aubrey quickly, slightly frustrated that she wasn't getting the answers she was looking for, feeling we were all united in our desire to keep her in the dark.

"Why is it a crime to be happy?" Nonna asked with a shrug. "I want my entire family to be happy." She turned toward me and shot me a barely perceptible wink, which made me smile even wider.

Mom threw up her hands, exasperated, and walked out of the kitchen to check on the few remaining patrons that lingered from the breakfast crowd.

Dad was amused by her frustration as he flattened the dough into ten oval shapes, then drizzled on our heirloom olive oil, poking it with his fingers until it took on the bumpy appearance of bread with cellulite. His hands returned to the spice rack before he dusted them with oregano and parsley, and then some of the ovals got cheese and jalapeños. After he did that, he pulled the gold St. Christopher medal suspended from a filigree chain on his neck, kissed it, and then blew a kiss in the air to the heavens.

Bumpo detested the cheddar and jalapeño focaccia. To him, that flavor profile was a kick in the teeth to our heritage. In his proud mind, it was a sacrilege to Italians everywhere to fuse our traditional recipes with South American flavors. But Mom was a businesswoman first, and when we offered it on a whim as a limited run, it was so popular it became a permanent fixture within weeks. Pops was stuck somewhere in the middle between not disappointing his traditionally-minded father and running a successful business to keep his wife happy. Bumpo was as stubborn as a mule, but he was also dedicated and loyal. I like to think of him in heaven, sitting on a cloud, watching all of us working together to carry out his dream and his vision of DeLuca's. Occasionally spitting and muttering under his breath, but overall proud of us and what we have accomplished.

At lunchtime, we sat down together. The fresh-baked

focaccia was served with a rich Minestrone. Nonna ladled out generous portions to each of us, only after we submitted to one of her trademark squishy hugs. No hug, no food. Ever since I could remember, it was this way. Food equalled love. There was never a point in fighting her methods. You just gave in and accepted the rules, and eventually, even Owen warmed up to it. The first day he spent at the bakery, she dangled out a cookie and then opened her arms. "Sweet boy, come give Nonna some sugar," she'd asked a wary Owen, who quickly reached for it, and she enveloped him in her fleshy arms, squeezing him until he laughed. He became her shadow, searching her out for treats, even knowing he was going to have to submit to a hug in exchange. Owen glowed when Nonna was around. Aubrey thought it was because of the sugar. I knew it was because of the love she showered on all of us.

"The boy is good for you," Nonna whispered in my ear. She squeezed me tighter, and I snuggled into her embrace. Nothing was better than a hug from Nonna. I closed my eyes, savoring the feeling; it was like putting on socks fresh from the dryer.

"He is," I whispered back.

"Lorraine loves you in her way," Nonna said in my ear. "But you know she is not going to give up."

"I know, I just want to keep it to myself for a little longer," I said. "I'll tell them soon, I promise. Thanks for keeping my secret."

She pulled back and squeezed my hands, and then picked up the white bowl filled with soup and handed it to me. Chunks of tomatoes and noodles floated in the steamy broth. I held it close to my face and inhaled its herb-scented deliciousness. "You're going to have to give me this recipe."

"It's a dash of this and a handful of that, just like my mama taught me when I was growing up in Sicily. Soups are very basic, *Mia Bella*. But next time I make it, you can watch."

Dad wandered over to her next, and her face lit up like he was the most beautiful soul on earth. For the first time, I wondered why she didn't have more kids. I would have loved a crazy aunt or uncle in the family tree.

"Marco." She kissed both of his cheeks, holding them in her satiny, wrinkled hands.

"Mama." He smiled broadly and accepted his soup before taking a stool next to me.

"Lorraine." She hugged Mom, and I saw Mom's stiff shoulders soften before a genuine smile broke out on her face. Aubrey and the kids were next, and finally, after Nonna had served everyone else, she ladled out a big bowl of soup for herself and shuffled to the table to sit down. I passed the focaccia to her, and we all took our first few bites.

The table was full of all the people I loved. Our daily lunch ritual was one of my favorite parts of working at the bakery, and I wondered if Foster would look forward to it as much as I did. I could see him in my mind's eye, spooning bites of soup and mopping up the juices with a thick hunk of focaccia. Maybe he *could* fit right in here with us. With me.

TWENTY

After another long, satisfying, and punishing night in the sack with Foster, I dragged my satiated and exhausted booty down to the bakery to open for Nonna. My limbs were soft and supple like I had just done an intense session of hot yoga, but I wasn't forced to meditate at the end. I stretched my neck from side to side until it cracked, and then smiled when the door opened and Nonna walked through it. A thin plastic hair bonnet was tucked over her hair and tied under her chin. Made from pink shower liner material, she untied and removed it, tucking it into her handbag. This bag was eerily similar to Mary Poppins' famous bag in functionality and design; it was a huge apparatus she never left home without that contained an entire powder room of accessories. Need tweezers? Nonna's bag. Need a mint? Nonna's bag. Need world peace or enlightenment? Check Nonna's bag. You think I am exaggerating, but one day, I watched her complete a sewing repair on a bride's dress, offer a lollipop to the flower girl, and then shoehorn her shoes back on her swollen feet in order to dance with the groom.

She donned an apron as I made her an espresso. It was the one act of kindness she allowed me do for her. She always rushed around serving her family tirelessly and never asked for anything in return. To show my appreciation, I endured a long educational session on the care and cleaning of our commercial espresso machine from Mom, but the smile I got from Nonna daily made wasting that hour of my life totally worth it. I made a latte for myself and carried our white cups to the counter in the kitchen, then pulled up two stools for us. This time was precious. It was one of my favorite rituals of the day.

"You are like ripe fruit." She wrinkled her nose and sniffed the air like she was choosing a cantaloupe.

I inhaled sharply, too, wondering if she could smell sex on me. Foster was insatiable, and I had to take a whore's bath in the sink instead of the usual full shower in order to get to work on time.

"Is that your gentleman caller?" she asked over the rim of her tiny espresso cup, her wrinkled pinky pointing up. She waved her head in the direction of the windows, and I turned around to see what she was talking about. Through the glass, I saw Foster pull his jacket tight against his body, stuff his hands in his pockets and start walking quickly down the sidewalk, and I blushed. I pressed my fingers to my nose and could still smell him there. "Your pink cheeks are betraying you, *Mia Bella.*"

"We've been sneaking around, because I'm not ready to put it all out there yet. When I go all in, things usually go sideways for me," I explained.

"Your fear stands in the way of your happiness." She

reached across the table and squeezed my hand. "Love requires a leap." She took a long sip from her espresso.

"How do you know when you've met someone worth leaping for?" I asked.

"Because it hurts more *not* to leap," she admitted. "You cannot live without the other. It's a true soul mate connection. That is what I had with Bumpo."

"I know." I nodded. "That's what I'm looking for, and probably why I am still single after all these years. I just never had the urge to leap until now. I thought I did with Brett, but I was so wrong about him, and now I don't know if I trust myself to make that kind of decision again."

"Love is about trust," she said. "You have to let go and trust that he will catch you."

"I've never really been into group projects, Nonna. I like to do things on my own."

"That's not how it works, *Mia Bella*." She tipped her head to the side, studying me. "You are a beautiful, strong, independent woman, and I am so proud of you. You've always known what you wanted, and you've gone after it with your whole heart." She took a little sip, and I felt she had more to stay so I waited, tracing the lines of the cup in front of me. "I see you on the ledge, wanting more, but your fear keeps you paralyzed. It keeps you stuck."

"What if I let go and it doesn't work out?"

"It might not," she acknowledged with a nod, "but what if you let go and it does?"

TWENTY-ONE

By mid-October, I was finally wrapping up the wedding season, but getting sucked into the Foster Valentine love bubble made it harder for me to see what was happening with Aubrey. I was so preoccupied and gushy, in the stage of a new relationship where you want to spend every waking moment together. Our friendship took a backseat as things heated up with Foster. Sensing I wasn't Tony's biggest fan, Aubrey kept me in the dark. When I finally checked in again, I could see I was going to have to pay more attention. Something about Tony didn't sit right with me.

"Just one more second," she said as she tapped out a quick text. "Tony gets really stressed when I don't text back. He's always so worried about me, wants to make sure I am okay."

In the land of red flags, that little nugget of information was grabbing my attention, and I couldn't stop myself from probing deeper. "That seems a little intense, don't you think? You're a grown woman and you have other more important responsibilities than texting him back. Are you sure he's being honest with you?"

"What do you mean?"

"He might be using your feelings to control you." I had to tread lightly because I wasn't totally sure about Tony's intentions. I also knew that Aubrey had a pattern of flying off the handle and then locking me out. Neither of those things was what I wanted her to do. It was always dangerous when Aubrey stopped communicating.

"He said he loves me G," she confided. "That he's never fallen so hard or so fast." She was so blissfully happy and lovestruck that I decided to keep my mouth shut —for now. I need to gather more information about Tony. Aubrey in love was as adorable as a box of puppies. She glowed with such fairytale joy that I was certain forest animals were being summoned to help her clean her apartment. Okay, maybe that is a slight exaggeration, but Aubrey loved to be in love, and that was her downfall. She ran at it headfirst, throwing caution to the wind, letting bad behavior slide.

"I thought you said this was strictly a catch and release program?" I reminded her gently.

"I thought it was, too, but sometimes you just have to go for it. He treats me like a queen, takes care of me. Makes sure I've eaten and am sleeping. This morning, he delivered my favorite bagel and coffee to my doorstep since he knows I am not comfortable with him meeting the kids yet. Isn't that the sweetest thing?" She dissolved into a puddle of sappiness. "He's really techie, and yesterday, he downloaded an app on my phone so if I'm out late at night and I need him, he'll be able to find me."

Hmm. He did what now? A tracker app? That's

disturbing. It's even more disturbing that Aubs thinks this is a good thing.

"We should double this weekend," I offered. It was the perfect way to see how he treated her in person and figure out his true intentions. The bite-sized interactions I'd had with him so far were off-putting, but I didn't want to judge him too quickly or too harshly. I wanted to give him the benefit of the doubt, but the little bits Aubrey was sharing were making my blood pressure rise. She wasn't great at seeing the red flags when it came to men.

She tapped away on the phone. "I'll ask." Instantly, there was another reply. "Oh no! He's got to go out of town!"

"Hmm. That's interesting. I never said what day." I wanted her to connect the dots without another awkward confrontation where she would feel attacked. They never went well. "How about Sunday evening?"

She tapped away again while I waited, knowing he would give an instant reply. "Oh, darn, he's got an early day on Monday and can't make it."

"Okay, how about Wednesday?" I asked, pushing to find one that would work, knowing full well Tony would come up with excuse after excuse, and I was right. Yet Aubrey still did not put it together. She didn't see what he was doing at all and continued to parrot his flimsy excuses back to me.

"He's on call at work," she answered.

"Well, he's got to be the most important man in Chicago with a schedule like that!" I mocked boldly. "Does he know the Obamas, or is he running a huge international conglomerate?" That last statement I should have kept to myself. I just couldn't. I couldn't sit there and let him manipulate her like that. I had to call bullshit.

She rolled her eyes at me. "Not everyone gets swept off their feet by guys like Foster Valentine," she muttered, frustrated by my line of questioning.

"You could!" I offered. "You're beautiful and deserve a man like Foster."

She rolled her eyes in response. "You've been with him for five minutes. Don't you think it's a little too early to be spouting off platitudes about relationships?"

She was right, but I recoiled, and the statement hurt. "Just because I don't have much experience doesn't mean I don't know what is healthy and what is abusive. I waited. Good things come to those who wait."

"Good for you, G," she said plainly, her voice pinched tight and accusatory.

"Yeah! It *is* good for me," I continued. "But I want you to find it, too, and I will give Tony the benefit of the doubt, but if he doesn't find time to fit me into his busy schedule soon, it's going to be hard to continue to do that."

She tucked her phone back into her apron and looked at me. "I am so happy for you, G. You deserve a good guy. We *both* do."

"On this point, we agree," I said and then stopped talking while I was ahead. My words always came from a place of love, but I had no filter. Most of the time, Aubrey loved that about me, except when it came to the men she was dating.

I pulled her in for a side hug and said, "I just want you to be happy. I've seen you get your heart broken over the years, and I want you to find the kind of love you deserve."

She relaxed into my hug, and I knew enough to let it go. For now.

TWENTY-TWO

Finally, the most important man in Chicago lowered his standards and was able to grant us an audience.

We decided to meet at Balls and Brews, a new Pinball Microbrewery that just opened up. Foster and I arrived a few minutes early, and he bellied up to the bar and got us a round of Blonde Fatale, a highly concentrated local beer we both recently discovered we loved during one of our Sunday Fun Days

"What do you know about this guy?" Foster said after he took a long sip of the amber-colored liquid. Foam coated his upper lip, making him appear like a little boy with a milk mustache as he licked it off.

"Not much. Aubrey has a tendency to sugarcoat things for my benefit. This is going to be hard to believe," I said, my voice thick with sarcasm, "but I haven't always been the most supportive of her choices of men."

"You? No way!" he said in an outraged, mocking tone that made me shove his shoulder and roll my eyes.

"Smart ass." I muttered as I took a sip and then said,

"There's been a few red flags already for me, based on some of the things she's told me about, but I am trying to go into this meeting with an open mind."

Aubrey rushed in, alone. I stood up to hug her. "He's running late, but said he'll meet us here."

I guess that's better than a blow-off, but still.

She pulled a compact out of her purse and glanced at her reflection in it.

"You look great." I offered, trying pre-smooth the feathers I would inevitably ruffle. She offered me a nervous smile and began to drum her fingers on the table.

"What are you drinking?" Foster asked.

She glanced over at our beers. "One of those looks good."

He walked away, giving me a second to chat with Aubrey, who looked a little rattled. "Everything okay?" I asked as I continued to study her.

"It's fine," she said. "I'm just nervous."

"What are you nervous about?"

"You breaking his balls. You know you can be intimidating, G."

I took that as a compliment. "Look, Aubs, I don't have any skin in the game. He has nothing to worry about with me as long as he treats you well."

"He does," she said vehemently, trying to convince me, then something caught her eye behind me and she broke out into a huge grin. "He's here!" She jumped up and ran over to him as Foster brought two more frosty mugs to the table and set them down in front of the two empty chairs in front of us.

Aubrey led him to our table, and they stood there awkwardly. An obvious gym rat, Tony's biceps stretched his black t-shirt to its maximum capacity. I could almost hear the cotton fibers screaming in protest. He thrust out a hand to Foster, who stood to shake it and grunted.

"This is Tony," Aubrey introduced him with stars in her eyes.

Foster's eyes widened as Tony's hand clamped down hard on his in a testosterone-fueled, competitive contest. "That's one hell of a handshake you got there." When they disengaged, Foster shook his hand out and wiggled his fingers, chuckling at his weakness, and Tony warmed right up seeing he'd bested him.

"Good to see you again," I lied and held out a hand and squeezed his back extra firmly, leaving no doubt in his mind that under all this chub was a fair amount of muscle. "Have a seat."

Tony settled himself into a chair with his hands in his lap.

"You must work out," Foster said.

"Thank you, Captain Obvious," I said with significant snark that I loved even more when Foster high-fived me. "Longtime listener, first-time caller," we chorused. Laughing, I hoisted the massive glass mug to my lips and took a long sip.

Tony was not amused but returned the focus back to himself without delay. "Four to six hours a day," he answered. "I am very disciplined and take my workout regime very seriously. The gym is my church."

"DeLuca's is mine," Foster joked and squeezed my knee, both warming my heart and providing such a contrast between himself and Tony it was alarming.

"You should join my gym. It will change your life."

"I feel the same way about this one's pastry cream." Foster grinned, hiking a thumb at me.

Looking at the beer in front of him he asked. "What's this?"

"Don't worry, we got the first round," Foster explained generously.

Tony held up the mug in the light and inspected it with a frown like it was diseased. "How many net carbs are in this?" He asked then pulled out his phone searching for the online menu. "I have to watch my macros religiously. I'm cutting for competition."

"Oh, I'm sorry," Foster interjected to smooth the uncomfortable conversation. "I'll drink that one, and you can ask the bartender for something that fits more within your macro requirements."

Instantly, the first word that came to my mind was douche. Second word, canoe.

"Come with me," Tony said, pulling Aubrey to her feet. He wrapped his arm around her shoulders possessively, and they walked off toward the bar.

Foster looked at me and sighed. "Well, it doesn't look like we are gonna be besties any time soon."

"Ha!" I scoffed as the burn of beer snorted up my nose. I yanked a napkin from the dispenser on the table and wiped it. "Definitely no danger of that." I watched them while anger bubbled up in my belly. "I hate the way she runs to fetch whatever he wants like a dog, and the whole alpha male caveman thing." I waved my finger in a squiggle in the air at them. "It makes me hostile."

"G. They are coming back. Be nice," Foster cautioned.

"I'm always nice," I said, sweet as pie, and to prove it, I pasted a warm smile on my face. "So, tell us more about yourself," I asked Tony, who returned to the table with a Budweiser Select. "Besides the fact that you prefer malt-flavored water."

Aubrey's eyes flashed a warning to me that I ignored.

"Do you have family around here?"

"Afraid not, it's just me," he said. "I work a lot. I'm in IT. I'm the guy they send in when no one else can solve the problem." He praised himself then chugged half of his beer.

"He's really successful." Aubrey leaned into him and gushed. "And really smart." Hoisting the bottle back to his lips he slammed it while we sat in awkward silence.

"Hey, Pretty, can you grab me another beer?" The way he called her pretty like it was her name irritated me. I sat up taller and felt Foster reach under the table and squeeze my leg in a gentle warning.

She popped up like she was taking an order at the bakery. "Does anyone else need anything?"

"No, I think we're good," I said.

She gave me a look and walked away. It got awkward really quickly after that. I leaned forward. "Tell me what you like about Aubrey."

"She's beautiful. Stays in shape. Makes a decent steak." He sat back in the chair sizing me up from across the table.

"Do you have any kids?"

"No."

"Do you like kids?"

"I can't say I've been around them enough to know. I was an only child."

"Are you close to your mom?"

"No. We haven't spoken in years."

His answers didn't surprise me at all, in fact they confirmed every fear I had about him. I leaned closer, about to really lay into him when a flutter of movement caught my eye. Aubrey rushed back clutching his fresh beer in her hand, and noticed the table was silent. "Everything okay here?" She asked, as her voice wavered.

"Absolutely." I turned to Foster eager to leave before I got myself in trouble. "Let's get some tokens and play pinball." I gulped fresh air as we left the table and anger enflamed my cheeks. We stopped at a 70s style Charlie's Angels machine where I inserted a token and aggressively yanked the plunger as far back as it could go and then released it against the metal ball. I snapped the flippers on the side of the machine just to dispel the hostile energy.

"I hate that guy already." I muttered under my breath. The ball rolled down to the flippers, and I smacked it hard with the right one, and then it rebounded to the top. It hit a bell and dodged against a bumper while the points chimed up on the machine.

"Maybe he's an acquired taste," Foster reasoned, trying to be Switzerland. "He's probably nervous. Maybe it just takes time for him to warm up to people."

"I love that you give everyone the benefit of the doubt, but I don't think Tony deserves it." The ball plunged down between the two flippers, so I turned the table over to Foster. "Your turn." He pulled the plunger back and sent the silver ball flying, concentrating on the game. I pulled the beer to my lips and took a longer sip. The buzz was the only thing making this night tolerable. I had to be careful because booze was my truth serum.

"I hate the way he calls her pretty. It's condescending. And all he did was talk about himself. He never asked a single question to get to know either of us better." I took another long sip and studied him with a scowl. "He's not good enough for her."

"You are right about that," Foster agreed. "She's quick to drop everything to cater to his needs. It's a little straight out of the 50s." He paused and reasoned with a shrug. "But maybe that is what she's looking for."

"I don't think even Aubrey knows what she's looking for. She thinks because she comes with baggage she has to lower her standards and accept any man who shows up. I told her she actually needs to set her standards even higher."

"That's good advice," he agreed. "Kids add an additional level of commitment and stress to any new relationship." He pounded the flippers, rocking on the balls of his feet, jerking the table, and then conceding and stepping over when his ball fell through the middle.

Aubrey and Tony were a few tables down from us. I watched them from a distance to see if they fit. Aubrey was playing first, and then she stepped to the side and let Tony take the next turn. She stood at the edge of the table watching when a semi-smashed guy tripped and bumped into her, grabbing her arm to steady himself. He was tipsy and apologetic as Aubrey's hands gripped his forearms in an effort to keep him upright. In an instant, Tony was in his face.

"You piece of shit. Watch where you're going. You almost knocked my girlfriend down!"

Aubrey tried to calm him, her little hands pushing his rippling forearms down. Her fists were tight balls against his muscular chest. She reached her hand up to his beet-red face and forced him to look at her. Tony pushed her away roughly and tried to get in the man's face again. Aubrey pulled him away, a difficult feat because he was double her size.

"Come on, honey, let's go." she said, and her eyes swung over to meet mine. Her eyes filled with fear as Foster ran over to her rescue.

"Come on, man. It's not worth it," Foster said, and finally Tony gave up the fight and let Foster lead him back to our table.

"I think we're gonna head out," Aubrey said as she gathered her purse and put her coat on. Before they left, she reached out to hug me and whispered with excitement in my ear, "Did you hear that? Tony called me his girlfriend."

My heart sunk. That's what she gleaned from the interaction? It was blatantly obvious she was in too deep already with this jerk. This did not bode well.

TWENTY-THREE

As a cake artist, when you get the chance to really do something outside the box, it's a huge win. During my phone consultation with Willow and Chase, I discovered they were painters and art lovers. They met when Willow was a docent at the Chicago Art Institute giving a tour of a new Monet installation and Chase dragged out the tour, making it last twice as long with his never-ending litany of questions. It was an over-confident move that got her attention but also got Willow written up for disciplinary action by the docent committee.

The couple arrived at the bakery dressed all in black, and they were rail-thin. Willow was rocking a dark, asymmetrical bob, contrasting sharply with her creamy white skin, and wearing a perfectly tailored long coat that was belted then flared at the waist, paired with tight black leggings with red stilettos. Chase's wavy blond hair gave him more of a surfer vibe, but his serious black cashmere sweater and perfectly pressed black pants with shiny black loafers killed that impression. His only accessory was a thick silver watch ringing his wrist.

I walked toward the couple with my hand extended. "It's so nice to meet you. I'm Gionna. Welcome to DeLuca's!" I greeted cheerily, beckoning them down the hallway. "Follow me. Let's get you settled in our tasting room. Can I get you an espresso?" I asked as they sat down at the round table, and they nodded enthusiastically. "Why don't you check out my portfolio while I prepare your coffee, and then we'll talk."

Willow and Chase eagerly began to flip through the album and study the cakes, page by page, pouring over them like they were fine art. This was the kind of client I adored, the ones who looked at my cakes as an artistic expression created out of sugar.

I glanced at my watch. Barely five minutes in and I could already tell, I wanted this commission.

They continued to flip through the photographs, murmuring excited comments to each other as I left the room for a few minutes, then returned with the coffees and settled in next to them.

"Your cakes are amazing," Willow gushed. "Each one is so unique. It's truly art, what you create. They are almost too pretty to eat."

"Thank you," I said, blooming in the warm light of her praise. "I'm glad you said almost because I've been told they taste incredible." I grinned. "Why don't you tell me more about the type of event you are planning?"

"It's an evening wedding at the Chicago Art Institute." Willow started.

"We've decided to return to the scene of the crime," Chase chimed in with a grin. "My persistence in chasing this one paid off. It's one of those full-circle moments the romantic in me can't resist." His hand found Willow's and clasped it in front of me. Some couples were naturally affectionate, no matter who was around, and some, you wonder if they ever touched each other at all. It was easier to get excited about a job when you loved the couple and were invested in their story.

Willow looked at him with the warmest smile. They genuinely liked each other. I know it is hard to believe, but some couples who get married *don't* actually like each other. After working with so many over the years, I could instantly tell if they were going to make it, or if the cake would barely be digested before they were running off to divorce court. These two were going to make it. I could feel it.

Willow turned back to me and continued. "We were thinking about a candlelight ceremony at eight pm. Intimate, around one hundred guests. We will have passed appetizers and champagne, but we really want the cake and dessert bar to be the star of the show."

"That sounds beautiful. Did you have any ideas in regard to the design?" I asked, poised with my notebook, scribbling notes as she talked. I took meticulous notes that I relied upon heavily during the design process. Any detail they shared, no matter how trivial I thought it was at the time was faithfully recorded in my folder. Willow looked over at Chase and squeezed his hand.

"What do you think, sweetheart?" she asked him sweetly and waited. "Do we have any ideas?"

"I think we are both in agreement." He looked over at Willow for confirmation, and she nodded her head eagerly. "We think artists work better and are more creative when they aren't micromanaged," he began. "Willow and I trust you, and you come so highly recommended, we thought we would give you free rein."

"Free rein? Are you for real?" I asked in shock as my desire for this commission quadrupled at hearing the words free rein. "I could kiss you both right now."

They laughed at my excitement, and ideas swirled in my mind. It took a minute to pull them together enough to articulate a concept. "There *is* a new technique I have always wanted to try that I think would be perfect for your event and tie into your story, but it *is* a bit risky," I said, formulating a plan as I drew a rough design on the paper in front of me.

They both leaned in, excited to discover what I had in store.

"Since Monet is how you met, I was thinking about hand-painting your cake impressionistically." The concept was starting to come to life in my mind already. It was a perfect expression of who Willow and Chase were, and that's how I knew it was a home run. "It would have a smooth ivory fondant base that the entire cake would be covered in, but on the day of the event, I would hand-paint the impressionistic design in lavender and purple and warm oranges and reds. The buttercream would become like paint, and the cake would be the canvas."

Their eyes widened, and I knew they were falling in love with the idea as much as I was.

"Could you give me some insight on your favorite Monet pieces? I will create a custom painting that is reminiscent of them on the cake."

I continued to sketch the concept. "The cake stand would be a modern fountain. A sheet of water around all four sides of the cake about a foot high would give it an audible component and would elevate the design, both visually and aesthetically." I crudely drew the elements, noticing their excitement grow with each stroke of the pencil. "On top of this stand, your cake would be a three-tier design. Since your event is smaller scale, I would suggest that the cakes be smaller but thicker to give us a wider canvas to work on. I was thinking an asymmetrical stacked rectangle design for you to cut into."

Willow flashed me a huge grin, feeding on my excitement. "I love it. What do you think, Chase?"

"Simply sublime." I smiled at his word choice. Sublime wasn't one I heard very often but fit this couple perfectly.

Savoring their praise, I continued to sketch as another new idea came to me. "Then, behind you on easels, we could also construct a vertical dessert bar. I could create two panels about 3 foot by 3 foot—a canvas of treats, cake pops, cookies, macaroons, even cannolis if you want, creating an abstract design that looks like two impressionist paintings."

"Interactive art you can eat!" Willow understood the concept immediately. "I love it. Amazing." She squealed a little in excitement, and it made me love her more.

"Are you ready to taste some flavors?" I asked.

"I've been looking forward to this part for weeks," Chase said, his eyes lighting up.

"I'll be right back." I headed out to the kitchen and started to put slivers of my sample cake flavors on a rose gold platter, buzzing on a high from their reaction. This was the part of my job that I loved—when a client trusted me enough to put the entire design into my hands.

"You're a happy girl today," Aubrey said. She was helping Nonna frost macaroons.

"Dream client." I smiled. "They are giving me free rein —the anti-Amara."

"That's awesome." Aubrey's distracted eyes darted away, and I followed them to where Tony was seated at a table hulked out with this open laptop facing us. His eyes narrowed slightly on mine. Aubrey smoothed her hair and washed her hands and then went over to his table.

"How long has he been there?" I asked.

"Since we opened," Mom answered with irritation edging her voice. "I'm going to have to have a word with Aubrey."

I observed her interaction with him. She was stiff and anxious, not her usual bubbly self. Mr. M. was watching them, too, since Aubrey was his favorite and he always kept a close eye on her. I hated seeing her conform and shape shift to fit the man she was dating. She had a tendency to take on a chameleon quality in an effort to keep the relationship together at all costs. It was frustrating to witness this woman I adored reduce herself and play smaller in order to find love, instead of looking for a bigger love that fit her properly.

Nonna was at the window, staring him down, shooting daggers with her eyes. Her lips were moving, muttering to herself under her breath and probably cursing in Italian.

I pulled the last of the samples from the case, added a sugar cookie, a few of our macaroons, and a couple of powder sugar-dusted Italian wedding cookies to the plate before walking it back to the tasting room.

I placed the tray carefully on the table and handed them a heavy silver fork wrapped in a cloth napkin.

Presentation during these consultations was everything. There was no detail that was too small. Willow unwrapped her fork and thrust it into the red velvet.

"Oh, Gionna!" She exclaimed, "It's so good."

"It's my most popular flavor," I said, soaking up their praise.

Twenty minutes later, I had a signed contract in my hand and a fat retainer. I can't explain it, but signing a bride was always a high for me. It validated my skills in a way that nothing else could. Power and competence surged through me, and I was in an unstoppable frame of mind. Deciding to use this power trip to my advantage, I waited until Aubrey dashed to the bathroom and crossed the room to pull out a chair at Tony's table.

He blatantly ignored me, so I cleared my throat. Since he was still giving me the cold shoulder, I leaned forward and gently pressed the screen of his laptop closed in a daring display of confidence and to get his complete attention. It worked. He was stunned. I got the feeling that not very many people stood up to Tony.

"I think you've had your fill. Why don't you move along now?"

"Is that right?" He leaned closer, trying to threaten me, but I refused to back down.

"Actually, why don't you move along completely? From the bakery, but most of all from my girl Aubrey."

"I'm not going to let a fat cunt like you tell me what I can and cannot have."

That word incensed me. The worst slur in the English language to call any woman. It was so terrible I couldn't even bring myself to say it. Instead, I abbreviated it to C-

U-Next-Tuesday. It was a word so vile, so nasty and repugnant, I saw red.

Mom and Pops appeared at the table and stood behind me. I was relieved that back-up had arrived.

"You are not welcome here anymore," Marco said, folding his arms across his chest. "I suggest you leave now."

Mr. M had found his feet and stood shoulder to frail shoulder next to Dad. "Get on out of here." He waved his finger at Tony, who could easily bench press him and break him in half.

Seeing he was outnumbered and we weren't planning on backing down anytime soon, he shoved his laptop into a backpack and stood. "Your cannolis taste like shit anyway."

He walked out of the door without a glance back, and we all sighed in relief when he was gone. I looked over to the kitchen where Nonna had run interference, distracting Aubrey with another task when she had come out of the bathroom.

God, I love my family.

Aubrey's face filled with concern when she came out of the kitchen and finally noticed Tony was gone. I knew I had only a few precious seconds before her phone would be blowing up with Tony's venom.

"We need to talk."

Her forehead wrinkled in confusion as she fished around in her pocket for her phone. I put a hand on her arm and said, "I think you should look at that later."

"Gionna… what did you do?" Her voice was stretched tight and wavering.

"Just hear me out," I pleaded. "He's not the guy, honey.

I know you want to believe he is, but he's not it. He's a despicable piece of shit."

"That was not your call to make." She shrugged my hand off her shoulder. "You don't get to decide who I let into my life. You were way out of line."

"Maybe, but he's a hateful human being."

"You don't know him like I do."

"I see how you are when you're with him. Running around to keep him happy, dropping everything to put his needs first."

"I don't do that."

"You can't even see what you're doing," I groaned, exasperated.

Mom and Pops took a step closer. "Aubrey, he's a bully," Mom insisted.

"He's just intense and misunderstood," Aubrey argued.

Customers began to flood the bakery for lunch, so we had to set it aside. Aubrey was quiet the rest of the afternoon, then gathered the kids and walked to the train, brushing off our apologies in her haste to leave.

TWENTY-FOUR

After our interaction with Tony, Aubrey was quieter and put up a wall. We had been friends long enough for me to know that she would eventually come around, but on her terms. She drifted away as I sat on the river bank, waiting for her to return. I'd see her at work, and at movie nights at Nonna's, but beyond that, she was a silent ghost. It wasn't her fault completely, because I was a terrible friend besotted and distracted by Foster.

Three months since our first date had passed in the blink of an eye, and we had developed a routine that fit perfectly into my life. He'd come over after work and cook dinner, I'd help him clean up, and then we'd snuggle in front of the TV for a few hours before bed. The November nights got darker earlier, and we spent them wrapped in each other's arms. The pressure was building for us to take the next step, but I tried to ignore it. I was delighted with the way things were, and didn't want to rock the boat. If it ain't broke, don't fix it.

Foster became a permanent fixture at my place. He

started staying over more and more, only going to his place to pick up mail and grab clean clothes. His toothbrush appeared in the holder one night, and there was a twinge of claustrophobia at seeing the blue toothbrush resting next to my purple one in the holder on the sink.

It's just a toothbrush. You're being an idiot.

Then it was a few white V-neck t-shirts that I found when I was doing a load of whites that tore me in two. On one hand, I loved seeing those t-shirts wrestling with mine in the hamper fresh from the dryer, but on the other hand, the sight of his personal items in my space tightened my chest and hit my panic button. It was a battle I fought daily inside myself, wanting to dare to fall in love, but terrified the fall would destroy me. It was a two steps forward one step back progression as I found myself giving in to him, but also verifying everything he said and testing him in little ways. He continued to pass my never-ending tests with flying colors, pretending not to notice.

Three little words. I love you. I loved Foster Valentine, and yet I couldn't say it. I tapped them out in a text message and deleted them endless times. You can't say something like that in a text. They were ever present on the tip of my tongue, filling my mouth, but I bit them back time and time again. Why were they so hard to say? I loved lots of things. I loved gelato and my dates with my dad. I loved Owen and Stella and Parmesano Reggiano. I loved dark chocolate and French bulldogs. I loved tattoos on a man and that little trail of hair from the navel to the goodies below. I loved so many things, but I couldn't admit that I loved Foster Valentine.

That night, the wine made me do it, or maybe it was the three beautiful orgasms he drew out of me with his fingers that were incredibly dexterous and nimble. They fluttered through my body, transforming me to a pile of quivering satisfied Jell-O laying in his arms. Sleepy and content with a sea of oxytocin washing over us, I drifted into the sleepy place between waking and dreaming where anything is possible and emotional revelations accidentally slip out.

His fingers tickled my back, tracing all the lines of my body. "Mmm. That's so nice," I mumbled. "G'night. I love you."

Oh shit, oh shit. I panicked, wishing I could take the words back. Instantly alert, I froze perfectly still, hoping he was sliding into sleep and didn't hear my post-coitus confession.

"I know you do." He grinned, his words low and lazy. Warmth rushed to my face and sweat prickled near my hairline.

I pinched his nipple.

"Ouchie, sweetheart." Foster laughed with his eyes still closed as he pulled me to him tighter. I pinched harder, anything to transfer the painful sting from putting myself completely out there. My chest flushed hot as he wrapped his strong hands around my wrists, preventing further pinches to his soft spots. "Under duress?" he asked. "Is that how you want to play this game?"

No. I want him to say it because he means it, not because of a perfectly timed titty twister.

He playfully rolled on top of me, pinning me down with his legs on the bed as I writhed, trying to get away. This just made him work harder to hold me down, and since he was incredibly strong, I eventually gave up and huffed in protest.

"Now, are you done fighting me?" He leaned down closer and looked into my eyes.

"I guess," I said, trying to sound bored. He let go of my wrists, and I wrapped my hands around my waist in defense.

"You don't need to protect yourself from me," he whispered into the air between us while still laying on top of my body. He felt like a weighted blanket and was oddly comforting. "Put your arms around me," he instructed. I bit on my bottom lip, considering his request, and then finally untucked my arms and wrapped them around him.

"See? That's better," he murmured.

Slipping his fingers into my hair, he steadied my face with his hands, propped himself up with his forearms, and looked deeply into my eyes. He leaned into me so close our noses were touching and said softly, "I love you, Gionna DeLuca. I have for a while now and was just waiting for you to catch up."

A sexy smile bloomed on my lips. His breath brushed across my cheeks, and then his lips met mine. Sweet and soft.

"I love you," he repeated a little more loudly and kissed me again.

"I *love* you," he insisted.

"I love you, too," I finally relented shyly. I pulled him tighter to me and nuzzled into the warm space between his neck and shoulder. The thrill in my belly blossomed like a rose in the sun.

He loves me. Foster Valentine loves me.

My fingers teased down his hip.

"More?" Foster asked. "Dear Lord, woman! You're

insatiable." He tickled my sides as I wriggled against him, his strong arms keeping me tucked in tight to him.

"What can I say, I'm over forty. I'm in my prime." Both my hands palmed his strong shoulders, squeezing them tight as he began to fill me.

"You are," he agreed as he sucked on the sacred space just under my earlobe.

And afterward, I fell asleep securely in my position as the little spoon and slept like a baby. Love is the most effective over the counter sleep aid there is.

TWENTY-FIVE

The bliss-filled magic of finding the right one was a little less sweet because I didn't get to rehash every sordid detail with my best friend. I wanted to shout from the rooftops. "I have found him, the one! True love *does* exist! I believe in happily ever after. I *be-lieve*!!!!" That's how I knew I'd watched one too many of Nonna's movies. I was in deep.

Foster said he loved me all the time, but I still struggled to say it myself. I responded with, "I know," and, "Mmhmm," a lot. I was stingy with the words he wanted to hear, but inside, I was fighting a battle. Love is scary. I wanted it, and Foster proved to me every day with every action and decision he made that he loved me. Sometimes, I was able to relax and enjoy it, and then other times, the fear set in. The paralyzing, soul-sucking terror that screamed, "You better hang on tight. Now that you have a good one, you can lose him!" I couldn't relax into the love bubble anymore. I was on high alert, looking for signs it was going to pop. Indications he was too good to be true.

He must have picked up on the energy because after a long, delicious dinner, he was rubbing my feet as we watched a documentary, and when the credits rolled, he asked, "Can we talk?"

Oof! Can we talk? The three most terrifying words a man can utter to a woman. Panic gripped my belly. Was this it? He was breaking up with me. I knew it. My heart dropped and a massive weight lodged on my chest. It was over. We'd had a good run, but it was time for him to move on.

Thanks for the memories.

"Sure," I breathed anxiously as our gazes tangled, and I scrambled to decode the intentions in his eyes.

"It's hard to read you sometimes," he started in. "You keep everything so close to your chest. I feel like you're always waiting for the other shoe to drop."

He was much more intuitive than I ever imagined. I swallowed hard and sat up to get my bearings, placing my feet on the floor. If he was breaking up with me, it would be much easier to accept without skin-on-skin contact.

He pulled out his phone. "I don't know if you know this, but I am quite a catch, G." He smiled and tapped the keys to open a screen. "Here's my credit report. It's a solid 787. I have a 401k and have been looking at real estate. I make decent financial decisions, most of the time."

I laughed at him but had to admit it was very calming to see his credit report. I tried to pretend I wasn't interested and pushed the phone away, trying to laugh it off.

"I want to be upfront with you. I know you haven't always had honesty in your relationships, and I want to show you that I am that guy. I love you, DeLuca. I want to build a life with you. I want you to know without a doubt that you can trust me."

"I do," I insisted, but the words were twinged with fear and coated in insecurity.

He shook his head and wagged his index finger at me. "You a liar," he joked. "I get it. I would be wary if I were you. I just want you to have some peace of mind. I want you to feel safe."

Safe.

Tears welled up at my lashes, and I looked down to hide my shame. In relationships, safety had always been elusive. It was a completely foreign concept to me. "Come here." He pulled me into a hug on the sofa.

"Your heart is safe with me. I promise." He snuggled in closer and breathed into my neck. "Your money is safe with me, and your emotions are safe with me. It is okay to open your heart and trust again." He spelled it all out. I wish I didn't need to hear him say those words, but when he did, my heart cracked open further, giving him more access, in spite of the terror that engulfed it.

———

A week later, I didn't want to hide anymore. I wanted him to meet my family.

"Do you have plans for Thanksgiving?" I asked.

"Thanksgiving?" His voice shot up an octave in surprise. We were tangled up in the sheets as his fingers traced along the planes of my back, and I was becoming drowsy. The question actually popped out accidentally, making the impossible seem possible after another earth-shattering orgasm, the only time my defenses were completely down. It was becoming a bad habit. My eyes remained closed as I continued to question him.

"What? Did you want me to hide you away forever?"

"Of course not. I just know that officially meeting your family is a big deal," he answered. "If you're not ready, we can wait."

"I'm ready, I just don't know how it's gonna go."

"Don't worry about it, baby. Parents love me, but Mom and I have a standing Thanksgiving date. The idea of her being alone on Thanksgiving doesn't sit well with me."

"Of course, it doesn't. I would never ask you to do that." I considered the craziest idea I'd had in a long time before forging ahead and asking him, "How about this? How about we just rip the Band-Aid off this bitch and meet each other's parents the same day?" It was said with more confidence than I felt as I waited for him to talk me out of it.

"Hmm," he said sleepily, and after a full sixty-seconds of silence where I wondered if he had drifted off, he replied, "That's ballsy. I like it."

"Really? Are you sure?"

"I've never been more sure of anything in my entire life." He leaned in to kiss me. "My mom is going to love you."

"Does she know I'm a million years old? How old is your mom anyway?"

"Fifty."

I winced. "Fifty? That's only eight years older than I am." I made a grimace "Ouch." The sleepy sexy afterglow was starting to fade in the bright reality of this sobering information.

"You worry too much," he said, dismissing my obvious

discomfort at the mere eight-year gap between me and his mother. "My mom trusts me to make good decisions. If you make me happy, she will be ecstatic you are in my life." He bent to kiss my forehead, his tone softening. "And I know without a doubt, Gionna DeLuca, you make me happy."

"Well, your mom sounds a lot more easygoing than my family. Are you sure you're ready for that?"

"Bring it, baby. I got this." He sounded self-assured and slightly overconfident, two qualities I loved about him. I was tired of sneaking around. I wanted to share my happiness and joy with my family. I wanted them to know who was lighting me up from the inside.

"Okay, then. It's settled. Thanksgiving with the parents." The idea pinched my heart with anxiety. "We can't go back, you know. This is a bell we can't unring. Once they know about us, it's over. We can't ever go back to our secret love cocoon. We will be out there loud and proud."

"I don't want to unring it," he said confidently. "G'night, DeLuca," he whispered into the dark as he pulled me closer and drifted off to sleep immediately while I lay next to him twisting in worry.

TWENTY-SIX

A few days later, Aubrey said she needed a night with a glass of wine and some Epson salts without the kids pounding on the bathroom door. Thrilled that she was done freezing me out, I jumped at the chance to have the kids stay overnight. I was a big fan of her self-care desire, especially since Tony hadn't made another appearance at the bakery since our confrontation.

Good riddance.

"Who wants spaghetti?" Foster called out as he sailed through the door with a canvas bag of groceries and the key I'd recently given him. Stella and Owen came running at the sound of his deep voice. "Can I help?" Owen didn't even wait for an answer. Cooking with Foster was one of his favorite activities. He was already pulling out the special stool Foster had bought for him to use in my kitchen a few weeks ago. It was collapsible and tucked into a corner, and he even knew how to unfold it and put it together himself. He jumped up proudly on it in a flash with a huge accomplished grin lighting up his usually serious face.

"Wash your hands, little man," Foster said as he turned to scrub his own. Owen jumped off the stool and dragged it over to the sink, and after squirting a ridiculous amount of blue liquid dish soap onto his hands, he was fresh and clean and ready to begin. I sat on the sofa with sweet little Stella, who wanted me to read *Pinkalicious* for the four hundredth time. I was so wrapped around her finger that I didn't even whine about it. I knew it by heart and recited the words and turned the pages like a robot, half-listening to Foster and Owen.

"So, when the head chef asks you a question, as a sous chef, you must always respond. You have to acknowledge the request. Communication is important in *any* relationship, but especially in the kitchen. Without solid communication, you can get burned."

Truer words have never been spoken.

Foster was schooling Owen on the correct etiquette and lingo used working in a professional kitchen, and it was adorable to witness. "You must repeat the head chef's command and then say, 'Yes, Chef.'" Foster instructed and Owen nodded solemnly, his eyes wide and serious. It was hard to stifle the giggle that set in as I watched them.

"Let's give it a try. Get the sauté pan," he barked at Owen, who was initially startled at his direct order, then jumped off the stool and scrambled to the cupboard that housed the pan.

"Sauté Pan. Yes, Chef," Foster prompted him when he said nothing.

Owen proudly repeated, "Sauté pan. Yes, Chef!" He

grinned and handed the pan to him, then climbed back on the stool.

"The secret to a good sauce is the sofrito," Foster disclosed, and Owen nodded like he understood what Foster was talking about. "*And* the secret to a good sofrito is a two-one-one ratio. That means two cups of onions to every one cup of the other vegetables. A sofrito has onion, celery, carrot, or fennel and parsley, and it's cooked in olive oil. In French cuisine, there is something similar, but it is called a mirepoix because instead of being cooked in olive oil, it's cooked in butter."

Owen continued to take Foster incredibly seriously, soaking up his culinary knowledge like a sponge. He was so serious and absolutely engrossed in the conversation it made me laugh because there was no way that he understood half of what Foster was explaining.

Foster pulled out a cutting board and a very sharp knife, taking the time to sharpen the blade. The knife sliced against the sharpener like a dramatic sword fight was taking place in my kitchen as he did five quick swipes across it on each side. It was a meditative habit of his that he never skipped out on, bordering on an OCD ritual, always beginning with freshly sharpened knives. Foster was like most chefs, logical and methodical in his thinking.

"Knife skills are very important for a good sous chef to learn," he said. "I'm not gonna let you handle the knife by yourself yet, obviously, because you are only seven years old and knives are very dangerous. But I do want to teach you the proper way to use a knife, so when you get a little older, you can do it on your own. Fundamentals are important."

"What are fundamentals?" Owen asked timidly.

"They are the basic skills you are taught when you first start learning a new activity."

Foster pulled out an onion and cut off both the top and the bottom and then lightly scored across the brown onion skin with the knife. The paper-thin skin was Owen's job to remove. His tiny little fingernails picked at the slit Foster had made, and finally, he was able to pull it off in one long pull that he waved in the air triumphantly as Foster clapped him on the back.

"Good work, my man!" Foster said and turned back to the cutting board. "Safety is really important. No one will hire a chef with three fingers." He poked Owen's side and the boy laughed. "See my fingers when I hold them straight?" Then he bent the fingers back at the first knuckle, curling the tips in toward his palms. "See the difference?"

Owen nodded again, completely enthralled with Foster's instructions. I had never seen him so engrossed in anything besides video games.

Foster pulled out the celery and the carrots and the fennel and chopped off the ends and handed them to Owen with a gruff order. "Wash the vegetables."

"Wash the vegetables. Yes, Chef!" Owen repeated, climbing down from the stool with his arms full. Foster helped by kicking the step stool closer to the sink, and Owen climbed up and washed all of the produce very carefully, taking the time to make sure it was squeaky clean. Then he brought them back to Foster one at a time.

"Now, we need to add the olive oil to the pan. This is called a cruet." He handed Owen the bottle with a metal spout, and Owen made quick work of swirling it around the pan. The oil dribbled out in a greenish-yellow stream that coated the stainless steel. Foster cranked on the gas burner, it crackled three times, and then there was a *whoosh* sound as it lit. He placed the pan on top of the flame to warm it up while he chopped the celery, carrot, and fennel.

"Dicing is one of the most important knife skills you can master." He chopped so quickly and with such precision that all the vegetables were quickly reduced to a pile of tiny, uniform squares. He scraped them into a cup to show Owen. "See how they are all the same size? That's very important. Your knife work will get you jobs. You can't be sloppy.

"Carefully pour this into the pan," he directed as he handed Owen the measuring cup. "Be careful about the oil. If you do it too quickly, the oil will spatter and can burn you." Owen poured it in slowly as instructed and smiled triumphantly when the glass was empty.

"Now, one of the other big differences between a mirepoix and a sofrito is that a sofrito has Italian parsley in it." He ripped a few leaves off the plant that I kept in a sunny bay window by the sink. Rolling it in his fingers, he held it in front of Owen's nose.

"Smell that?"

Owen nodded again.

"Fresh herbs are mandatory. They add complexity and a burst of freshness to any dish you are preparing."

Foster bent over the cutting board again and minced the parsley and garlic into tiny uniform pieces, then scraped it all into the sofrito bubbling on the stove. The house was beginning to smell incredible.

"Yum!" Stella said.

I tucked one of her curls behind her ears, marveling at how soft it was. "Are you hungry, Stella?"

She nodded eagerly. "Me too!" I said. Foster pulled the artisanal sausage out of the fridge and began to break it into small pieces with Owen. "Animals do us a service when they become food. Did you know that you can taste a huge difference in the meat from a pig that has been humanely raised versus one that has been confined to a tiny stall at a corporate farm?" I cleared my throat in a warning signal that Foster's quick glance told me he received, not wanting them to get too in-depth about the real origin of meat. The kids could be picky eaters, and I didn't want to be the reason they suddenly became vegetarians.

"Rigaldi's Meat Market is just a few doors down from the Bakery," I offered, changing the subject from the slaughterhouse. "You love their bacon."

"Everyone loves bacon, Auntie G."

"True." I couldn't disagree with that logic. He was right; everyone does love bacon.

"Okay, now we need the pasta pot," Foster said as he scooped the sausage into the sofrito and then added two cans of crushed tomatoes and all the herbs. Parsley, basil, and his secret ingredient, dill, went into the simmering mixture, and then he put a lid on it to let it bubble.

"Pasta pot. Yes, Chef!" Owen climbed down and got the big pasta pot from the shelf and handed it to Foster, who filled it with water and added it to the cooktop.

"And now, we wait." Foster smiled. "Let's go see what cartoons we can find." He walked to the living room and flopped down on the sofa, putting his feet up on the coffee table. Then he laced his fingers across the back of his neck and rested his elbows on the wall behind him. Owen struck the same exact pose, and it was so cute, I had to take a picture and send it to Aubrey with the caption, "Twinsies."

She sent a flurry of heart emoticons back.

Twenty minutes later, we were sitting at the table with the kids, who were twirling their noodles into their spoons using the proper technique like Pops had shown them. No adopted grandkids of his were going to resort to cutting their pasta. It had to be twirled and slurped up like God intended.

"Great job, boys!" I praised and gave them a chef's kiss. "So good. In fact, after dinner and the dishes get cleaned up, you might be able to talk Auntie G into walking down to the corner for gelato."

TWENTY-SEVEN

At the time, the mutual meeting of the parents on Thanksgiving sounded like a good plan—a one and done situation. But that afternoon, reality set in deep in the pit of my stomach. My anxiety was off the charts after picking Wendy up at the airport on our way to my parents' house. Making small talk and trying to impress my boyfriend's mother was not my strong suit, reducing me to a stuttering pile of blushing nerves. I babbled on endlessly as we drove, spending way too much time analyzing the forecast and the possibility of snow. Something I never usually gave a rip about, but my brain was blank, scanning and searching for common topics to discuss, desperate to fill the silence with words. Any words. Words that would convince Wendy to like me. I was clearly out of my element. I was hyper-aware she was sitting next to me, calmly looking out the window, while I started to sweat as the anxiety climbed. I saw Foster's eyebrows raise once or twice in the rearview mirror, enjoying seeing me on the hot seat while trying to make a good impression on his mother. I felt my phone vibrate and pulled it out at a stoplight.

Foster: *G. Relax. If I love you, she will too.*

I caught his eye in the mirror, and when he winked, I finally was able to exhale.

———

I stood outside of my childhood home taking a breath to center my nerves before opening the door. Foster stood next to me, and reached out to give my hand a supportive squeeze. Thankfully, he had covered up his tattoos in a long-sleeved navy Henley shirt. Mom could be really judgmental about people with tattoos, and right out of the gate, I didn't want to give her anything to pick apart about him. I turned the knob and called out, "We're home!" as we walked into the house that I grew up in. The familiar scent of roasted garlic and basil hit my nostrils, and I heard Wendy say right behind me, "Wow. That smells incredible."

"I probably should have warned you, lasagna is our turkey," I said over my shoulder as I led them down the hall.

"I'm a big fan of *any* meal I don't have to cook. To be honest, I never really liked turkey anyway," Wendy commented with a warm smile. Carrying a bottle of wine, a bottle of sparkling juice for the kids, and an arm full of flowers for Mom and Nonna, both Foster and his mother were identical bottles of nervous energy. I walked further, following the sound of my dad's warm booming voice singing in Italian, and every step closer ratcheted up my anxiety.

Why am I so nervous?

When Nonna laid eyes on us, she walked over with a big smile, her eyes alert and snappy. Kissing both of Wendy's cheeks, she said, "Hello, welcome to our home," and pulled them both into a warm hug.

"Nonna, this is Foster and his mother, Wendy," I introduced them as Mom and Pops came forward next. "This is my mom, Lorraine, and my father, Marco," I said. "And my best friend, Aubrey." The kids were right behind her, and Owen took up residence at Foster's hip as Foster's hand ruffled his hair.

"Mom, this is my sous chef, Owen. He cleans and peels carrots like no one's business." Owen burst with pride and looked up at Foster like he was a god.

Wendy stuck out her hand to shake Owen's much smaller one and said very seriously, "It's nice to meet you, Owen."

"And this is his lovely sister, Stella."

Wendy squatted down to say hello to Stella on her level, making the little girl practically glow from the focused attention.

Aubrey's gaze met mine as I noticed dark circles and a forced smile pressed into her lips that didn't quite make it to her eyes. She walked stiffly back to the island where she was slicing a loaf of bread into thick, chunky slices.

Wendy followed Mom to the stove to tackle any last-minute meal preparation duties. Pops's eyes shot over to Foster, studying him, measuring, sizing him up, and drawing conclusions before words were ever spoken. He blamed himself for missing the truth with Brett, and now I could see him carefully scrutinizing Foster, trying to see around heartbreaking corners to try to save me from heartache because he thought he failed last time.

"Sir, I am a huge fan of DeLuca's and a sous chef at the Ivy." The corners of Pop's mouth twitched up at this news. The Ivy vouched for him more than any words I could ever say. Pops was close with the owner, and he surprised me by clapping the Foster on the back and giving him the task of mincing the herbs while immediately launching into restaurant and culinary speak. It was a test, and a few minutes later Foster's finely minced parsley passed with flying colors. I said a silent prayer of thanks to the gods who aligned me with a chef, knowing that out of all the boys out there, a chef would be the one that might actually earn Pops' approval.

I followed behind them, marveling at how much pent-up stress I had been feeling leading up to this meeting and how effortless it was actually turning out to be. I had built this moment up in my mind by overthinking and worrying from the start.

The table was set, and the tapered candles were lit. Mom's best china was laid out on top of an ochre velvet tablecloth. The wine was poured into all the glasses expertly by Foster, who pretended to be a sommelier. He forced Owen to swirl his sparkling grape juice in the glass and taught him to fan it toward his nose and say big words like bouquet and finish. Foster had become Owen's idol almost overnight, and Owen worked hard for his approval. It was like watching the Pied Piper weave his magical spell.

Foster was vocal and full of accolades for Bumpo's cannolis and for the daily espresso he admitted he couldn't live without. Even Mom was won over by his lavish praise for the organic coffee beans. Carefully explaining the roasting method to his poor mother who, bless her soul, actually acted interested in the tedious process. The lasagna was passed around the table family style, followed by bowls of asparagus and thick beans, buttered and glistening, roasted carrots and prime rib, and crusty bread slathered with butter and parmesan garlic knots.

Foster gave a rousing impression of his culinary instructor that had wine even shooting out of Mom's nose. He got extra points for jumping up to do the dishes and clean the kitchen with Nonna because it was a massive undertaking. In the span of just a few hours, I wasn't the only one under his spell anymore. It was impossible not to love Foster Valentine, and we all had it bad.

An hour later, all the dishes were washed, dried, and put away, and I sliced thick, creamy squares of tiramisu for everyone. Artfully, I presented them on pretty plates with whipped cream and mint. Foster helped me carry them back out to the dining room, where we all settled down to take a few more bites to top off our already overstuffed bellies.

Foster looked right at my dad and then stood, raising a glass. "I'd like to make a toast if that is okay with you?" Pops nodded eagerly, and Mom was so enamored with him she raised her glass, eager to toast anything he deemed toast-worthy. My brows crinkled in awe as I watched the room captivated again under his spell.

"This has been an amazing day for my mom and me. Gionna has told me so many stories about you, but she didn't even come close to conveying the warmth of this family. You are so lucky to have each other. Family truly is the only thing that really matters."

"Here, here," Pops sang out in agreement, and I watched a sweet knowing smile creep across Mom's face.

He said the magic words, successfully wrapping them all around his finger.

A few hours later, Nonna loaded us down with left-overs, packed carefully into easy one-serving containers, and we left after giving a round of hugs. Mom squeezed me tight and whispered in my ear, "I like him." And I melted. I hadn't realized until that moment how much her approval mattered to me.

"Me too," I whispered back.

Mom hugged Wendy like she was a sorority sister, and when they exchanged phone numbers, you could have knocked me over with a feather.

I walked to the van and opened the door for her while Foster got our leftovers situated in the back.

"Gionna, this was a perfect Thanksgiving! Thank you so much for inviting me to share it with your family. They are incredible."

"I'm so happy to hear you enjoyed yourself."

"It gives me a lot of peace of mind to know this one is surrounded by wonderful people." She hiked a thumb back toward Foster, who smiled and nodded. "Makes the phys-ical distance between us easier to endure."

I drove us back to the apartment and set up a cozy bed for Wendy on the couch.

"Do you have any really good Foster stories?" I asked her. "Like really embarrassing ones I can save for later, and trot them out at inappropriate times?"

"Hmm. Let me think." She paused before continuing. "There was that time in his fourth-grade art class when he got sent to the principal's office for painting a girl's hair purple that sat in front of him," she said, her brown eyes dancing.

They have the same eyes.

"No way!"

"Hey, I was just overflowing with creative energy that yearned to be expressed." He smirked with a shrug leaning against the countertop in my kitchen.

"Oh, And once, he stole the neighbor's lawn ornament."

"What? You mean there's a thief in our midst?" I asked in mock outrage.

"I can't believe Mr. Pollack even noticed. His lawn was covered in flamingos." Wendy started laughing so hard and grabbing her stomach, struggling to get control over herself as she held up one finger and breathed between fits of giggles. "He got caught..." Another burst of giggles made it hard to understand her next words. She squeezed her legs together.

"Mom, get a grip," Foster cautioned, laughing at her.

"He got caught because he shoved his fingers so far up the flamingo's behind...they got stuck." She mimed the action with two fingers, looking like she was performing a prostate exam, "we had to call the fire department and have them saw it off him." She leaned forward, laughing so hard that I couldn't help but join her in her merriment.

"Okay, that's just funny," I said gleefully. "I don't care who you are. What else you got?" I said as I pulled three mugs out of the cupboard and set a pan on the burner. "Who wants some hot cocoa?"

"Me!" Wendy raised her hand like a kindergartener does in school. It was endearing.

"Me too!" Foster said. "If you guys are going to insist on taking this painful trip down memory lane, can you at least pour a shot of mercy schnapps in mine?"

"Ooh! Great idea, babe," I said, standing on my tiptoes to try to reach the liquor cabinet. Foster popped up and pulled the bottle from the top shelf and handed it to me. I added heavy cream and half and half to a pan and then broke heavenly chunks of Ghiradelli dark chocolate into it and stirred slowly until the chocolate melted. Then I swiftly poured the warm cocoa mixture into the three mugs before adding a shot of peppermint schnapps and a handful of miniature marshmallows. I set them on a tray and added biscotti and a couple of sugar cookies, then walked over to the table.

"Thank you, dear," Wendy said. "This is such a treat."

"More, I need more stories," I begged.

"Once, when he was about fourteen, I think, he had a big test coming up, so he rolled in some poison ivy so he didn't have to go to school for a week. The joke was on him though. The doctor told me to get him hemorrhoid cream for the itching, so he had to coat his entire body with it a few times a day." She sipped again, laughing. "I spent a small fortune on Preparation H and had to change pharmacies. The looks I got checking out at the drugstore with four tubes of it every few days!" Her eyes widened as she laughed.

I laughed until my stomach hurt.

"Go ahead, darling, laugh at my expense," Foster said dramatically as he bit into a cookie. "You guys are already ganging up on me." He shook his head in mock annoyance, but I could tell he secretly loved that we already liked each other so much.

TWENTY-EIGHT

The end of November rolled into the Windy City, and I had another draining meeting with Amara. She came solo this time with so many changes to the cake design and new ideas I was beginning to wonder if she had a split personality.

"Oh my God. Aubrey, she is *killing* me." I sighed after my meeting with Amara. "She's the worst. The only thing that is keeping me from calling her and breaking our contract is her upcoming feature with *The Knot*." I collapsed dramatically onto a stool at the counter. Working closely with Amara was soul-sucking and exhausting, and trying to corral her insane expectations and edits to the design was making me lose my mind. "I am never getting married. Weddings turn normal people into crazy nutballs."

"Never say never," Aubrey cautioned. "Absolutes like that always come back to bite you in the ass." For once, she wasn't glued to the phone, and I took that as a good sign.

"Mommy!" Owen burst through the door and ran straight into her arms, and she winced when he hugged her. "Hey there, buddy. Good day?"

"Yeah! We learned about rocks today and got to go on a field trip."

I pulled a fresh cannoli from the case and added extra chocolate pastry cream and a sprinkle of pistachios and brought it over to him. His little arms squeezed around my middle. "Got any homework, stud?"

"No," he answered, looking up at me and grabbing for the plate.

"I guess I'm going to have to call your teacher and tell her she needs to assign more homework then."

"No!" he wailed. "You can't, Auntie G!"

I ruffled his hair and then smooched Stella's chubby cheek before setting a cookie in front of her.

I walked back to the case and waited for Aubrey to return once she got the kids settled. Watching her carefully, I noticed she was moving a little more slowly than usual. "Everything okay?" I asked her.

"Just tired." She pressed her lips together. "Single momming isn't as easy as it looks."

"Are you still seeing Tony?" I asked, not wanting to bring his name up, but afraid not to. I had a feeling she was still seeing him on the sly, but since he hadn't made any more appearances back at the bakery, I was hoping it was fizzling out.

"Sometimes. He's been quiet and acting weird. I'm not sure what I've done to piss him off lately, but he always runs hot and cold," she said sadly.

Let's put him in the cold position permanently.

"You haven't been happy since he came into the

picture. I know you, honey. You can't fool me." The words tumbled out before I could censor them and sound more accusatory than I wanted them to.

She bit the inside of her cheek, considering my statement, and I recognized her shoulders stiffening. She was feeling attacked.

"Sorry," I apologized quickly, trying to smooth her ruffled feathers, knowing she would tune me out if I took it too far. "It's just that I love you, and I think you deserve someone who lights you up and makes you feel safe. You don't have to take the first one who shows up."

"Wow." She pulled away. The truth stung, and I could tell it hurt by her one-word response.

"Aubs…" I took a step closer to her.

"At least I am putting myself out there," she retaliated, her hands balled up into tiny fists that she rested on her hips in defiance. "You hold a guy like Foster out at arm's length. A man who wants to give you everything, and you are so far up your own ass trying to avoid being hurt that you let it destroy the practically perfect love he is trying to give you."

"You don't understand."

"You're right, I don't. If I had a man like Foster, there is no way I'd hold anything back," she shot at me like a little dictator. "Do you love him?"

"I think so."

"Think so? What hoops is that man going to have to jump through to get you to go all in?"

I blinked and swallowed hard. She was turning the tables, and the spotlight on my deficiencies as a girlfriend burned. Aubrey took another step closer.

"Do you tell him you love him?"

"Sometimes," I mumbled uncomfortably. When I thought about it, I actually said the words far fewer times than he did. Rarely was more accurate. They still stuck like cotton balls lodged deep in my throat.

"How long do you think he's going to put up with that?"

Panic surged up and knotted in my chest, and tears welled up in the corners of my eyes as she voiced my biggest fear. I dug my fingernails deep into my palms to keep them from flowing down my face.

"Keep Foster out of this," I said quietly.

"You know what I think?" She shot back, her eyes flashing in anger. "I think you love it when I'm a mess. It gives you something to focus on, so you don't have to dig too deep into your own failures."

"That's not true," I countered weakly as warmth walked up my neck into my cheeks, slashing crimson across my cheekbones. A biometric lie detector that even I couldn't deny.

"It looks like neither one of us is killing it in our relationships right now." She argued, "I love you, G, but I don't think you're really qualified to give relationship advice." It was another zinger that hit me in the solar plexus, and I knew enough to keep my mouth shut. Continuing down this path would just be useless and painful for us both.

I studied her as she quickly looked away and went back to the table with the kids. Owen threw his arms around her, and I thought she winced again when he squeezed her. It was a flash of agony that splashed across her face and disappeared so fast, I wasn't sure it happened at all.

She was quiet the rest of the day, taking care of customers and sitting with her kids, and I stayed out of her way. I spent the afternoon in the kitchen working on sugar shapes again, making crystallized nests with spun sugar and dusting them with edible silver glitter. I waved goodbye to them as she rushed out the door to get on the train home. Grasping Owen and Stella's hands and half-running, half-skipping down the sidewalk with her mouth set in a hard line.

TWENTY-NINE

December was always one of our busiest months at the bakery, so whenever Foster wasn't at work, he became a fixture at DeLuca's. Showing up when we were slammed or when we had a big order to fill, he was an effective buffer between me and Aubrey since we were at a best friend stalemate. The words we said to each other still hung heavy, but we were both too stubborn to apologize, so we ignored any topic of conversation that touched on our relationships and tucked it away for another time.

Foster had an amazing work ethic, something that Pops immediately approved of, and as a result, he won over my parents in record time. Foster was also incredibly disciplined and tireless. He never did anything halfway, he got up early to help out at DeLuca's for hours before his own shifts at The Ivy with a smile on his face the entire time. He was getting so accurate at scooping out cups of flour, he could almost do it blindfolded and nail it on the scale every time.

Having Foster around was good for everyone, but no one benefitted more than Stella and Owen. Foster was happiest in the kitchen, whipping up pastry cream and letting Owen lick the beaters. One day, Owen came to the bakery sporting a mohawk just like Foster's. Aubrey even let him tint the tips of it blue like Foster was currently wearing. Owen warmed up to Foster in a way I've never seen him warm up to another man. Always jumping to help, begging to go on deliveries, anything for one more minute with him. It was adorable, and I'm not sure which of them loved or needed it more.

"He's so good with Owen," Mom remarked softly with hope blooming in her eyes that I tried to ignore. I shot her a look that immediately discouraged her from continuing on this topic.

Foster was deep into negotiations with my dad. On Thanksgiving, he shared an idea to add hand-tossed pizzas to our menu, and we had everything we needed to pull it off. Pop's was so excited he fast-tracked the idea. He had pretty much gotten up every day for the last fifty years and done the exact same thing, but here was Foster with new ideas and creative flavor combinations he wanted to try, and his excitement rubbed off on everyone. Even Mom got sucked into it. There was an energy Foster brought into a room I felt that very first day, but it wasn't just something *I* experienced. Foster entranced them all—Mom, Pops, and Nonna. They were his biggest fans in record time, and jokingly I commented more than once, "This better work out because I think they might love you more than they love me." Foster never had a real dad, or at least a dad that gave a shit, but my dad *loved* him. Mine called him son, pulled him in for hugs, and listened with great respect to the ideas that filled his mind. He even helped concoct plans to carry them out.

Foster finally had a father figure that loved and approved of him, and my dad finally had the son he always wanted. For a week, they stayed up late drinking bottles of wine and debating flavor combinations until the wee hours of the night. Foster would stumble upstairs to bed after one of those sessions, smelling like a winery and singing to himself, and then fall asleep thirty seconds later and begin snoring softly in my ear.

To market the newly expanded lunch offerings, they decided to hold a blind tasting event at the bakery. Foster worked and worked for days in my little kitchen because he didn't want Pops to discover his secret formula. He stood at the stove for days, simmering his secret sauce, using ingredients that he never disclosed even to me.

"After all this is over, I'll tell you, G, but not a second earlier." He brought a spoon out and swirled it through the sauce, blowing on it to cool it.

"Look who has trust issues now," I teased, brushing away the hint of truth that was hidden in humor and had become my coping mechanism.

He laughed at my huge pout and then pressed it to my lips. "Only when it comes to this." I licked the spoon, and my eyes lit up. It was so rich and complex. The basil and peppery notes hit my tongue first before finishing with a slight sweetness. Sweet heat has always been a weakness of mine.

"Are you sure you're not even two-percent Italian? This sauce tastes like you are. There's got to be a little Italian in you somewhere."

"Someday, I'd like to put a little Italian in here." He

laughed, pointing to my belly, a cute off-handed comment that stunned me speechless. I expertly deflected and ignored it, using sex as my weapon. I kissed him and pushed him up against the wall, playfully nipping at his neck. He made a *mmm* sound and then pushed me away.

"I see what you are doing woman! You are working for the enemy. Trying to distract me with your hot rocking body so my sauce scorches. I am onto you!" He shook his finger in my face as I laughed at him. "You will not distract me with your kisses."

"I won't?" I said as I pressed my body against him again and rubbed my hand down the front of his apron, feeling him harden against my hand. "Are you sure about that? Feels like you might be lying."

He grabbed my hand. "Get off of that unless you plan to let me use it."

"Oh, I plan to." He glanced at me as I bit my bottom lip. He pushed the pan to the back of the stove and clicked the knob off quickly before chasing me to the bedroom, leaving a trail of clothing as he went.

———

Two days later, we had a packed house. Customers spilled down the sidewalk and around the block in a long line, braving the single-digit temperatures to sample our new pizzas.

"All those flyers and social media posts worked!" Mom exclaimed, clapping her hands excitedly. The sound of the cash register ringing was always music to her ears.

"If I could get your attention." Pops whistled into the

crowd, and everyone quieted quickly. "On behalf of my family, I'd like to welcome you all to DeLuca's on a momentous day in our history. We've been serving pastries, coffee, and sweets for decades, but now, with new inspiration from our friend, Foster Valentine," he waved at hand at Foster, "we are venturing out into handcrafted artisanal pizzas. We thought the best way to let you in on this new development was to engage in an old-fashioned throw down!" He stopped as the room broke out in applause. "It is your very important task to taste test two of our most delicious pies and to decide which one is the victor." He smiled wide, sure of himself, and puffed up with pride at the turnout. I loved seeing my dad in his element.

"There are ballots on the tables, so please only vote once. This is not a presidential election."

Laughter bubbled from the crowd, and then a voice piped up, "You're right. It's *more* important than that!" Pops's deep booming laugh rang out.

"There are two choices, a chorizo, pineapple, red onion, manchego pizza, and a mozzarella and pecorino margarita style with fresh basil and heirloom tomatoes grown in Nonna's garden." The audience clapped at the mention of Nonna's name. She was a beloved fixture in the bakery, and many people came just to see her. Every day, after the rush was over, she would make her way out onto the cafe floor and sit at each table, chatting with our patrons and hugging the children. It wasn't just the cannolis they came for.

Aubrey, Mom, Nonna, and I grabbed trays filled with samples of both pies to pass out to the crowd. Cut into tiny squares, they were the perfect bite resting on white napkins. Foster and Pops weren't allowed to pass out samples because neither of them could be trusted to keep the fight fair. Even I didn't know whose pizza was whose. Pops stood proudly next to Foster, earnestly watching the reaction of the crowd. Their smiles were infectious as they stood arm in arm, ribbing each other as our customers devoured their creations. Foster shifted back and forth on the balls of his feet, unable to contain his excitement. He was competitive, as most chefs are. He wanted to win, and was willing to crush my Pops to prove himself.

An hour later, the ballots were counted. I stood in between them. The energy was electric, popping back and forth—they were dying to know. "I want to thank everyone for coming and celebrating this new venture with our family. This has been a hotly contested title, and I am torn. On one hand, I want my Pops to win." I turned to him and smiled as the audience clapped. "I *am* a daddy's girl," I admitted as Pops glowed next to me.

"But on the other hand, I'm rooting for my boyfriend, the incomparable Foster Valentine." I turned toward him. His eyebrows raised, and he took the opportunity to pull me into his arms and dip me into a deep kiss in front of the crowd as the entire bakery erupted in applause and hoots and hollers. Landing back on my feet, a little breathless, I hammed it up, fanning my face with my hand as I composed myself again.

"It was a close contest, but the results are in. There were eighty-four votes for the new margarita pizza." Everyone clapped again, and Pops beamed. It must have been his. "And eighty-seven votes for the chorizo!" Foster leaped into the air, both fists punching with excitement, and then he hugged my Dad tight and hard as Pops clapped him on the back.

I grabbed Foster's hand and launched it in the air with mine. "We have a winner!" Mom snapped a photo that I knew was going to find a permanent home next to the sun-faded one of Dad snapped so long ago, and my heart smiled.

"Pizzas will be available for carry-out and by the slice starting tomorrow. Thank you for supporting our new adventure." The crowd clapped and descended on our pastry case like locusts, leaving nothing but crumbs behind.

Foster was floating on cloud nine, so thrilled and happy with himself. He visibly puffed up his chest with pride from the win, walking straighter after proving himself to Pops. The good-natured gloating would never end, but he was careful not to rub it in too much while Pops licked his wounds. That night, our family gathered to try them both in the kitchen after we closed to decide for ourselves.

"The sauce is magnificent," Pops conceded and offered his hand. "If I was going to lose, at least I lost to a man I respect." He pulled Foster in close and kissed both his cheeks while I melted from the obvious acceptance and the warmth of the wine.

Mom opened another bottle and poured us all fresh glasses. She raised her glass and said, "To our burgeoning pizza empire. Foster, Marco and I adore you."

Nonna cleared her throat.

"And Mama too," Dad added obediently.

Foster lit up and winked at Nonna.

I cleared my throat, and Pops laughed.

"Yes, of course, Gionna too."

"I like to think I am responsible for bringing him into our lives. You guys owe me," I bragged.

"Here, here," Pops said, and the glasses chimed against each other. "Now, son," he switched into a bad mafioso accent, "I want to make you an offer you can't refuse." It so badly butchered an iconic movie like the *Godfather* it elicited an eye roll from me instantly.

"I love you too, Marco, but I'm not gonna whack someone for you," Foster teased and waited.

"We want to offer you a position at DeLuca's." His eyes burned with excitement at the prospect. "It was your idea to expand our offerings, and judging by the crowd's reaction today, it looks like we are going to need to hire extra staff." Mom smiled widely at his suggestion, acting like it was new information, but I knew it was her idea. She called all the shots at the bakery, but she allowed Dad to be the figurehead. He was a traditional man, and she loved him so much she let him be the public face. To everyone else, he was the leader, the businessman, but behind the scenes, we all knew Mom was the puppet master pulling the strings.

"Really?" Foster said. "In that case, I accept. But as long as I can still give the Ivy two days a week."

———

He folded into our life like egg whites into meringue. Airy and light, simply and easily like he had always been there the entire time. It amazed me how everyone jumped to accommodate him. How he could get even Mom to bring him an espresso with a smile. He had her wrapped around his finger. I've never seen that phenomenon in real life, where my mother's defenses were completely down in the presence of someone that wasn't my father.

We all loved having him around. Foster was always cooking up something new, pushing the culinary envelope, daring to try new things. He wanted to create a line of spicy and savory cookies, something that I had long ago tried to get mom and dad on board with. When the words came out of my mouth, they sounded ridiculous and foolish, but when they came out of his, they were Avant-garde and cutting edge. He was the bakery's golden boy, and everything that he suggested was taken seriously. If I didn't love him as much as I did, I would've been offended.

His first full week of work at the bakery, Mom swept him into the dining room and took him from table to table, introducing him to our regulars like he was a mayoral candidate. He warmed right up to the task, enjoying meeting the people that were obsessed with DeLuca's pastries.

I was sitting on a stool cutting out gum paste petals when I felt him behind me. "I have an idea," he breathed into my neck, sending shivers up my spine. He pointed over to Mr. Manzetti still sitting at his regular table. We watched as he got up to go to the bathroom and stopped by Miss Sophia's table, then bent down to pick up Clifford. Miss Sophia's wrinkled face lit up with a huge smile as Clifford licked Mr. Manzetti's.

"See that?" he whispered. "They are both so lonely. They come here every single day. Maybe they just need a nudge."

"What are you planning?" I asked, and he just winked

and washed his hands and then began to spread out a pizza crust onto a pan in the shape of a heart. My eyebrows lifted as I watched him spoon on the red sauce with a ladle and then spread it around evenly, adding basil and toma- toes, a sprinkle of parmesan, and liberal chunks of fresh mozzarella he had recently learned how to make. Then he slid it into the oven.

A few minutes later, he pulled it out, set it on a tray, and walked it over to Miss Sophia's table. Nonna and I watched as he placed it in the center. Then he walked over to Mr. Manzetti and helped him to his feet, gathering his newspaper and coffee cup and settling him down with Miss Sophia.

"Why didn't I think of that?" Nonna said with a smile as we both watched them looking at each other with fresh eyes. Mr. Manzetti served Miss Sophia the first piece and then offered her the parmesan and peppers. The cheese pulled so high it made them both grin like teenagers.

Foster breezed into the back and stood behind me.

"Playing matchmaker?" I asked as we all watched them soaking in the sweetness of what we thought might be a first date. Miss Sophia became more animated as she sat up and cut her pizza into small squares with her knife and fork. She chewed slowly with a huge smile on her face that lit up her eyes. When Mr. M. reached the crust, he broke off a little piece and offered it to Clifford, who defied gravity, sitting back on his haunches with his thick belly extended. He jumped high to retrieve it from Mr. M., and they started laughing. It was like watching one of Nonna's black and white movies; I couldn't take my eyes off them.

An hour later, Mr. M. offered her his coat and his arm

and walked her out of the bakery. Warmth flooded my heart, and I glanced over at Foster, who was smiling as sweetly as I was. My little cupid was so proud of himself that my heart burst, cracking like a dam does in a torrential rain event. Flooding me with love, gushing into every pore and synapse. It was a beautiful thing.

THIRTY

We were alone closing the bakery one night late in the second week of December because Mom, Dad, and Nonna had theater tickets to *Jersey Boys.*

"Taste this." Foster was simmering something on the stove. He pulled a tasting spoon from the drawer, dipped it in the pan, and coated it. Holding his hand underneath, he blew on it to cool it off and then slipped it into my mouth.

"Oh my God." I covered my mouth with my hand. "I think I just came."

Foster laughed as I pulled him in for a kiss. "Well, in that case, my work here is done." He made a little bow.

"What is that?" I asked. My mouth was still dancing with notes from the creamy white sauce.

"Tomorrow's Valentine Special." Since the launch two weeks ago, Foster's pizza line was doing such swift business that Mom decided to capitalize on his name, and so the Valentine Special was born. Thanks to social media, people would start lining up at ten am. By design, he only created ten pies for the daily special. When Mom protested because it physically hurt her to leave money on the table, he stood his ground and said, "Lorraine, scarcity is everything. It will get buzz and word of mouth popping like nothing else will." He was right, like he was about everything. The Valentine Special was picking up steam, and he charged more per slice since it was a limited edition. When the ten pies were gone, they were gone. He had also taken on the task of blogging about it on our website where he shared behind the scenes photos and logged a running tally of the past flavors.

"We can do a contest in about six months and get customers to vote on which three should be in the regular rotation."

He was a genius at social media and won Mom over almost immediately. Facebook and Instagram were things that didn't make sense to her, but she *did* understand their power. She uncharacteristically offloaded the control to him. I literally shared her DNA, and she never trusted me enough to post anything without permission on social media. He just broke down all her defenses, and she caved and gushed his praises.

I helped myself to another taste. "God, this is so good you can eat it with just a spoon."

Foster's arms wrapped around me from behind, and I leaned into him. "I could eat you with a spoon," he whispered into my ear, sending shivers down my spine.

I turned toward him and pressed my lips into the hollow of his neck, the spot I knew made him weak in the knees.

"Gionna?" he breathed into my hair as his fingers seared heat into my skin.

"Yes?" I asked, continuing to rub my fingers up his back.

"Think we could take a little break and go upstairs to discuss the finer points of my culinary genius?"

"Again?" I deadpanned. "You have to be so sick of that topic by now. We've beaten it to death." My hand moved down the front of his chef coat and landed on the growing bulge in his pants. "How about I beat this instead?" I infused sex into my words. I pulled him up the stairs and pushed him against the wall, the need intensifying, my kisses passionate and searching. I pushed him to the bed and climbed on top of him, his hands on my breasts, in my mouth, and in my hair. I wanted to consume him, to draw him closer to me, to prove my worth to him and bind us more tightly together. I used my body to prove my love to him because the words were so hard to say. A tiny seed of fear had taken root and started growing. I couldn't shake the feeling that Foster was borrowed, loaned to me, and that someday, I was going to have to give him back.

THIRTY-ONE

I didn't realize how fragile my relationship was, delicately and falsely held together by preconceived ideas and conclusions drawn until one sentence detonated like a nuclear bomb. "I can't wait to have a little girl who looks just like you," he mentioned offhandedly as he was mincing garlic one night at home while I sat on the sofa cruising through documentaries on Netflix. His statement paralyzed me. It resurfaced like a shark in the deep that I had ignored, but now, the monster was back and there was blood on the water.

A lump rose in my throat, and panic gripped my belly. I had erased that possibility from my future years ago. I'd donated the eggs I'd stored when my financial world crumbled after Brett because I couldn't justify the expense. I mourned the loss. Completely. Motherhood was no longer an option for me. It was a truth that I accepted at face value.

"Kids?" I croaked out. "I'm a little long in the tooth for that, don't you think?"

He stopped chopping. "What do you mean?"

"I mean, my eggs are ancient. I *mean,* the risk of birth defects in babies born to women over thirty-five is astronomical. I *mean,* the chances of us getting pregnant in the first place at my age are minuscule." My words came out harsher and faster than I meant them to, and I instantly regretted it.

He walked over to the table a few feet from me and sat down on a chair. He was so quiet, stunned, and speechless. My heart dropped.

"But you're so good with Owen and Stella," he remarked, dumbfounded by the truth.

"I love them dearly, but they are not mine. At the end of the day, they are Aubrey's responsibility." I reached out to grab his hand, desperate to physically connect as I felt him slipping away, floating away from me on an iceberg, and I shivered as though I could feel the cold. "I don't see myself as a mother, or with kids in my future. It's not something that I have a burning desire to do."

"But what if it's something *I* have a burning desire to do?" he asked softly.

I exhaled a long breath. "I don't… I don't know what that means." The answer terrified me. The tone of his question wasn't an ultimatum, yet it felt like one.

"I need some time to think about this," I told him.

"Of course," he said as he stood up, returned to his cutting board, and finished cooking dinner in silence. It wasn't the kind of passive-aggressive silence that filled the spaces of most relationships; it was the quiet of self-reflection. I quickly turned on a documentary just to fill the dead air. It hung heavy and thick like fog between us, obscuring everything from view. I lost myself in it and zoned out to the neon green tree frogs laying eggs in the pond water that filled the screen. It was the first time I felt truly afraid in our relationship. It was the first time I knew we had arrived at a fork in the road moment. A moment where we could part ways and go forward separately and alone, or we could choose a path and continue together. It was crystal clear that his path was going down a road that I had long ago closed in my heart.

I walked over to him at the counter and hugged him from behind, wrapping my arms around him and nestling into his back. His warm hands wrapped around my arms, and I closed my eyes, breathing him in. Fabric softener twinged with sweat, a scent that was quintessentially Foster that I adored. It crossed my mind that this could be one of the last times I would ever smell it.

"Let me figure this out," I whispered into the warmth of his shoulder blade. "If being a father is something you really need to do, I don't think it's fair for you to deny yourself. I think you would grow to resent me. Maybe not right away, but eventually, you would regret being with me and what you had to give up in order to do it. I just need some time. I honestly don't know what I think."

We ate quietly that night, our minds distracted by indecision and what it would mean for our relationship. The truth was suffocating, sucking all the air out of the room. Having lived several blissful months in the warm cocoon of Foster's love made the idea of living without it now an impossible future to accept. But wasn't sure we wanted the same things anymore. I didn't know if I wanted to be a mother at all, especially this late in life. The closer you get to old age, the harder and more solidified you become. You no longer have the willingness to compromise and the moldable stock of youth—you are harder and unyielding. As you age, the compromises you are willing to make are fewer and further between.

I tossed and turned that night, unable to find comfort knowing that the real possibility of losing Foster was on the table. I had come to love and depend on him and saw an amazing future with this man I adored except for one really big thing. He was born to be a father, and I couldn't take that away from him. I couldn't ask him to give that up for me and I knew this truth immediately. I just didn't know if I had the ability to compromise and give him what he wanted without compromising myself too much. My brain worked on overdrive, sorting out both realities, weighing the pros and cons. It was heavy, time-consuming thinking that I focused on as the minutes turned into sleepless hours that ticked endlessly by.

On my queen-sized bed, he seemed so far away, though he was sleeping just inches from my fingers. I rolled toward him in the middle of the night, wanting to put my arms around him, to navigate the distance between us that seemed suddenly so vast and expansive. He snored softly next to me, and I wiggled into his back, burying my face in his shoulders and burrowing into his warm knee pits, needing to feel his skin on mine. As the morning sun started to streak the walls in its pre-dawn color palette, I fell into a fitful sleep.

———

I nuzzled him in the morning, knowing that morning make-up sex usually got me out of the doghouse, but he grabbed my hand and pushed it away. "Not now," he said calmly and then sat up on the bed, firm in his resolve to continue the conversation we started yesterday.

"I want kids, Gionna. And I want them with you." His voice was steady and absolute.

"I know," I said quietly, looking down, unable to meet his eyes.

"Would that be the worst thing in the world?"

"Maybe… I don't know… I don't think we are on the same page," I started to explain.

"Then get on my page," he begged. "Please, G." I gathered the strength to pull my eyes toward his, and the intensity I found there startled me.

"I don't think I can," I said, my voice breaking.

"Why the hell not?" he asked, the first vestiges of anger appearing front and center.

"It's too late for me." I slid across the bed and tried to rub his forearm.

"Women in their forties have babies all the time," he argued.

"Not women like me."

"Don't blame your age, or your circumstances, or the shitty relationships you've had up to this point. Why can't you just admit that you are afraid?"

I sat up in the bed, my heart hammering in my chest.

"You can't even tell me you love me," he accused. "Do you know what it feels like to be head over heels in love with a woman who can't verbalize her feelings? It makes me doubt everything. It makes me feel worthless as a man."

"But I *do* love you."

"Do you realize you only say it after your third glass of wine?"

Stunned, I swallowed hard. I couldn't dispute it because he was right. I struggled to say the words. To open my heart enough to let them flow. Until that moment, I thought I had hidden it well and distracted him enough with sex. The hurt on his face, which deepened in his warm brown eyes that were locked on mine made me see that was a lie.

"I know you're not the kind of woman who is going to say I love you every day. I understand who you are, but sometimes, I need to hear it. I am starved for it. I shouldn't have to wonder."

The floor was dropping out from under me, and the sinking sensation made my stomach flip. My insecurities rushed forward, filling me with fear. I was failing him, and the truth was soul-crushing, constricting the air in my throat and rendering me speechless.

"I love you, G. In order for our relationship to work, we need to move forward together. We need to grow *together*. For me, that includes marriage and family."

"Why do we have to label it?"

He was exasperated and raked his fingers across the morning scruff on his jawline, sighing in frustration. "Why *can't* we label it?" He ran his hand through his hair. "You want to play house and play games and stay in this place where you never have to grow up. You're selfish, Gionna DeLuca. You've had everything in your life handed to you on a silver platter. Your career, this apartment… You've never had to fight or work hard for anything a day in your life."

His revelation stung. I felt it like a slap, and my cheeks burned in shame. "I think you might want more than I can give you." I whispered.

"That's the first truthful thing you've said all morning." He stood up and pulled his wrinkled clothes from the floor and stepped into his jeans. "I can't do this anymore, waiting for you to come around, waiting for you to decide to let yourself love me." He was shaking, and his voice was wavering. "You said you wanted a love like your grandparents had, and here I am, showing up to give it to you, but instead of jumping into my arms, you hold back, waiting for the other shoe to drop."

"Love is like a bungee jump," he said. "You either grab my hand and we leap into the unknown craziness together, figuring it out on the way down, or you sit paralyzed in fear on the edge, watching me jump without you."

He pulled his shoes out and started to lace them up. "I know what I want. I have never wavered from that. I convinced myself that you'd come around, that you just needed a little more time. But now, I can see so clearly that you were never going to be able to give me what I need."

Tears rolled down my face.

Say it. Tell him you love him. Tell him you're sorry.

I sat there frozen, the words I wanted to say dead on my lips.

"Wow." His voice was tight. "You have *nothing* to say?" He paused, waiting for me to respond, to reach out and bridge the widening gap between us. After a full five minutes, he silently gathered up his things. Walking around my apartment, he hunted for his chef knives and his jacket. I wrapped the blanket around me and trailed behind him, following him like a shadow from room to room. The unsaid words taunted me, screaming in my head, but I was unable to vocalize them. The fear clamped down on my mouth hot and heavy, holding me prisoner again. The warning bell bleated, clamoring in my ears so the only thing I felt was panic and fear.

"I deserve more than the scraps of love you want to give me. I want it all or nothing at all." He strode to the door, then hesitated with his back to me and his hand on the door. The silence was thick and suffocating. After a long pause, he turned around. "I don't think we should see each other anymore."

"Wait," I croaked out.

He paused. The silence was dense between us, and my mind was racing. I couldn't put two thoughts together. The words simply would not come.

"Argh. I give up." He sighed. "Take care of yourself, Gionna," he said sadly and then opened the door and walked through it. In a trance, I walked to the picture windows and watched him walk away, his shoulders hunched together from the cold air of the morning and holding the box in his arms. Each step created a larger gap between us, pulling his heart that had been fused with mine for months apart. The total agony as it ripped away made me tremble.

I traced one shaking finger down the window on his body as he became smaller and smaller and finally disappeared, and when he was gone, I finally broke down and sobbed the tears that hovered on the surface. There was crushing weight on my chest. I cried until I hiccupped and then laid down on the sofa in a pile.

He was gone. Foster Valentine was gone, and I had no one to blame but myself.

THIRTY-TWO

I called in sick to work and never left my bed. In a daze, I watched the headlights from the cars driving below shoot across the walls for hours, begging sleep to release me from the heaviness in my chest. My mind spun out as I sat alone in my apartment. I checked the phone over and over. Looking for a missed message, desperate to hear his text notification tone ring. Nothing. The screen remained blank and mocked me. I typed out a text to him, then promptly deleted it. Then two more and deleted them, too. At noon, Pops delivered soup and a sandwich, and I couldn't face him, so I made an excuse about not wanting to get him sick, and he left the food on the welcome mat. When the coast was clear, I opened the door to grab the delivery and sipped on the soup without tasting it.

I finally fell asleep in fits and starts, only able to patch together cat naps of twenty-minute stretches. I'd wake up, and then the truth would flood in and the sadness would well up again, deep in my chest.

What is wrong with me?

Why can't I let go and love Foster wholeheartedly?

When did I become so close minded and unwilling to compromise?

The questions cycled repeatedly in my brain, and they were punishing, pounding me with despair again and again. I ruminated in self-loathing that flooded over me in waves. After three glasses of wine, I whispered in the darkness, "I *do* love you. I do," as fat, warm tears rolled down my face. I numbed out to the TV, and eventually, my body gave in and I fell asleep.

Waking with a slight headache in the darkness of the next morning, I stumbled down to the bakery and turned the lights on. The wintry dawn left teardrops of melted snow scattered on the front window panes. The street lights made them sparkle and glisten in an achingly beautiful way.

The back door opened, and in a rush of cold air, Nonna shuffled in, and my heart leapt to see her. I didn't want to be alone anymore. She came inside and hugged me tightly, making fresh tears well up again in my eyes. She pulled back and studied my face. "What is wrong, *Mia Bella*?"

My voice cracked, and I clung to her. She wrapped her arms around me again, comforting me with soft shushing noises and rubbing circles on my back. "He's gone. Foster and I broke up." I choked out the explanation. It was painful to admit.

"Oh my." She led me out into the dining room where she pulled two chairs down for us and patted one for me. "Tell Nonna," she said softly, and I did. The story spilled out, and the truth of what I had done gutted me.

"Only you can know your heart, little one. If you are

sure this is what you want and need, then you made the right decision." She patted my hand to comfort me.

"I don't know *what* I want. He's right. I *am* selfish." I wailed. My nose was congested and I developed a sniffling whistle. My head was throbbing, so full and tight with tension that pinched my forehead.

"It is true you have been given opportunities, but they have not come without work," she said softly. "It is easy to make accusations in anger," she continued. "He was hurt."

"I want to run to him and beg him to come back."

"Then do that," she nudged gently.

"That's a selfish act, too," I said.

"What do *you* want?" she asked gently. "Is this life you've built enough for you? Are you fulfilled by working in the bakery and making your cakes? It's okay if you are. That is a full life, but it can be lonely."

"Is that how you feel without Bumpo?"

"Sometimes." She smiled a sad smile, and continued. "But I am surrounded by people who love me." She reached out to squeeze my arm.

"*Mia Bella*, the most important parts of your life will be the moments you spend with the ones you love."

Her declaration welled up fresh tears at my lash line. "But this fear is suffocating. The idea of children and a husband makes me hyperventilate, and is a completely different life than the one I am currently living." A breath shuddered out of me, "To be responsible for the happiness of another human being terrifies me."

"It shouldn't, Gionna," she said quietly. "You are not responsible for the happiness of others. You simply have to show up and do your best. Love the people in your life the best way you can. People are responsible for their own happiness. It is not your job to provide it for them."

"What do you mean?"

"Foster doesn't expect you to make him happy. He is happy on his own. Sure, you can contribute to his happiness by bringing joy into your relationship with him, but at the end of the day, a person's happiness is their own responsibility. If you think you can control it, you are mistaken."

You know the truth when you hear it. It rings true. She squeezed my hand again and continued. "Fear is a liar and is so paralyzing. Before Brett, you were fearless. To see that *Jabroni* harden your heart was one of the most painful things I have ever had to witness."

I smiled faintly at her sweet Italian insult. Nonna was as tough as nails; you couldn't let the little old lady act fool you.

"It took me a long time to pick up the pieces and put myself back together," I admitted, looking down at the table in leftover shame.

"I know, *Mia Bella*, it was heartbreaking to watch." She looked at me and tipped my chin up to meet her eyes again. "That takes courage, but so does love. Putting your heart out there again, giving someone all the tools they need to destroy you. Knowing from experience how much that can devastate you and still deciding to do it anyway? Well, that's the most courageous act of all."

I nodded. I couldn't disagree.

"Can you tell Mom and Dad?" I asked her. "I just can't," I said, my voice hoarse. I couldn't walk through the pain again and see the disappointment register on their faces. Foster had become so ingrained in our lives it was like he had broken up with all of us.

"Of course," she said and hugged me one more time.

We heard the key rattle in the lock, and then Mom and Pops's voices, so I got up quickly. I wiped the tears from my eyes and spent a quiet early morning rolling out dough and making heart-shaped sugar cookies, deep in thought. Nonna delivered the news, and Pops started in on prepping the pizza dough without a word.

At six am, Aubrey came in with the kids for her shift. She wrapped the white apron around her waist and got the kids settled in the back at their table. I poured a glass of milk for each of them and brought out a small plate with doughnuts and a small clump of green grapes. I set the plate on the table next to the kids and sat down quietly with them. They were munching on the doughnuts as the bakery began to come to life. The first bleary-eyed coffee addicts were starting to shuffle in as I got up to help our customers. I was grateful for the steady stream of patrons. The time flew and took my mind off the events of the previous days. Hours passed as I handpicked and filled cannolis, macaroons, and cookies from the case and put them in kraft boxes. I was grateful to have simple tasks to occupy my busy brain, when a white-haired, older woman was next in line with a sweet teenage boy. He'd bowled me over with his polite remarks and incredible vocabulary.

"Your grandson has impeccable manners," I remarked. "Teenagers can usually be a handful, but he's a delight! So smart."

She laughed. "Actually, he's my son, but thank you just the same. As a mother, you never get tired of hearing strangers sing your child's praises."

My cheeks pinked up. "I'm so sorry."

"Don't be," she said putting me at ease right away. "He's my miracle. I never thought I'd get the chance to be a mother, but I can't imagine my life without him." I watched them walk away and marveled at how he held open the door for her.

My eyes kept flitting over to the kids, who were behaving like angels.

What was I so afraid of anyway? Look at them.

Instead of a mom, you'd be more like a grandma. A geriatric parent, going to football games and shopping for prom dresses. Stop torturing yourself! That ship has sailed, and you refused to get on the boat.

There was an internal tug of war that played out over and over again in my mind. On one side was Foster, yanking me toward the finish line to love, family, and commitment, and on the other side, I sunk my feet into the ground and struggled against him. Fighting to keep things the same, battling to remain in the life I had always known because it was safe. The idea of being dragged kicking and screaming into the unknown scared the hell out of me, cueing up my fight or flight instinct to unseen levels.

At lunchtime, I finally slowed down and sipped on the meatball soup Nonna made.

"You've been so quiet today. Is everything okay?" Aubrey asked. The bakery had been so busy it was the first time we got to chat.

I crumpled. The break in the action gave me pause enough to crack. A tear fell fast and furious down my cheek, and I swiped it away quickly so no one would see.

"G? You're scaring me."

"You'll be happy to hear you were right about Foster, after all," I said ruefully, and she leaned in closer.

"He broke up with me." I barely got the sentence out before I fell apart.

Owen's ears perked up. "No! Oh, Auntie G., say you're sorry," his little voice begged, shattering what was left of my heart into even finer shards. "Just tell him you're sorry. Please. I love him." Owen began to howl so loud Aubrey had to carry him out of the bakery and into the back. Nonna took over and helped comfort the sobbing child.

The guilt was a sea that I was drowning in. It smacked at me and sucked all the air out of the room. Owen loved him, and I had sent the only good man who had shown up in his entire short life away—forever.

"I did not expect that reaction," Aubrey said when she returned, still shocked by Owen's outburst.

"It's the Foster Valentine Effect." I labeled it. "I know exactly how he feels."

"Then fix it."

"It's not that simple."

"Yes, it is," she insisted. "A guy like Foster is rare. You don't let a love like that walk out of your life."

"It's not that simple," I told her sadly. "We want different things."

"Then change what you want."

"I'm not built like that." I looked at her with my eyes teary.

"What was it?"

"Kids. He wants kids, and I am not able to give them to him."

"Unable or unwilling?" she asked, pushing me already.

"Unwilling, I guess is the most truthful," I stammered. "I don't think I'm mother material."

"I'll fill you in on a little secret. No one thinks they are mother material. You have a kid and you figure it out." She looked at me. "You could if you wanted to. I'm here, and your family would be over the moon in love with your baby. The only one standing in the way of what you want is you."

She was right, but I was too stubborn to admit it. Aubrey wasn't going to let me get off that easily. She started in again. "I'm going to tell you the truth. You are making a huge mistake, and someday, you will wake up and see that, but it will probably be too late. Men like Foster Valentine who want to settle down and commit don't stay single for long."

The rest of the day passed slowly, and with every jingle of the bell, my pulse raced. I yearned to see him walking through those doors, to see him saddle up to the counter and sass me sweetly, but he never came in. I continued to check in vain, riding the hope and loss roller-coaster while pieces of my heart disintegrated jingle by jingle.

THIRTY-THREE

A day later, Pops met me at a new fondue restaurant that just opened up. I stood when he came to the table and hugged him, holding on for an extra second and blinking my eyes hard to keep tears that hovered at my lashes at bay.

Our fresh-faced waitress came by with menus, and Pops turned his attention to it, looking down for a minute, and I was thankful it gave me time to get myself together. I felt fragile, delicately held together as deeper cracks began to spread through my heart. Destroying any illusion I had that I was the strong, capable woman I prided myself to be.

"A bottle of Erath Pinot Noir," he said to her confidently with a smile. "And can we start with the Chef's Fondue Platter and Skirt steak tips?"

"Absolutely." Then she left us blissfully alone.

His eyes met mine, a weak smile sitting on his lips. "You look tired, *Bellissima*."

"I am," I said. It was true. Sleep was elusive; I struggled to string more than three hours together in the days since the breakup. The waitress appeared at Pops's shoulder with two glasses and the wine, giving me a moment to collect myself. She opened it and poured a sample for him. I watched him circle it around the glass and then sip and nod his approval.

"Very good."

She poured our glasses and then left. I heaved mine up and nearly drained it in one gulp as Pops' eyes widened in shock, but he said nothing and even poured a little more into my glass.

"Sorry." I licked my top lip, the cherry notes making my tongue tingle. He offered his hands to me on the table face up, and I placed mine in his, as was our ritual. I closed my eyes to savor the warmth I found there.

"I can see that I don't need to ask my question. It is obvious you are unhappy," he stated as I looked down at our hands, unable to look him in the eyes. "Do you want to talk about it?"

I took a deep breath and started in. "I feel guilty."

"What? Why?"

"Foster... the pizza dynasty... I know you loved him."

"Look at me," he asked gently and then waited for me to swing my sad eyes toward his concerned ones. "It's true, I liked Foster a lot, but I *love* you. You are my priority, not the bakery or the pizza dynasty—you."

Tears welled up in my eyes, and one broke the surface tension and slipped down my cheek. I brushed it away quickly and then returned my hands to the safety of his. He squeezed gently. "I want you to be happy, but only you can decide what that means. Marriage is hard enough when love is the foundation, but it's definitely doomed to fail when it's obligatory or built to please other people."

"I *was* happy with him."

"Then what was so big that it drove you apart?"

"Kids. He wants to have kids, and I don't know if I do."

"Ahh." He picked up his glass and took a long sip, thinking for a minute before asking, "What are you afraid of?"

"So many things." I paused and then gave voice to my fears recounting them to him in a quick laundry list. "I'm old. I don't know what I'm doing. I'll look ridiculous pushing a stroller around, and there's the unlikelihood of a healthy pregnancy at my age. All of it, it's terrifying."

"Parenting *is* terrifying."

"You're not helping," I said with a pained smile. I sipped at the wine again but slowly this time.

The waitress appeared with the fondue and the steak on skewers. A pot of water was set down in front of us, and she added sliced mushrooms and scallions to it. Then she poured tiny bowls of flavoring in to make a broth, and it sizzled then simmered away.

"Thank you," I said as she nodded and left.

Pops picked up a skewer and dipped it into the pot of water, and in a few minutes, it was cooked through. He let it rest on the edge of the pot to cool and looked back at me.

"I thought I knew what love was, but the second they put you in my arms, my heart had the biggest growing pains. It stretched and opened in such a profound way I doubted I even knew what love was before I met you." His sincerity choked me up as he continued, "I was given another chance to experience everything in life through your eyes. What a beautiful gift that has turned out to be, and I would not trade it for the world."

He popped the meat into his mouth and chewed thoughtfully for a minute as I thought about what he was saying. I stabbed a piece of fried potato and swirled it through the cheese, then did the same with a dill gherkin. The bright, tangy combination woke up my taste buds.

"Oh my God," I said in spite of myself, covering my mouth with my hand. "It's so good. The gruyere melting into the buttery notes of the gouda and then the vermouth, you gotta try this." I was temporarily distracted and blissed out in my cheese coma.

He smiled. "See? This is exactly what I am talking about. Sharing time like this together, if I didn't have you in my life to experience moments like this, it wouldn't be as sweet."

He stabbed a gherkin and dragged it through the cheese sauce and then to his mouth. In seconds, a huge smile broke out across his face. He pressed his fingers together and kissed them. "You are correct." He pulled out his phone to take a photo for his review as I stabbed a round pretzel bite and then coated it in the sauce. I popped it into my mouth, and my eyes widened in delight.

"Okay, that is my new favorite," I said gleefully, covering my full mouth.

He laughed and followed suit. We continued to talk about anything but Foster Valentine as the bits of bread, circles of sausage, and bunches of cauliflower on our plates disappeared. The wine dislodged the lump in my throat, and for the first time since the break-up, I felt at ease. After we destroyed the dinner, the waitress brought a pot of molten dark chocolate to the table, along with chunks of strawberries, angel food cake, and rice crispy treats. Dad poured the last of the wine into our glasses and then held his glass up to me. I chimed mine against his and took a sip before diving into the chocolate with a ripe red berry.

While I chewed, his eyes met mine one more time. "We love you, Gionna. No matter who or what is in your life, we will always love and honor your choices. Let go of the guilt, sweetheart. It's too heavy." He paused then added, "Your heart is bigger than you give it credit for. Don't sell yourself short or get in the way of your own happiness out of fear."

THIRTY-FOUR

The longest week of my life ensued as the final countdown to Christmas began. I was shocked that texting Foster the everyday minutiae of my life had become such an ingrained habit it was almost physically painful to stop. It was like I'd lost an appendage. There was a hole in my heart that deepened and eroded, creating a sinkhole of suck, and thrust me into a depression that was worse than when the truth about Brett was exposed. The aftermath of my life after the break-up with Brett was fueled by rage. Hate sustained me and gave me the energy to forge ahead. This was far worse. Now, I was suffering from a self-inflicted bullet wound. I had decided to sabotage something that could have been amazing. I chopped it off and stunted it before it even got the chance to grow into the beauty it could have been. I was to blame. My current state of agony was one I came to honestly, and I had to look at myself in the mirror every night before bed while I brushed my teeth and acknowledge that I had done this to myself. I couldn't blame Foster. I couldn't blame fate or timing. It was my decision, and I had to learn to live with it. I tried to take comfort with the small concession of "Hey, at least you didn't put it all out there." But the more I explored that thought, the angrier I got. I protected myself, but at a tremendous cost.

Seven groundhog days came and went as I survived the same day over and over. My world was gray. I craved his presence and the sunshine and safety that I always felt when I was in his arms. I continued to look at the door every time the bell rang, begging God to let him walk through it, but he never did. Each day, it felt a little more final. Each day, the reality that he was gone settled deeper into my bones, and the fact that he would move on without me became more concrete in my mind.

We all felt the loss. The bakery was more somber, and Mom and Pops kept quiet. Even with all the forced glee of Christmas, the season felt hollow and cavernous, an echo chamber that I shouted into and heard nothing in return.

Foster had taken the time to email my parents his pizza recipes—something that he did not have to do, but he was invested in our success with a project he spearheaded, with or without him. His obvious integrity made the painful reality I had chosen even harder to accept.

"Are you sure?" Pops asked when he had me to himself. "Absolutely sure you can be happy without him?"

"I am not," I admitted as more ever-present tears rushed to my lashes. "I'm not sure I'll ever be happy again." My voice cracked, and he pulled me into a hug. I breathed in his cedar-scented aftershave as he held me until I stopped shaking. He never doubted my decision or tried to convince me to change my mind, even though the idea of becoming a grandfather was a dream I knew he held deep in his heart. He trusted me to know what I wanted in my life, even if it didn't match up with what he wanted for his.

On a Monday morning, I finally said to myself, "You've wallowed for a week. It's time to suck it up now." I was desperate for Aubrey to come in. Time passed more quickly when she was around. I wanted to walk her through my latest self-analysis to have her talk me off the ledge of reaching out and texting him.

An hour later, Aubrey hadn't called in and she hadn't come to work. I texted her repeatedly, but after receiving no response, I was getting anxious. It wasn't like her at all. In the five years she had worked at DeLuca's, this had never happened.

"Pops, Can I take the delivery van and see if Aubrey is okay? It's not like her to go radio silent."

Mom immediately grabbed the keys from the ledge and threw them at me, and I caught them sailing across the kitchen in one hand. "Yes. That's a good idea. I'm worried about her, too. Go check it out and report back."

Having Mom confirm my feelings made the fear surge in my belly. I tossed my phone in my bag and started up the DeLuca's delivery van. When I wasn't in a hurry, I didn't mind taking the train; people watching on it was one of my guilty pleasures, but today I knew I needed to get there as fast as possible. The anxiety gave me a lead foot and my road-rage was in full effect as I whipped through traffic changing lanes. Finally arriving at her apartment, I ran up the stairs two at a time and waited breathlessly in front of the door, hearing the TV through it. Someone was inside. I knocked on the door, pounding on it with my clenched fist until it turned pink.

"Aubrey! It's G. Let me in."

Through the door, I heard footsteps cross the floor and then saw a shadowy figure underneath.

"I know you're in there, and I am not going away," I barked.

I heard the door unlock, and when it opened, I saw Owen's pale face. I knelt down on the ground and opened my arms, and he ran into them and hugged me tightly. "Where is your mama?" I asked him.

"She's not feeling good. She told me to take care of Stella," he said and then pulled me into the apartment. It was cluttered yet clean, like spaces typically are that have small children living in them. The sheer quantity of stuff that came with the care and feeding of little people always astounded me.

Stella was sitting in front of the TV eating a bowl of cereal.

"Nice job, Owen," I said. "Proud of you, little man." He brightened with the praise, and I knelt down to his level again. "Stay here. I need to see your mama for a minute."

He walked back to Stella, and I watched him pour a little more cereal into her bowl. At Aubrey's bedroom door, I knocked softly and then turned the knob and entered. "Aubs?" I whispered her name; it was dark in the room with the shades pulled shut, but I could make out a lumpy shape on the bed. I sat on the edge of the bed and heard her sniffling. "Hey, you," I whispered and reached out to touch her, and she flinched. "You're scaring me."

She faced the wall, but her body was trembling. I reached over and opened the blinds, and the light flooded in. Her face was tear-stained and pale. She was forlorn, like a puppy that had been beaten. It was heartbreaking.

"You have two seconds to start speaking or I am calling Mom and telling her to come over here. She is worried sick about you. We all are."

Aubrey sat up with a painful moan and shifted in the bed. My eyes caught a glimpse of a black bruise across her back, and I gasped in surprise. I pulled her shirt up slightly, my eyes slowly walking up the sides of her stomach where a network of dark bruises had formed. "What in the hell?" I whispered. She quickly straightened her shirt, wiped her face with her hands, and then crumbled into pieces in front of me. I had never seen her fall apart like this. I squeezed her arm, and she whimpered. "Tell me," I whispered to her.

"I can't."

"Honey, you have to."

"I am so ashamed."

"There is nothing to be ashamed about. Did Tony do this?"

She started to cry again, but this time it was a wail that she muffled with the pillow so her children wouldn't hear. I stroked her hair, trying to calm her down, but it was proving impossible.

"Things were so good, G. I promise. So good and then there was this shift in him. He went through my phone while I was in the bathroom and found a Facebook message from some rando I went to high school with, and he went ape shit."

"He shouldn't have been going through your phone, to begin with. No healthy man is ever compelled to do that."

"I think it's pretty obvious I'm not that great at judging the health of a man, G," she said sarcastically, with an edge of self-deprecating snark that was one of the qualities

I have always loved about Aubs. "He pushed me up against the wall and demanded I give him the guy's contact information, and when I refused, he froze me out. I decided to let him have his hissy fit and ignored him, which just added fuel to the fire. He was inside my apartment waiting for me when I got home last night."

"You gave him a *key*?" I asked, shocked that she had given him access to her apartment with her kids here.

"No," she said quietly as her voice began to calm down.

"That's breaking and entering," I declared. "We need to call the police. We need to press charges."

She started to cry again.

"Asshole," I whispered under my breath. "He can't get away with this."

"I'm stuck." She looked at the door. "He said he's going to make my children pay if I get out of line one more time."

"Jesus." I wiped a hand quickly over my face.

"Owen..." She whimpered his name. "He's already been through so much."

"Piece of shit." I had to think. "Did you get medical attention?"

"No."

"Okay, that is the first order of business." I stood up and continued. "We will drop the kids at the bakery and then go get you checked out."

"He'll know," she cried. "He always knows."

"You don't have to press charges right now if you don't want to. But I think we need to document what has happened in case you change your mind later. You need to preserve the evidence."

"I can't."

"You have to. Get dressed," I said a little too brusquely and walked out into the living room with the kids.

"Hey, guys, let's get your backpacks packed. You're going to stay with my mom and dad for a while, while your mom and I work on something."

Owen's huge eyes met mine. "It's okay, buddy. We will hang out every day at the bakery," I said, hoping it would put his heart at ease, and it worked. Pulling out a hamper, I tossed in all the clothing I could find for the kids. Mom would sort it out later, taking the time to carefully launder it all. "Make sure you bring your blankies and any toys or stuffies you want to have with you because we won't be coming back here for a while," I instructed the kids.

I walked back into her bedroom to see Aubrey moving slowly to get dressed, her arm protectively crossed around her torso. My guess was cracked ribs, and it incensed me. Breaking someone's ribs took a level of detachment and violence that turned decent people's stomachs. Small grunts and painful whimpers left her lips.

"Sit. I got this." I pulled the pair of socks from her hand and tugged them onto her cold feet and then carefully twisted her shoes on until I successfully got them in place.

"The kids are ready. I'm taking them to my parents' house. They have a lot more room than I do, and Pops is good at distracting them. You are going to stay with me while we figure out what to do."

Aubrey nodded weakly. The fight was gone from her eyes. She was a shell of what she had been.

———

A few hours later, after dropping off the kids to a surprised Mom and Pops, we were waiting to be seen at urgent care. Aubrey was changed into a paper robe, hyper-focused on her phone that kept vibrating in her hand.

"See? He won't ever leave me alone." She held it out to show me. A string of messages filled the lock screen.

"This isn't helping. Why don't you let me hang onto it for a bit?" She finally relented, and I tucked it away in my purse.

A doctor breezed in, and I cringed. Male, mid-forties, kind eyes behind glasses. He looked at the sheath of papers in his hand.

"Can you tell me what brings you in here today?" he asked, his eyes glancing up finally.

Aubrey tightened the robe around her body, and the paper under her legs crinkled as she shifted in embarrassment.

"I was... I am... My ribs..." she stammered, unable to complete any sentence. Her eyes filled again as she swung them to me. Her bottom lip trembled.

"She was the victim of an assault," I spoke for her. "Can you check her out and see if she needs treatment for her injuries?"

"I'm sorry to hear this." The doctor asked, "Did you want to be seen by a female doctor?"

"No," she said dully. "I just want this to be over."

"I understand."

"My ribs hurt. It's hard to breathe."

"I'm going to have you open your robe," he said to her, gently encouraging me to stand next to her on the other side of the examination table. She opened it, shaking, and in the fluorescent sterile lighting, the bruises were even worse than they looked in her bedroom just hours earlier. His eyes blinked slowly. "I need to press on your body in a few places. Is that okay?" he asked gently. "Lay back on the table." I helped her lay back onto the flat pillow as he pulled out the footrest for her feet. I gently squeezed her hand. Her eyes rolled over to me, terrified hazel discs framed in long lashes that were identical to Stella's. I forced a smile on my face to reassure her, but it was tight and stiff.

The doctor uncovered her body one section at a time and ran Aubrey through a bunch of movement exercises, noting when she winced. He wrote down notes and then covered her up and moved to the next section, documenting the location and size of her bruises. "Are you going to press charges?" he asked gently.

"I don't know."

"You need to. It is the only way monsters like this guy will learn," he answered. "If you don't, another woman will show up in another doctor's office like this someday after tangling with him. Guys like this never stop."

Her panicked eyes met mine.

"What if we just called the police and at least had a record of it, in case it's needed down the road? Then you can think about it and decide if you want to press charges," I asked, trying to bridge the gap that was the source of Aubrey's terror.

"That's a great idea," the doctor agreed.

"Okay," Aubrey said weakly. I pulled the phone out of my bag and called the non-emergency number. Then I fished out Aubrey's and saw fourteen missed calls and a string of angry texts on her home screen.

"We are going to take some x-rays and see what we're

dealing with." He pressed lightly on her tummy. "Any pain there?"

"No."

"That's good." He covered her back up and added a thin blanket. "I'm writing you a prescription for pain meds. My guess is fractured ribs, but we will have to see the film to be sure."

"Thank you," I said, and the doctor nodded and then slipped out of the exam room. "We need to go to the station after this and file an official report."

"I don't know." Aubrey said, "I just want to go home."

"We will right afterward, and I'll make you anything you want for dinner."

She wanted to say something but stopped herself.

———

An hour later, with the exam records in hand, we sat at the station. They allowed me in the room, and Aubrey was photographed by a female officer. Each flash from the camera made her flinch. Seeing her tremble and shake, my stomach was in my throat, rage coloring everything red.

I kept my eyes glued on Aubrey. She was so thin. So frail. It's hard to sit by and watch your best friend be destroyed by a man. I wish I had spoken up earlier. I wish I had gotten her to run away from this guy when the red flags first went up for me. I should have tried harder. Guilt flooded me since I felt partially responsible.

After the photographs were taken and the exam records were copied, we were sitting down with the female officer, giving a detailed account of what happened. After a quick search, the officer discovered a rap sheet on Tony that was a mile long.

"He's on parole," she admitted painfully. "There are multiple charges against him currently, assault and battery, aggravated assault, breaking and entering. Impersonating a police officer."

"Oh my God," Aubrey wailed. "I brought a monster into my life—into my kids' lives. I feel sick." She clutched her stomach, and I slung my arm over her shoulder to comfort her.

"Can she get a restraining order on this guy?" I asked and pulled out her phone. "Look at this!" I scrolled through several screens of infuriated messages screaming horrible names.

The officer shook her head, as frustrated as I was. "She can do the paperwork, and the judge will likely issue one, based on his history. But we all know that restraining orders are just a piece of paper. And when someone is a predator like this man appears to be, a piece of paper isn't going to protect you. It will give you the ability to legally pursue him, but in terms of physical protection, it's flimsy."

Aubrey cleared her throat and said softly, "Then what is the point of all of this?"

"That's not to say that reporting an assault is not worthwhile. It becomes part of his criminal history and creates a bigger legal picture of his behaviors. So, when he does commit a more violent crime, the judge is able to give him harsher and stiffer penalties than he would've gotten otherwise. Look," she said, "I know you're terrified. I know that you want to just crawl in your bed and hide and forget any of this ever happened. But if you do that, he will do this again. And can you live with yourself knowing that you could have helped stop him from hurting another woman?"

Aubrey brushed the tears from her face. "No. I don't want anyone else to feel this. But the smallest selfish part of me wants to pretend like it never happened. And if I sign my name at the bottom of this report, I can't deny that it did."

"Pressing charges doesn't change the fact that it happened, Aubrey," I said, trying to encourage her.

I pulled her in closer to me again, putting my arm around her, feeling terrible when she cried out in pain. She was cold and shaking. The officer offered her a pen, and she thought about it for a solid minute before scrawling her signature on the bottom of the report.

"I am so sorry this happened to you," the officer said gently. "But you have done the right thing."

"How come it doesn't feel like it?" she answered sadly, then looked at me. "Can we go now?" Her hand trembled as she set the pen on the table.

"Absolutely." The officer gave us a card and a copy of the report and said that we would need to wait for the court to contact us.

We walked back to the car. It was getting dark outside as Aubrey pulled her jacket tighter around her body, wrapping her arms around herself.

"I'm so proud of you," I told her. "I know it took a lot of guts to do that. No one expects you to save the world. But if this report helps one less person get victimized, then it was worth it, don't you think?"

"That's the only reason I did it," she admitted, defeated, and leaned against the van that looked like it was the only thing holding her up. "I just seem to go from one shitty man to the next. I don't know why I do this to myself. I feel so stupid, G. You were right about him. I feel like such a fool."

"You're not a fool to want to be loved. Everyone wants that," I said softly as tears began to fall down her cheeks. She wiped them away impatiently, exhaled loudly, and I pulled her in for a hug. I opened the door and tucked her into the passenger seat, fastening her seatbelt and tucking the harness carefully behind her, then settled myself behind the steering wheel.

"It is what every woman really wants, truly, deep down inside. The ones that tell you they don't are lying," she agreed sadly.

"I am jealous of your ability to be wide open and love with your whole heart. I've always been so closed off and wary, but you need to learn not everyone deserves unrestricted access to your heart. Make them earn it."

She nodded. "I know. I give people too many chances, and I fall in love way too fast."

"I know that you want to think the best of people, and I love you for that, but you have to protect yourself. It's not just you that's affected by the men you bring into your life. It affects Stella and Owen, too."

Hearing her children's names, she crumpled up into a ball and began to sob. I leaned over to put my arm around her. "You have a big heart, Aubs. There's nothing wrong with that."

"Why doesn't anyone love me, G?"

"Oh, honey, that's simply not true. So many people love you, Aubrey. All your regulars at the bakery missed you today. Mr. Manzetti and Miss Sophia were asking about you. You may think you just serve coffee and it doesn't matter, but it does. And what about Stella? Would you want her to feel like this? Would you want her to hurt like you're hurting right now?"

"Of course not, but this is so hard. I don't know if I'm strong enough."

"You *are*, and when you start to think that you're not, you can lean on me. You have so many people that love you and want to protect you. You are family. We are all here for you." I put the van in drive and drove us home silently, turning on the radio just to have a little back-ground music. Aubrey laid back and was silent the rest of the trip.

Back at the bakery, I opened the side door and helped her out of the van as she winced. "Ouchie. Oh my God! This hurts so much, which is saying something because I had two childbirths without epidurals." She whimpered as she climbed the stairs to my apartment slowly.

"I know, honey. We are almost there, and then you can rest. What can I make you for dinner?"

"I don't know if I can eat anything right now. My stomach is upset."

"You have to eat something. We need to keep your strength up."

Aubrey was gasping for breath at the top of the stairs.

"Lean on me," I said to Aubrey, and she wrapped her arm around my waist as I led her into my apartment and down the hall to my bedroom. "Let's get you settled, and I'll make us both some comfort food."

'Thank you," she whispered.

"Of course." I settled Aubrey into my bed and tucked her in with three blankets. "Why don't you try to take a nap? I'll wake you up when dinner is ready. She smiled weakly and then closed her eyes, and I tiptoed out of my bedroom, shutting the door behind me.

I pulled out my phone and opened iMessages, then tapped on Foster's name. I typed out a message. Then deleted it. Then typed out another one. Then deleted it, too. We were no longer together. He didn't owe me a comforting response, but I would have given anything to have him to lean on tonight. To have him in the kitchen, whipping up something delicious and taking Aubrey's mind off the pain. That's the kind of thing that a husband does, and it was clear that I had refused to let him be one of those. The regret surfaced again, sucking the air out of my lungs.

It's so strange when you find a home inside the arms of another person. When they become a safe haven during the brutal storms of life. I wanted to cling to him again and feel his arms wrapped around me. I yearned to bury my face in his chest to be comforted by the slight thump of his heartbeat next to my cheek, but I was never going to feel that again, and that bitter reality took my breath away.

THIRTY-FIVE

I was mentally and emotionally exhausted after the events of the last few days. Christmas Eve was bittersweet and deathly quiet in my apartment as Aubrey slept. I sipped warm apple cider hit with a shot of rum and stirred it absentmindedly with a cinnamon stick, looking out the window. Large snowflakes fell from the sky and collected on every flat surface, floating peacefully down. It was like living inside a snow globe. I loved the snow. I loved nights like this where the usual hustle and bustle of downtown was put on pause as the world transformed into a winter wonderland. I pulled a soft chenille throw across my shoulders as I watched a few people scurrying on the sidewalk below me. My tipsy eyes played a trick on me when my heart raced at the sight of a Foster-sized man walking toward the bakery. Then my stomach dropped to the floor when I realized it wasn't him.

I wondered if he was at home with Wendy. Or if he had met someone new and was... My mind created a movie that I couldn't bear to watch, and jealously reared its ugly head in my belly. I wanted him to be here. I wanted him to be kissing me under the fake clump of mistletoe that Nonna hung every year in the bakery. I wanted to wake up Christmas morning with my legs wrapped around him and then drive over to Mom and Pops's for eggnog and French toast.

A stab of loneliness crushed my heart.

You're too late.

Regrets surfaced again and again, and I drank them away, wanting to soften the agony of my broken heart. Being tipsy actually made it worse. I missed him more and craved his touch. I pulled out my phone and scrolled through all the texts and the pictures. Reading and re-reading a hundred hours of flirty banter. I swiped through the photos of us I put in a special folder on my phone. I watched the goofy video snippet of us in the Ferris Wheel pod at sunset at Navy Pier. The screen became blurry as tears coursed down my face, and I stared into lights on the Christmas tree, dreaming about what could have been.

I checked on Aubrey, who was sleeping soundly on my bed, then I laid down on the couch to watch a documentary, anything that would occupy my mind that kept circling back to him. Finally, I fell asleep and gave in to the dreams, and when I woke up, my face was tear-stained and my eyes were swollen from crying.

We gathered at Nonna's house for breakfast and presents, smelling warm gooey cinnamon rolls the moment we walked in.

"Mommy's here!" Owen said, running to Aubrey and squeezing her as she pinched her lips together to stop a groan from the pain.

"Yes, buddy. Merry Christmas!"

"Hey, O!" I said cheerily, but he ignored me. For a seven-year-old, his grudge-holding ability was remarkable. I bent down anyway and tried to connect with him. "I know you're mad, but I still love you and want to give you a hug."

His eyes filled, and after a slight hesitation, he took a step into my arms and hugged me tightly. "I miss him," he whispered into my neck.

"I do too," I said and stood up quickly as my own eyes filled.

"Stella Bella!" I shouted out as Stella ran over to us and launched herself into my arms.

Like an observer, I watched everyone open presents, unable to feel anything but loss and regret. The holidays were flat and morose, magnifying the loss, giving me too much time on my hands to focus on my mistakes. I couldn't wait until they were over so I could bury myself in work again.

THIRTY-SIX

Two weeks into January, we got an incredible gift. Tony was arrested for breaking and entering, having been caught on camera kicking down the door of Aubrey's old apartment after the locks had been changed. He violated parole and was facing jail time. The news flooded Aubrey with relief; she had been on pins and needles for weeks, but now she could let herself relax and begin to heal.

I breathed a sigh of relief, too, when the holidays were finally over. Spending New Year's Eve at home and lonely, I was ready to take tentative steps forward. We sprang into action and rallied around Aubrey. Mom hired a mover, and we spent two days packing up her things. Pops leaned on his neighborhood connections to find an apartment above the cheese shop just two doors down from the bakery and secured it for Aubrey and the kids in his name.

I was so happy to have something to do, something to focus on and push the work of healing my broken heart off onto another day. I went into full-on Lorraine-mode and focused all my attention on getting Aubrey's new place set up. The kids were already at the bakery with Mom and Pops, so we shopped for groceries, and I was planning on getting the bunk bed set up. I wanted to get sheets, their stuffed animals, and blankets on the bed, so when they slept in the new apartment for the first time, it would feel a little more like home.

Opening the trunk, I looped my wrists through canvas bags of groceries and loaded myself like a pack mule, trying to one-trip it.

"G," she said weakly, "let me help. I'm not an invalid."

"No way," I said. "You know we can't risk you re-injuring yourself. The doctor put you on a fifteen-pound weight restriction." Aubrey walked ahead of me, slowly clutching the handrail and using it to pull her up the stairs one at a time.

"How are you feeling today?" I asked, watching her wince as she walked up the stairs to her new digs. Fractured ribs were painful and took a long time to heal. The bruises had faded from an eggplant purple to a greenish-yellow, and then a barely perceptible gray. Her body was healing, but that was the easy part. I was more worried about her heart and her mind.

I heaved the heavy bags up the stairs one at a time, a workout that made me short of breath and was clearly the most cardio I had done in a week as Aubrey opened the door to the bright apartment. Cardboard boxes were stacked to the ceiling in every room. Seeing the chaos, she burst into tears. I quickly dropped the bags on the floor and scooped her up in my arms gently.

"I'm sorry," she cried. "It's just so overwhelming. I

don't know if I have the energy to do everything that needs to be done."

"The hard part is over, honey. I know it looks like a mountain of work, but the reality is that everything you own is in this apartment. No more living out of a suitcase, no more looking over your shoulder. Once we get you unpacked and settled, you'll love it here. And I'm so close by, you or the kids can pop over anytime you want. You have support here. This will be a great place to heal yourself."

"I'm so grateful, G. I don't know how I will ever be able to thank you."

"We're family, Aubs. It's what family does, like it or not, you're stuck with us."

"Well, I made out like a bandit, but you guys got the poopy end of that stick." She laughed.

"Why don't you relax, and I'll make you a cup of tea and then put the groceries away."

"I feel guilty accepting, but that sounds amazing." She yawned. "I've been so tired lately."

"You might be depressed. If it sticks around, you should go get a screening." I pulled a tea bag out of the plastic bag of groceries on the floor and scrounged a mug out of one of the boxes, then started heating up the water in the microwave. "Have you ever thought about trying therapy?"

Shock washed across her face. "Who are you and what have you done with my best friend?" she teased. "Gionna DeLuca is advocating for therapy? I never thought I would live to see the day!"

I flushed pink. "I'm really good at advocating therapy

for *other* people, just not so good at recognizing when I need to go myself."

"Actually, it has crossed my mind," she admitted. "I feel so broken and empty. Like I am running around aimlessly from nightmare to nightmare, oblivious to the dangers that everyone else can see. And the worst part is that I'm dragging two kids along for the ride. It's not fair to them. They don't deserve any of this."

"That's true. They don't," I said softly. "But neither do you."

She brushed a tear away. "I'd love to finally figure things out. I feel like I'm taking a test that I'm not prepared for, but everyone else already knows all the answers. I'd love to understand why I pick men who hurt me. I am tired of giving my all to the wrong guys who never reciprocate."

The wrong guys who never reciprocate.

It hit like a dagger. Pangs of regret stabbed me, and I cringed and closed my eyes as I breathed through the pain.

"Enough about the hot mess express over here." Aubrey reasoned, "How are *you* doing? Have you heard from Foster?"

"No," I answered sadly. "I think he's done with me." I continued to busy myself putting away the groceries, drowning in the sea of self-condemnation.

"Can't you work it out?" she asked. "There was so much good between you two. If you and Foster can't seem to figure it out, no one can."

"We aren't going the same direction," I answered. "Sometimes, it can be so close to perfect, but still not work out. He wants kids, and I don't think that I do."

"Sometimes, you have to make concessions for the

person you love. You can't have everything the way you want it."

"That's a *big* concession," I pointed out. "Besides, my life is so full with work and getting you and the kids settled."

"Whoa." Aubrey winced as she rose from the chair to walk closer to me. "I truly appreciate everything you have done for me and Stella and Owen, but you don't get to distract yourself with my problems. I am not your excuse to hold back and ignore your own issues."

"Why do you always have to hit me with the truth bomb?" I mumbled.

"Real friends tell you when you're screwing up, and you are screwing up." She insisted, "You *are*."

"Thanks," I muttered as I continued to put groceries away.

"I know Brett ripped your heart out. I know the humiliation and pain you suffered, but you can't let that shitty relationship stand in the way of the happiness you deserve." She paused and then continued. "Nothing is perfect, G. But when you find something that is *practically* perfect, you hold on with both hands and you don't let go. He is good for you. You light up when he's around. Foster brings out the best in you; you can't deny that."

"He does," I agreed.

"Then what are you waiting for?"

"I'm not sure I am ready."

She laughed, and I stared at her, confused. "Newsflash! No one is!" she shouted. "But when you find someone like him, you hold on and you figure it out. Kids are a huge responsibility, but you have support. You won't be alone. We will all be here fighting over who gets to hold that little one while you fight Foster to make sure he doesn't end up with a baby mohawk. You know Stella would be over the moon with a real baby to dress up."

"She would."

I considered her words. A flush of hope rushed up my chest. She was right. I hate it when that happens. What was I waiting for? Why was I content to shrink and play small and settle for a life that didn't include love? Playing it safe would only numb down everything. I wouldn't be hurt, but I also wouldn't know the fullness of life, the excitement of love, and the passion of a man who worked hard to build a life with me. I *did* deserve that. Even if the life he wanted didn't line up exactly with mine, maybe I could still adapt. Maybe I could open my heart to the idea. Maybe I could be a mother if that was what it took to make him happy. Maybe I could.

"You might have a point," I relented. "But what if it's too late?"

"Then it's too late," Aubrey answered. "And that will be really painful," she paused and then continued, "but what if it isn't?"

What if it isn't? My heart raced as adrenaline surged through me.

"I'll think about it," I conceded, it was the best I could do.

THIRTY-SEVEN

Thinking about it mandated a doctor visit. I needed real information, to know the pros and cons of having a baby when you're over forty. One bright morning the first week of February, I sat in the ill-fitting examination gown on the cold metal table, waiting in my doctor's office as thoughts raced through my head. *Am I really doing this? Do I want to be a mother? Am I even fit to be one in the first place?*

Dr. Cahill strode in and shook my hand. Her bony grip encased my sweaty one.

"Gionna, I have to say we were at the Wellington wedding last month, and your cake defied gravity. It was spectacular. It almost felt wrong to eat it."

"I hope you got over that quickly," I offered, blushing at her praise. "Thank you so much. I was really proud of that one. The iridescent, large-scale sugar sculpture took a full week to create."

"Oh, we did, and it tasted as good as it looked." She closed her eyes, remembering. "That chocolate buttercream? Dreamy. My mouth is seriously watering right now thinking about it."

"You should bring your kids to the bakery on Thursdays. That's when our Death by Chocolate cupcake is featured."

"If I'm going to die, that is the way I want to go out." She smiled. "Okay, enough about my sugar addiction, let's get to it. Tell me why you're here."

"Well, I'm on a fact-finding mission, I guess you could say." I looked down at my stockinged feet that were nervously jiggering up and down on the table. "In your professional opinion, what are the chances of someone like me having a healthy pregnancy at forty-two? I mean, it's insane, right? The likelihood of it happening is a long shot."

"Well, actually, this is where freezing your eggs works in your favor. It basically acts to stop the clock. We can screen the health of the egg, fertilize it with healthy sperm, and implant it, and if you have a successful implantation, you can go on to have a healthy child."

The stab of regret was physically painful, and I hung my head. "I donated my eggs a few years ago, I hit a financial bump and couldn't afford the storage fees."

"Oh." She said as she added notes to my chart, then met my eyes as I asked the most important question.

"Could I still conceive naturally?" I asked.

"That is still certainly an option, but you may have to be open to in-vitro or a surrogate. Fertility decreases rapidly as you age, but it is not out of the question. Why don't you lay back, and I'll conduct your examination?"

I wrapped my arms around my waist, hoisted my legs into the stirrups, and laid back on the table. She continued to chatter about my cakes, and I couldn't say a word; it's weird carrying on a conversation with someone while they're rooting around your uterus. She inserted the ultrasound wand and after studying the screen for several long silent minutes said, "Your egg follicles look healthy."

"But it's risky at my age, isn't it?"

She pulled off her rubber gloves and tossed them in the trash can and then offered me a hand and pulled me to a seated position.

"It's true, there are more risks, but there is no medical reason I can find that you would be unable to conceive." Her eyes softened. "I wouldn't say this to just anyone, but we've been to DeLuca's so often you feel like family."

I waited, unsure of what she was going to say next.

"It sounds like you are trying to talk yourself out of it."

"Oh, no… Yes… I don't know. Maybe…" I burst into tears, and she handed me a tissue. "I feel like I'm running out of time."

"Well, let me remove that worry from your shoulders," she said. "You have plenty of time to have a healthy baby if you choose to have one. Now, you just have to decide if that is what you want."

———

That night, I looked around my apartment, the place that had been a sanctuary for me after Brett. It had been enough for a very long time, but it wasn't anymore. The truth was I was stagnant and root-bound here. I had healed myself, but there was no room for growth if I continued to close my heart off to the possibility of love. I studied the photos of Nonna and Bumpo, the pure unadulterated joy on their faces smiling at me from the frames on my shelf.

Once in a lifetime, every person gets a chance to find a perfect love.

Love requires a leap.

Let him love you.

I picked up the photo of Mom and Dad on their wedding day, her adoring eyes lit up and smiling into his, a 70s vision of lace and ruffled organza.

Love is about finding someone you can't live without.

It is a risk worth taking.

Real love is quieter.

I burst into tears. Every real relationship in my life was conspiring to help me learn what true love was, and I'd ignored it all, selfishly thinking that I had all the answers. Cynical and untrusting, I had been holding on to pain and grudges and choking out any chance love had to show up in my life.

Nothing is perfect.

You figure it out.

What if it isn't too late?

All the voices of all the people I loved converged into one, and suddenly, I knew what I needed to do.

THIRTY-EIGHT

The next day, I stood in front of a glassed window at the jewelry store, working up the nerve to go in. Spotlights shone down on sparkling diamonds and platinum bands encased in red velvet. I considered them one by one, trying to talk myself out of it, but I couldn't. It was do or die time. I had to prove to Foster I was committed, that I wanted a life with him and everything it entailed, and I needed a grand gesture to make that happen. I exhaled slowly, blowing the tension out through my cheeks, then opened the door and walked inside where a pretty brunette greeted me.

"Are you looking for something special?" she asked, immediately understanding that I was so far out of my element, still dressed in my chef coat and black clogs.

"Actually, I am." I explained, "I'm going to propose to my boyfriend on Valentine's Day, and I wanted to have a ring to make it official."

She clapped her hands together as a big smile spread across her face. "Oh! Surprise proposal? I love it!" she gushed. "You have come to the right place. What's he like?"

"He's simple, a sous chef, so I was thinking of a plain band."

"Okay." She unlocked the case and pulled out a box containing nine thick bands in gold and platinum.

My hand shook as I pulled one from the velvet. This was a life-changing decision, and I trembled in fear and excitement, but without doubt. It *was* a risk worth taking. "Can you tell I'm a little nervous?" I joked, trying to lighten the tension.

"Don't be. I'll help you make the right decision." She smiled at me, and I relaxed.

"I think I like this one." I held a thick, platinum band in my hand.

"That's a great choice," she said. "Here's an idea! How about custom engraving a message on the inside to make it extra special?"

"I love that!" I said, getting pulled into the anticipation and excitement of the occasion. I thought about it for a second and then I knew. "I want it to read, *I love you.* It's been hard for me to say those words, and I want him to have a constant reminder."

I paid for the ring, and the clerk said the engraving would be finished in a week. Leaving the store, I felt a rush of relief. The decision made, I felt the tension melt and the worry and fear dissipate. Soft snowflakes peacefully fell from the sky as I walked home. I was content and happy for the first time in months.

THIRTY-NINE

On Valentine's Day, I sat in the chair in my apartment as Aubrey finished curling my hair.

"Are you nervous?"

"Yes," I admitted, sipping on the champagne she'd brought. A second bottle was in the fridge chilling and would be coming with me to The Ivy. I walked to the drawer and pulled out the red velvet box that held the platinum band, opened it, and handed it to Aubrey.

"It's beautiful," She said, looking at it for a minute before handing it back to me.

"I had it engraved." I stared at the band for the longest time, mesmerized by what this metal circle represented. My index finger stroked the smooth surface as I imagined what it would look like on his hand. Praying it would find its home there instead of being shamefully buried in the back of my closet later tonight. "There's no turning back now." I flashed her an anxious grin.

Aubrey picked out my dress—a long, flowing, cobalt blue number that flared at the waist and had a pop of creamy cleavage. She paired it with gold wedges she loaned me, one of the best perks of having the same shoe size as your best friend.

"You'll bring the kids to The Ivy at ten?" I asked, running over the timeline one more time in my head to calm my nerves. "Mom, Pops, and Nonna are driving me there. I have everything set up with Andre. Foster thinks they are closing for a private party at ten." I breathed out the anxiety that was filling me through pursed lips. "What if he says no?" I asked, panicking. It was a real possibility, and I wanted to be mentally prepared.

"Then it's his loss, and we will pick up the pieces and go back to our lives." She paused. "But don't you think it's better to live in sadness than regret?"

"True," I agreed. "Man, my stomach is flipping!" I pressed my palm to my belly where the horde of butterflies was making its presence known.

"G., you're really putting yourself out there. I am so proud of you. It takes guts to pull off a surprise proposal."

"I would be lying if I said I wasn't terrified," I admitted. This was either going to be the best night of my life or the worst. Knowing I would have an answer one way or the other in a few hours made me pace around the apartment to dispel the nervous energy.

"Okay, honey, I've got to get the kids ready. Owen is going to lose his mind." She hugged me before she left. Her ribs had finally healed, but her heart would take longer.

I flashed her a smile. "See you there."

———

I rode with my family over to the Ivy. Nonna sat in the backseat holding my hand, smiling and caressing the back of it with her thumbs, a calming gesture I desperately needed.

"You always did love to rock the boat and do things your own way," Mom said. "So stubborn, just like your father."

"It's not my fault. I come from a long line of stubborn Italians," I answered.

"We're not stubborn. We are simply a passionate and fiery people," Pops teased, winking at me in the rearview mirror.

I went over the details again in my head, giving them the rundown for the fourth time today. "So, Andre is going to sneak us in and settle us into the back room. Then, he is going to bring Foster out, and..." I hesitated. This was where the rubber met the road.

"And then you will live happily ever after." Nonna smiled, squeezing my hand, ever the romantic.

"I think you've watched one too many of your movies," I said, secretly hoping she was right.

Pops pulled up to The Ivy, an antique bricked building with an adorable yellow awning. A nearly century-old establishment, it collected three Michelin stars and was booked solid for nearly six months. When we walked in, Andre greeted us and then whisked us into the back room that was exclusively lit with almost a hundred candles. Dark red rose petals lined the tables, and soft, swoony, big band music was playing in the background.

"Oh, Andre, it's beautiful!" I exclaimed. I felt like I was living inside an episode of *The Bachelorette*, a show that Aubrey and I endlessly mocked, but secretly wished some of the romance would spill over into our real lives.

"You can thank Lorraine and Marco," Andre admitted with a smile.

"Really?" My eyes shone in the candlelight. "You did all this for me?"

"Yes, sweetheart," Mom said. "It was your dad's idea."

I opened my arms wide. "Get over here and hug me." They wrapped their arms around me and squeezed. "Thank you for making this so beautiful for us."

"No matter what happens tonight, we love you and are so proud of you," Mom said.

"He is a great man and would be lucky to have you," Pops stated.

"He would be lucky to have *us*," I corrected. "Like it or not, I'm a package deal."

Andre returned with Aubrey and the kids, who joined my parents in the back of the room. I exhaled loudly, shaking my arms and cracking my neck to dispel the nervous energy.

"Are you ready?" Andre asked.

"As ready as I'll ever be," I said, and he left to get Foster from the kitchen. I ran over the words I wanted to say in my head. I'd practiced them in the mirror for days, and again in the car heading over in my mind. Trying to select the right words that had been always so elusive for me, but so effortless for him. I wanted to tell him all the things I had been afraid to say.

"Can you record this for Wendy?" I asked at the last second. "You know, in case things go well?"

"Of course." Mom pulled out her phone as she, Dad, and Nonna found a place near the back wall.

I heard his laugh before I saw him, and my stomach dropped and my palms dampened.

God, I've missed that sound.

The door opened, and there he stood. My eyes drank him in eagerly, from head to toe, taking in his white chef coat, the sharp spikes of his hair, and the tattoos that ran up his forearms. My mouth was instantly dry, my tongue felt thick and wooden, and the words I had memorized for days disappeared. In a panic, I searched my mind for them as the butterflies fluttered in my stomach. He took steps closer until he was so near I could smell the lemon on his fingers.

"What the... Gionna?" He looked confused as his eyes adjusted to the low light of the candles. "What are you doing here?" I tried to read the meaning of his tone between the lines, but he was neutral. His eyes moved around the room, taking in the candles and the rose petals and my family. His forehead knitted, trying to put the pieces of what was happening together. I had surprised him.

"Happy Birthday," I mumbled softly with a nervous smile, "Foster." "Someone told me once that love is like a bungee jump." My voice trembled as the seriousness of the moment strained it drum-tight.

He smiled. "Sounds like someone incredibly brilliant."

"Yes," I agreed with a shy smile. "Someone incredibly brilliant. Someone loving and smart, and sweet and funny. Someone I learned to trust. Someone who taught me that it is okay to put your heart out there and love people fully." I looked down for a minute and then back up into his eyes that were warm chocolate, crinkled at the edges.

"You told me that I had a choice. I could grab your

hand and we could leap into the unknown craziness together and figure it out on the way down, or I could sit in fear on the edge, watching you jump without me." My voice broke. "I obviously chose the latter and I have to say, I am not a fan of that experience. Zero stars, do not recommend." I chuckled nervously. My hand went inside the pocket of my dress, fiddling with the ring box anxiously. I exhaled deeply and pulled the velvet box from my pocket. Then I lifted my dress and got down on one knee in front of him, opening it as his eyes widened in shock. "I decided we needed a do-over."

Seeing the ring surprised him again. "I love you, and I am not afraid anymore. I do not want to hold back. Wherever you are going, I want to go, too. You make me feel safe and loved, and I want to give you everything you want in this life."

"Even kids?" he asked, and his eyes pierced mine, searching for the truth.

"Even kids," I repeated as Nonna and Mom gasped in the background and Aubrey squealed.

He pulled me to my feet, kissing me deeply. I had forgotten how sweet his lips tasted and the exquisite contrast between his soft lips and the stubble on his chin. He folded me into his arms and held me, cupping the back of my head and cradling me into his chest.

"Hey! You never gave me an answer," I said, muffled into his chest. He laughed as I pulled back to look up at him.

"Yes, silly woman. Let's get married," he answered as he wiped his eyes. Relief flooded in, and joy unfurled from my belly to my limbs.

I showed him the ring again. "I had it engraved. It says

I love you. I never want you to go without knowing how much you mean to me ever again. You will never have to wonder." I kissed his smile as his eyes became glossy in the candlelight.

"Are you crying?" I teased him.

"Must have some pepper in my eye." He rubbed them again and then he pulled me close and kissed me again.

"I love you." I breathed into his kiss. "*I love you,*" I said more urgently, and the words came easier each time I said them.

Mom, Pops, Andre, Aubrey, and Nonna all applauded and rushed toward us with hugs and kisses of congratulations. Owen ran to Foster, who bent down and scooped him up.

"Who wants some champagne?" Andre said, "It's time to celebrate."

Joy flooded me as the cork popped and flutes were poured. I was engaged to Foster Valentine on Valentine's Day—it was the sweetest day.

———

Thank you for reading "The Sweetest Day." So many readers fell in love with Gionna, Foster, and the whole DeLuca family, I have decided to turn it into a series. There are three more books coming in 2024.

This Sweet Life
Bittersweet
The Sweetest Dream

———

While you wait for them to become available, check out "Up in the Middle of Nowhere." A mother daughter duo embark on a Smoky Mountains adventure to heal their relationship.

Inspired by True Events

One mother. One daughter. One adventure of a lifetime that will change their relationship forever.

When her troubled teenage daughter, Nova, is hell-bent on self-destruction, Tessa Donahue makes a desperate bid to save their future.

Together they will leave behind the familiar and step into a world of whimsical wonder. Nestled amidst the lush greenery of the Great Smoky Mountains, four unique treehouses offer a breathtaking escape as they embark on a journey filled with self-discovery and reconnection.

Tessa and Nova will be forced to face their demons and fight for understanding as they realize this may be the last chance to repair their relationship before Nova graduates from high school.

This poignant and heartwarming tale of a mother's unconditional love and a child's fight for independence will remind you that life's greatest adventures are often found in the most unexpected places.

Order here.

Also Available on Amazon, BN Nook, Apple iBooks, Kobo, Google Play.

———

Like FREE Books? Enter to Win a Gift Card to My Bookstore https://tealbutterflypress.com/pages/join-our-email-list-and-win

There's a new winner every week!

READ MORE BY THIS AUTHOR

Use the QR code below to access my current catalogue. **Teal Butterfly Press is the only place to purchase autographed paperbacks and get early access.** Buying direct means you are supporting an artist instead of big business. I appreciate you.

https://tealbutterflypress.com/pages/books

Also available at Barnes and Noble, Kobo, Apple books, Amazon, and many other international book sellers.

Find My Books at your Favorite Bookseller Below.

Books by Ninya

Books By Blair Bryan

ABOUT THE AUTHOR

 I've always been a risk-taker, so at 44 I decided to write and publish my own books. It has been a roller coaster ride with a punishing learning curve, but if it were easy, everyone would do it. I write under the pen names of Ninya and Blair Bryan.

I love to travel and a trip to Scotland with a complete stranger was the inspiration for my memoir. I also seem to attract crazy experiences and people into my life like a magnet that gives me a never-ending supply of interesting storylines.

If you love a good dirty joke, a cup of coffee so strong you can chew it, and have killed more cats with your curiosity than you can count, I might be your soulmate.

Visit me online www.tealbutterflypress.com

Let's connect in my facebook reader group, **The Kalei-doscope: Teal Butterfly Press' Official Author Fandom**